KITE MAKER

By Candace Lee Van Auken

KITE MAKER

By Candace Lee Van Auken

New Victoria Publishers Inc.

Epigram quote from *East of Eden* by John Steinbeck (pg. iv). Copyright 1952
by John Steinbeck © renewed 1980 by Elaine Steinbeck, John Steinbeck IV
and Thom Steinbeck. Used by permission of Viking Penguin, a division of
Penguin USA Inc.

Published by New Victoria Publishers
P.O. Box 27 Norwich, Vermont 05055
Cover Design by Ginger Brown
ISBN 0-934678-32-4

                    Library of Congress Cataloguing-in-Publication Data
Van Auken. Candace Lee. 1953-
    Kite Maker / by Candace Lee Van Auken.
        p.   cm.
    ISBN 0-934678-32-4 $8.95
    I. Title
    PS3572.A 4164k57   1991
    813′ .54-- dc20   91-8271
                                            CIP

This book is dedicated to
Christina Maria Sparich,
for whom it was written,
and to the memory of our friend,
Bodil "Mimi" Schmidt-Nielsen

Laughter comes later, like wisdom teeth, and laughter at your-self comes last of all in a mad race with death, and sometimes it isn't in time.

—John Steinbeck, *East of Eden*

Prologue

When Julie accepted Ramona's invitation to dinner, she figured something was up. And being a sophisticated woman who was no more immune to Ramona's charms than anyone else she knew, she thought she knew what Ramona was planning.

But no. The dinner was lovely, Ramona was beautiful, the tension was electric—and now here she was, sitting in a bar while Ramona poured coffee down another woman's throat. Not exactly a magical evening.

Julie drummed her fingers discreetly on the table. "Um, Ramona?" she inquired sweetly.

"Sal? Come on, wake up and drink this," Ramona said, seemingly oblivious to Julie's presence.

May, the bartender, came over with a damp cloth and wiped up the coffee that had spilled on the table. "They're gonna pull my license yet," she muttered irritably, pausing to dab at Sal's chin with a tenderness that contradicted her words.

Philosophically, Julie wondered how many of May's new bar stools Sal's insobriety had paid for. But all she said, her voice cheerful, was, "Sal'd have a fit if she knew you were mopping her face with a dishrag."

"I'm sorry," Ramona said to May, looking at her helplessly. "It just hits her all at once."

Sure, it does, thought Julie, exchanging a knowing look with May. *Ramona's always making excuses for Sal. Now she's telling everyone that she's just drinking so much because of how Carla died.* Julie shook her head. *Like hell.*

May rested her hand momentarily on Julie's shoulder before she headed back to the bar. She gave Julie a quick sympathetic smile and shook her head. There was a world of meaning in that gesture, and Julie struggled to understand it. She was at a decided disadvantage. May had known Ramona and Sal, and Carla, way back when. She already knew all the things that Julie had had to piece together, a little at a time.

Julie leaned back in her chair, watching Ramona coax coffee into Sal. There was a lot of history there. When Julie had first met Ramona, several years before, she had felt more at ease with her than she usually did with white women. Part of it was Ramona's friendship with Sal. Julie had figured that Ramona had to be pretty relaxed about race if her best friend, Sal, was black. Julie smiled to herself. Little did she know. She was a little put off by Sal's style, her very white manners and elocution. *Affected academic,* she had thought at first. But no, she quickly found out there was more to it than that. As far as Sal was concerned, Julie was the only woman of color in Ramona's circle of friends.

Julie pursed her lips. Sal was an odd one. She had been brought up with wealth and privilege, and she acted for all the world as though she had only one parent, a white one. When Julie finally asked Ramona about it, she had said that she and Sal had never discussed Sal's race. Sheepishly, Ramona admitted that she had never had the nerve to bring it up.

That had raised Julie's eyebrows. From what she'd heard, Ramona and Sal, years and years ago, had been lovers. And to think that they'd never talked about it! Julie had had to battle mightily to suppress the urge to deluge Ramona with questions. Ramona was very reticent about some things, protective of both Sal and herself. Julie knew, for instance, that Ramona had been studying medicine when she was involved with Sal, but Ramona never talked about why she had left medical school.

And finally, there was Carla. Julie had only known Carla near the end—a bitter, moody woman obsessed with her own failure, a hypertensive who refused treatment and died of a massive stroke. From little things Ramona said, Julie knew that wasn't the way Carla had always been. Once upon a time, she had been wild, madcap, the bon vivant who had first introduced Ramona and Sal.

For a moment, just a moment, Julie felt sorry for the two of them. She hadn't known Carla very well. It wasn't until after the funeral, several weeks ago, that she understood how hard Carla had worked on that stroke, the neglect, the self-abuse that had verged on suicidal intent. Ramona and Sal were the survivors, the old friends left behind with all the guilt.

Julie sighed, deciding that once, just this once, she'd cut Ramona a little slack. Maybe the evening could still be salvaged once Sal was straightened out. Resignation was not Julie's strong point, but loyalty was. She put her reservations on hold and waited to see what was going to happen.

Leaning back in her chair, she surveyed the bar. A quiet night, and yet there was a kind of electricity in the air. Like anything could happen, like.... Over at the door, Bets, the bouncer, startled and leapt back. Julie wondered what was going on. She had this uneasy sense that whatever it was, she would find out about it soon enough.

La Casa Sappho

What it was, was a Cadillac convertible. The car was customized—that much is unarguable. A gross understatement, but a kind one. Aesthetically, the car was neither kindly nor restrained. It impinged, it exploded, it crashed onto the reef of one's sensibilities, a neon Flying Dutchman.

Bets, the bouncer, saw it first. She was peering through a rectangle of wavy glass, set chest-high in the door. "I've always found it useful to know what's coming," she would say. What was coming this time was that big, gaudy car, a candy-apple-orange Queen Mary nuzzling up to the curb in front of the bar.

In fact, the boat was nuzzling *over* the curb, onto the sidewalk. In a moment of cowardice most unbecoming to the professionally brave, Bets stepped back from the door. She regained her nerve just in time to watch the right front wheel drop off the curb. *Clunk.* "There goes the front-end alignment," she muttered, practical as always, perhaps even seeking to mask her moment of doubt in a firmly delivered opinion.

The car came to rest. Bets pushed open the door to confirm the vision she had seen through the glass. "Jesus," she murmured. The car was very new. Every bit of paint and chrome announced this to the world. There were few signs to suggest this vehicle had traveled as far as its license plate proclaimed. In all its poor taste, from the long horns, real ones, mounted on the hood, to the flames and pin stripes swirling down the sides, to the oversized antennae curving graciously over the back end, her eyes had not betrayed her. It was awful, it was ridiculous, and it was parked smack-dab in front of her bar.

Bets reeled from the door, letting it close ungently, and called to May behind the counter, "How about a beer over here?" Bets was not one to overreact. When overwhelmed on any level, by any particular feeling or impulse, her reaction was the same. As soon as possible she would step back, take a deep breath, and offer herself a fundamental choice: "Do you want another beer, or is it time to go throw up?"

• • •

May pulled a Shlitz out of the cooler, took a tender swipe at it with her towel, and set it on the counter. Bets did not reach over to take it.

After a few minutes, May retrieved the beer, removed the cap, placed a cocktail napkin on the counter, and set the bottle down again. Bets did not seem to notice.

The next time she was free, May picked up the beer, walked the length of the bar, ducked the gate, circled around, threaded between tables, and stopped before Bets' staring eyes. Waving the bottle like a wand, May demanded, "Okay, what is it?"

"Pimp-mobile, I guess," said Bets, taking the bottle and lapsing back into reverie.

May shook her head, put her hands briefly on her hips, and went back to the bar. Sometimes she wondered whether this woman, love of her life, was a dreamer or a dullard, a poet or a parrot. People who knew Bets would have laughed at descriptions of her that veered anywhere near the poetic, the profound, but May knew better.

At that moment, Bets was, by a whimsical thread of free association, lost in the mists of a fantasy about a lesbian whorehouse: Out of that customized Cadillac (now painted a modest shade of deep, flaked purple) Bets imagined a mysterious and provocative figure stepping. She was about three inches taller and forty pounds lighter than Bets, but with only minor modifications, she looked flatteringly similar to the humble bouncer.

She was dressed simply in black leather, silver chains, and ruffles at cleavage and cuff of finest lace. She affected a silver-headed cane and a fetching black fedora. She was sleek, she was chic, she was *très élégant*. She was the Madam of La Casa Sappho.

Feared by some, adored by others, she administered her enterprise with a firm but velvet hand. Her concern did not discriminate on the basis of race, color, creed, or place of national origin. Fees were on a sliding scale, tailored to income and number of dependents. The physically handicapped were not turned away or made to feel other than the fine Amazons they truly were. Same for those who were short or tall, skinny or heavy. Oh, sure, the radical lesbian feminists reviled her establishment, spray-painted "P.I." on the back door, but that was

2

only when, after collective meetings, they were not sneaking off to avail themselves of her exceptional facilities.

At La Casa Sappho women lined up, dressed to the nines, to wait eagerly for their private audience in the elegantly appointed apartments of Madam Bets. With a mysterious smile the Madam handpicked their partners for an evening of sensual delight. Only she knew that, actually, there were no women for sale or rent at La Casa Sappho. Lovingly, Bets paired off the lonely, the shy, the bereaved, the proud, and the desperate, customer with customer, vicariously sharing in their happiness—and picking up her fair share of pin money off the deal....

Bets sighed, taking a swig of her beer. She paused, startled, to stare at the bottle and wonder how it came to be in her hand.

• • •

While Bets dreamed, the gaudy Cadillac was beyond her sight, if not her thoughts. She did not wait, straining to see through her little window, struggling to peer through the tinted glass of the car, to discover what would emerge. She may have thought she knew what kind of person would drive that car. Indeed, the driver started out promisingly enough, pausing after the car was parked to unwind a snow-white fur from around her neck, taking time to lay it gently on the seat. But there all resemblance to Bets' fantasies ended.

The woman who climbed out of the driver's seat was no match for the car itself. On a hazy day with a brisk breeze fluffing her auburn curls, she might have passed for five-foot-two. With a valorous working over by a gifted makeup artist, it is possible (if the downy line of the lower jaw were covered, if dark glasses were added to hide the changeably green and youthfully undefeated sparkle in her eyes), it is just possible she could order a drink without getting carded.

Her clothing made her look even younger. She wore a cotton plaid shirt, the tartan scaled down to match her size, and her jeans were old and unfashionable, boot cut. Perhaps least helpfully, her feet were clad in blue-black-and-gray argyle socks and a worn pair of low-cut basketball shoes. The sneakers were an unusual shade of ultramarine tinged with battleship gray.

Having climbed out of the Caddy, she stretched her legs gratefully, ran a nervous hand through her curls, and reached into her hip pocket. She tilted a scrap of paper toward a street lamp, scrutinized it carefully, and looked at the name over the

3

door of the bar. She then cast unhappy glances up and down the deserted street, sighed, sniffed, pushed the paper back into a pocket, tucked in her shirttail, and pulled open the door.

In an instant she had her first glimpse of a lesbian bar and wondered whether it might be her last: a long and consequential arm was thrust gently but firmly in front of her chest.

"ID?" demanded Bets.

The woman dug out a fat wallet and produced a Kentucky driver's license.

"Can't take it," said Bets. "Gotta have an L.C.B. Card."

"What?"

"You have to have a State of Pennsylvania Liquor Control Board ID. That's the only one I can take."

"But I just got here."

"Doesn't matter."

"I mean, I just this minute got here. I've come all the way from Kentucky. I just arrived. Just now. How could I possibly have a whatever-you-said?"

Bets sniffed. "Doesn't matter. You can't come in anyway."

"Why?" asked the woman in the miniaturized tartan.

"Jeans." The woman stared quizzically at Bets. "Jeans," repeated Bets. "Dress code. No jeans."

"Oh," she said, taking a step back. Abruptly she rallied. "Now wait a minute! This is ridiculous. I came all the way from Kentucky just to come *here*. I drove all that way..." her voice was getting louder "...so you can tell me I've got the wrong piece of paper and the wrong pair of pants!"

Bets had a moment of sympathy, but heads were turning, challenges being defined. "Look, sister, I'm sorry. That's just the way it is."

The stranger was desperate, that was clear. She scanned the women sitting at the tables, made eye contact with an attractive older woman, and proclaimed, "IS THIS FAIR?"

Ramona sighed. After a moment's hesitation she shoved back her chair resignedly and marched over to Bets, hands in her pockets, head down, eyes level. "Hey, Bets," she began, "what's going on?"

"Nothing," said Bets, raising her arm again. "No problem."

"Why don't we discuss this reasonably...."

"Forget it, Ramona. No card, no jeans."

Ramona sighed. "Now Bets, I don't think we should pass judgment so quickly. I mean, how much can anyone expect? If

4

she's got other proofs of age, and you think she's old enough, then under the circumstances, admitting her would be entirely justifiable."

"Yeah? *You know* there's a dress code."

"C'mon. It's a week night, a slow night, Bets," began Ramona, then stopped, seeing Bets' eyes narrow. She turned to the stranger. "Have you got other clothes with you?"

"*With* me?"

"Well, you know, you said you just arrived. Didn't you...."

"This is all I brought," said the woman, gesturing defenselessly at her person.

"Huh," said Ramona. She turned back to Bets. "Look, you made your point. Why don't we just show this girl from Kentucky how hospitable we City-of-Sisterly-Love folks really are?"

Bets scowled.

"Okay, okay," said Ramona wearily, "are flannel slacks all right under the dress code?" Bets nodded. "Well, then," she said, undoing the top button of her pants, "shall I give these to her here or would you rather we stepped outside?"

"Stop that!" barked Bets, flushing.

"Aw, come on, Bets. Surely, with or without pants you wouldn't turn *me* away?"

"Cut it out, Ramona, I'm warning you," muttered Bets, now a deep shade of maroon.

A crowd began to gather and someone yelled "Go, Ramona!" just as May elbowed through.

"All right," intoned May, "that's enough. Bets, drink your beer. Ramona, pull up your pants. You, come on in. And everybody else, GO SIT DOWN!"

Smiling, the stranger from Kentucky took a relieved stride forward—only to be halted by Bets' capable arm. "What is it?"

"Two dollars."

"What?"

"That'll be two dollars. Cover charge."

"Oh," said the young woman, biting her lip. "Cover charge, huh? Well, uh, do you take MasterCard? Visa?"

Bets emitted an ominous throaty sound.

Ramona turned back, fishing in her pockets. "That's okay, Bets. Here, that takes care of it. All right? Good. Come on, kid. Consider yourself welcomed." Ramona grabbed the arm Bets released and steered the woman to her table. "Whew. Sit down," said Ramona solicitously, pulling out a chair, "and tell us how you first discovered this talent for inciting riots."

"Oh, no, Ramona," remonstrated Julie, seizing the opportunity to reclaim Ramona's attention, "*you* tell *us* where you discovered this talent for, shall we say, creative clothing removal."

"You see," said Ramona in a patient kindergarten teacher voice, "this is a black person. I know they don't let them sit at the same tables down in Kentucky. Now you see why."

With that all hell broke loose. The stranger began, "But they do too...." Julie started in, "Now hold on, paleface...." And Sal, impressing the stranger as a woman both genteelly attired and generously intoxicated, perked up and tried to intercede, but her protests came out sounding like "Ip, ip."

"I think things are getting out of hand," said Ramona. "Why don't we settle down."

"I'm okay," said Julie, "but I think Sal's needle is stuck."

"Sal, Sal! It's okay. You can stop now," commanded Ramona.

"Ip," said Sal, but very quietly.

"There," said Ramona. "I think we're all set. I'm Ramona Stevens and you're...?"

"Melvina. Melvina Skittle," said the stranger, solemnly shaking hands.

"Melvina, huh? Well, it's nice to make your acquaintance, Melvina. This is Julie Farragut, and this is Sal Deevers."

"But she'll answer to 'Ip,'" added Julie.

"That's *enough,*" said Ramona.

"Your friend got a problem?" Melvina asked Julie in a whisper.

"Sal doesn't have a speech impediment, if that's what you mean. She's drunk. And Ramona is not on the verge of a coronary. She just looks that way when things get crazy, usually her doing. And you, you have just set the land speed record for shortest length of acquaintance required to get Ramona to drop her pants. Let me shake your hand, I'm impressed. I like your style, even if you do have a funny name."

"Funny name?" said Melvina.

"Wait a minute," said Ramona, "this is by no means the strangest name I've ever heard. Just the other day they brought in a kid named, honest to God, 'Nowax Fleurs.'"

"'Honest to God No-Wax Floors'? That *is* peculiar, still...."

"Boy, they do carry on," said Melvina, more or less addressing the semi-catatonic gaze of the woman beside her.

Sal shifted her stare toward Melvina with some effort. She

6

shook her head sharply, drew herself up, and blurted, "Well, actually, it's-a-rather-poor-attempt-to-diffuse-some-portion-of-the-preencounter-sexual-tensions- that- tend- to-arise- between -the-presently-acquainted-but, let-us-say, not-yet-familiar, possible-sexual-intimates."

Eyes wide, Melvina thought for a moment. "Yeah, I got that. You mean...."

"Banter," said Sal flatly, "pre-canter banter." She chuckled at her joke. "The thing that amazes me," she added, more slowly, "is that people always choose such predictable and meaningless things to argue about. I mean, if one really wished to criticize those two, one should single out, say, Ramona's obsession with controlling everything or Julie's tendency to lose bladder control during fits of high hilarity. Those are *real* shortcomings. But no. Instead, they're having at it over the socially momentous question of the absurdity of names."

It took Melvina time to digest this. She furrowed her brows and then raised one uncertainly. "And you're saying they do this because they're hot for each other?"

"Crudely put, but to the point. My funny name is Sal Deevers. What's yours?"

"Melvina Skittle."

"That *is* funny. So's your accent. You know what, Melvina Skittle? I'm afraid all this is starting to make sense to me. It's time for another round."

There was a lull in their conversation as Melvina and Sal tried to get Ramona and Julie's attention. "This is silly," Julie was saying.

"You just noticed?" Sal pushed back her chair. "I don't know whatever gave *Homo sapiens* the idea she was ready for speech." She stood up and steadied herself. "Let me ask once more, is anyone ready for a drink?"

"You're not," observed Ramona, aiming for a conversational tone.

The look Sal gave Ramona was brief and to the point. Julie noticed it and laid a gently restraining hand on Ramona's arm. While Sal was taking Melvina's order, Julie exchanged a series of looks and grimaces with May across the bar. May shrugged and nodded. Julie patted Ramona's arm.

Melvina took it all in. She threw her elbows out wide and sat back, interlocking her hands behind her head and stretching her legs. She seemed to gather about her the air of ease and obvious

7

comfort of a homeless cat settling herself on a hearth. "Well," she announced, "this sure isn't like what I was afraid it would be."

"What do you mean?" asked Ramona, her eyes on Sal at the bar.

"I don't know. I guess I sort of pictured, you know, tough women, smoking cigars. That sort of thing." Ramona pursed her lips and glanced down at the table. Melvina went on quickly, "Oh, please don't be offended. I mean, I don't really know anything about...you know...lesbians."

Ramona drew her brows together, "Wait a minute. I'm confused. Didn't you tell Bets you drove all the way from Kentucky just to come here?"

"Uh, yes. Well, not directly. I mean, I figured I ought to check out a, uh, lesbian bar. Well, uh, actually, I'm looking for someone. An old friend. I mean.... Look, let me explain. Years ago, you know, when I was little...."

"You still *are* little," whispered Julie confidentially.

"When I was litt*ler*. I used to go to Farm Camp in the summer sometimes."

"Yeah," said Ramona, chin in hand, looking skeptical.

"Well, there was this girl, Laura Maynard. I never saw her the rest of the year. Just at camp. Anyway, we were real good friends and, uh, I decided to look her up."

"And she lives in Philadelphia?" asked Ramona.

"And she comes here?" added Julie.

"Well, I don't know if she lives here," said Melvina. "Not for sure. I know she came here to go to college six years ago."

"You mean you just got up one morning and said, 'Gee, why don't I drive all the way to Philadelphia and look for my friend who I haven't seen in ten years?'" demanded Ramona.

"No, wait a minute," said Julie. "Why did you come *here* to look for her? And how did you know about Peaks?"

"And how did you get here?" asked Sal, returning with drinks.

"I just wanted to look her up," said Melvina to Ramona. "And I just...borrowed a car," she said to Sal. "And I...had this idea she might be here," Melvina said to Julie with an uncertain shrug.

"Doesn't wash," said Ramona, shaking her head. "I don't think you're being straight with us."

There was an ominous silence at the table. All eyes bored

8

into Melvina, now nervously peeling the label off her bottle of beer. "Straight?" said Melvina tentatively, her smile wan.

Julie chuckled graciously. Ramona gave her a dirty look. "Start at the beginning. We only spank if you lie."

Melvina sighed. "This is embarrassing."

"Uh-huh," said Ramona, leaning forward, chin on her folded hands, elbows on the table. "Come on."

"Give it up," whispered Julie. "Once Ramona's dug in she won't budge till she gets her way."

"Hush," said Ramona, still staring at Melvina.

"Okay," said Melvina, "I guess it started with the car." She paused. "My uncle got this new car. He's, uh, real rich. Showoff. I can't stand him. Anyway, he brought the car over, you know, to show it off. The car's sort of overdone, but, you know, it's a Cadillac. A real, honest-to-God, Cadillac." Melvina paused again, looking around the table and then down at her label peeling. "So I asked him if I could try it out. You know, drive around the block. So he said 'Yes' and I took off."

"Only you didn't drive around the block?" suggested Ramona.

Melvina licked her lips. "Right. I mean, I did, but it was so neat. I mean, boy, a Cadillac convertible. Neatest thing I ever drove." Melvina shrugged. "So I kept going. I don't know. I didn't want to be there. I was bored." She paused again. "I wanted, you know, adventure, romance...."

"So you stole your uncle's car," said Julie.

"Yeah, well, he's a real turd. He had it coming. And anyway, he'll be mad as hell, but, after all, he knows I'll bring it back. I mean, it's not like stealing. We're *family.*"

"You sure about that?" asked Sal.

"Oh, yeah," said Melvina, nodding her head. "My cousin once took half the credit cards in the family. Went all over the country charging things. Everybody was mad as hell. But it gave 'em, you know, hot gossip for weddings. They took it out of his hide when he got home. But that was all, and it sure livened up a few weddings. I guess I thought, 'Hell, if Ollie can do it, why can't I?' I mean, I'm young. You only live once, right?"

"So you hopped in your uncle's Cadillac and took off," said Ramona.

"Yeah, and then, when I was driving, I had to think of some place to go. So I thought of someone I wanted to see and here I am."

Ramona glanced from Julie to Sal and back. Melvina caught

her eye momentarily and tried to smile. Ramona frowned at the table and cleared her throat. "Okay," she said, "but why here?"

"Yeah, why'd you think your friend would be here?"

"Oh, boy," said Melvina. "You guys don't give up, do you? All right. When Laura and I used to go to Farm Camp, we palled around. We were really good friends. But...." Melvina stopped, sighed, wiped a hand across her mouth. "This is embarrassing, you know." She paused for sympathy, got none. "Okay. One day, the last summer of camp, we went to camp together, we were coming back from a hike and...well, she kissed me behind the latrines." Melvina hid her face in her arms on the table. Julie patted her back. Ramona smiled behind her hand and rolled her eyes.

Sal shook her head vehemently. "I *knew* it. This drink is watered!"

"Oh, come on Sal," admonished Julie. "Have a heart. This kid is here, pouring out her...."

"So somebody kissed somebody behind the latrines. So? I'd rather kiss 'em on the mouth."

"So you think Laura's a lesbian?" Ramona paused to scowl at Sal. "Because she kissed you?"

Melvina nodded her head, still buried in her arms. Julie was rubbing her back and Melvina was leaning into it.

"Hm," said Ramona, "so you came here.... Do you realize how remote the likelihood of her being here, now, is? I mean, even if she did turn out to be gay, which is not very likely, and even if she still lives in Philadelphia, which...."

"Yeah, I know," mumbled Melvina. "But it was someplace to go, something to do."

"Uh-huh. And what about you? Is your interest in finding her, well, did you just want to look her up and say 'Hi'?"

"None of your business," snapped Melvina, pulling her head up, moving away from Julie.

"Oops, I think you hit a nerve, doctor," said Sal, gazing at Ramona over her drink.

"Well, look, it doesn't matter. If we can help you find your...friend...we'll be glad to," said Ramona, trying for a light-hearted tone.

Melvina was quiet for a moment. "Thank you. Really. I'm sorry. You guys have been really nice."

"That's okay," said Julie, tousling Melvina's curls. "Listen, have you got a place to stay?"

10

"Yeah, how are you fixed financially? That's a long trip to take on a whim."

"I started with fifteen dollars," said Melvina, "but then I found my uncle's wallet. I guess it fell out of his pocket. He didn't have much cash, but, boy, does that man collect credit cards!" The women at the table gaped at the cascade of charge cards that Melvina produced.

"Plastic heaven," observed Sal.

"So you got here on a sudden impulse, one set of clothes, fifteen dollars, and a pile of plastic?" asked Ramona.

"You got it," grinned Melvina.

"Amazing," said Julie. "Will wonders never cease. Wait a minute. You still haven't told us how you found Peaks."

"Oh, that was easy," said Melvina, "I just asked a cop."

"You mean you pulled up by one of Philly's finest and said, 'Pardon me, sir, could you direct me to the nearest lezzie bar?'"

"Well, not *exactly,*" demurred Melvina.

"Close enough," said Julie, shaking her head. "We've got to take care of you, child. You are a rare find."

"Yeah," said Ramona, resting her chin on her hand and furrowing her brow. "Definitely."

• • •

The night was almost over. Behind the bar May indulged in a heartfelt sigh and a luxurious yawn. There was no doubt about it, some nights were crazier than others. *Often as not,* thought May, *Ramona's responsible.* Not that anyone would have guessed. Ramona appeared the soul of reason, maturity. *Hell,* thought May, *she livens things up.* And for most people, that was what the bar was there for. Some place to go, some vague hope of finding excitement, companionship. *At night, when everyone goes home,* thought May, *most of what I sweep up are shattered dreams.* She thought of Carla and pressed a knuckle into her upper lip to keep the tears at bay. She'd been doing altogether too much of that lately. Even watching Ramona waltz into the bar with yet another woman on her arm made May want to cry. *We're all getting older,* she thought, *and we keep on going around in circles.* May shook her head, watching Ramona gaze at Julie. She still liked Ramona, pants at half mast and merry-go-round of women and all. *We are too many sheep and not enough hellcats,* thought May, and she silently raised her glass to Ramona.

11

"It's getting late," said Ramona. Julie had answered the call of Donna Summer's *Last Dance*. Sal appeared to be asleep. Melvina was playing with another beer bottle, as happily preoccupied as a four-year-old.

"Yeah," said Melvina significantly.

"I guess the question before the board is, where are we going to put you for the night?"

"Oh, I don't know," said Melvina, clearly more interested in her bottle. "I don't want to put anyone out. I could go to a hotel, sleep in the car—anything's fine."

"Like hell. I would be tremendously honored to invite you to share my humble abode, except...." Ramona trailed off, glancing over her shoulder at the dance floor. "Well, I'm just getting to know Julie. And—you never know when it might be a good idea to have space available for a relaxed heart-to-heart talk."

"You mean you're hoping she'll go home with you," observed Melvina, leering at her beer bottle.

"Well, let's not jump to carnal conclusions, shall we? It's just that—I want to be able to offer her my—I just want my accommodations to be available should she wish to avail herself of them. That's all."

"Sure."

"Look, sweet stuff, my cultivation of Julie is no whim. For years I've kept my eye on that woman, watched her lovers come and go, prayed for an opening. By my calculations, her relationships last an average of five-point-three years, with a fairly small standard deviation. I have plotted my entrance into her life with infinite care. This is, I figure, my last chance before the end of menopause—and that barely—for a meaningful liaison with that wonderful person. Do you understand? I've had my ups and downs, ins and outs, little quickies and this-is-forevers. It's time for the old girl to settle down, consummate the mature love fermented from a lifetime of loving and losing, never the leaver, always the leftover...."

"Okay, I get it. Enough! So, what do you plan to do with me?"

"Well, Julie and I are out. That leaves Sal."

"Sal? I don't think she likes me."

"*C'est la guerre.* It's the best deal. Sal's got room, no one else around, and anyway, she could use the company."

"I'd say Johnny Walker was her favorite company."

"Watch it. That's not nice. You don't know Sal like I do. She's not always like this. She's a very respected prof over at Cathedral. It's just—well, we both lost a friend a while back. A good friend. She's taken it pretty hard."

"Too bad," said Melvina disinterestedly. She shrugged. "Happens all the time, though."

"Very profound. Look, I can tell you're not keen on each other, but that doesn't matter. It's expedient, and it'll be good for both of you."

"Yes, Mom."

"Oh, shut up."

They watched the ineffectual shots of weary pool players for a few minutes before Melvina said, "You know, if Sal hadn't told me you were hot for Julie, I would've thought you and she...."

"Us? No way. We're just very old, very dear friends."

"Huh. You never...?"

"No, never. Oh, once, a million years ago. We both got drunk one night and landed in bed. Once. Didn't work out."

"Too bad. You didn't like her as a...lover?"

The merest shadow of a smile played around Ramona's mouth. She inclined her head just a little as she replied. "Oh, it wasn't that. In fact, it was probably one of our better nights. I wonder who started it, what started it? I can't remember. Anyway, it was funny. We were both so shy, so young," Ramona smiled and shook her head. "I remember, the next morning when we woke up—embarrassed? Whew! She took off so fast—I just sat there and thought, 'Wow, I'm in love with my best friend....' So, being a mature and forthright individual—as one tends to be at that age—I wrote her a note, told her how I felt. I left it on the bedside table."

"What happened?" asked Melvina, still peeling her label.

"Nothing. She just pretended nothing happened. She got the note, it was gone, but she never mentioned it, or me, or us. So that was that. I was hurt, but—we've got a pretty good friendship. We survived that. We'll survive this." Ramona gestured at Sal, presently slumped over the table. "It'll be okay."

The overhead lights went on, capturing a few lingering couples clasped together on the dance floor. Patrons winced and cried out at the sudden burst of light. The woman running the pool table startled and sank the eight ball. Her audience groaned. Suddenly, everything looked, and everyone felt, shabby.

"This is a first for me," announced Julie, stumbling back to the table. "First time I've ever closed Peaks on a week night."

"Come on, Sal," said Ramona, shaking her friend's shoulder. "It's time to go home."

"Is she going to be okay?" asked Julie, helping to sit Sal up.

"Yeah, I think so," said Ramona. "I've seen her worse."

The women who had done battle at the pool table were shaking hands. Melvina heard names offered, telephone numbers. There was the rustling of coats, the slinging of purses over shoulders. May came out from behind the bar to gather glasses. Bets pulled her little table back from the doorway.

The dancers, the drinkers, the pool-table fixtures all made for the door, some reluctantly, some as if pursued by paparazzi. Ramona and Julie took their time with Sal, making sure there was someone on each side of her.

"Everybody got everything?" asked Ramona.

"Has everybody got everybody?" echoed Melvina.

"Good night, May," called Julie as they neared the door.

"Good night, girls," called May. "Be careful now."

Melvina cast one last look around the bar before she left, hurrying to catch up to the others. Just as she went out the door, she paused, thinking she heard something behind her.

"Good riddance, Kentucky," muttered the Madam of La Casa Sappho.

Sinking Ships

When Melvina was a little girl, her father used to take her with him on scavenging trips. Together they would ramble around the countryside on Sunday afternoons, looking for junkyards or dumps or junk shops—or the collections of things that farmers way out in the sticks assemble over the years. She remembered best one crisp fall day when her father saw a Model A pickup, rusting in a hay field, and turned in at the next driveway to make inquiries about it.

"Even if he doesn't want to part with it, he's probably got more where that came from," her father said with a wink, enjoying the idea that he was a shrewd old haggler.

The house and barn they found around a bend in the dirt drive looked about as decrepit as a house and barn could. The barn's clapboards had weathered to an unhealthy gray, while the house was barely white from the chalky residue of the paint that had once graced it. The rooftrees sagged like the backs of old farm horses, and the gutter pipes, broken, hung down like abandoned reins.

Only weeds and a few unpresentable hens graced the dooryard, and the old man who came off the front porch to greet them looked himself rather like a chicken with hominid pretensions. With effort he jutted his chin out past his Adam's apple and, hands in the pockets of his overalls, cleared the fender of Melvina's father's truck with the chaw he spat out.

"Mornin'," said the farmer.

"How do," said Melvina's Dad.

The two men came face-to-face about four feet apart. There they stood, shoulders hunched and hands jammed indifferently in pockets, sizing each other up, squared off like boxers about to go at it with their elbows. Melvina stood over to one side of her father, just as intently working at a small caricature of the old men.

"Saw a junker in the field back there," said Melvina's father,

15

pointing. "Yours?"

The man looked at his feet, pushed a little dirt around with one toe. "Yes?" he said, not really answering Melvina's father's question, just giving him permission to go on.

"Well, I thought...." her father paused to cough, a process that consumed almost a minute. "Excuse me. I just thought I'd stop and find out about it. Does it run?"

The farmer sniffed and cocked his head to one side, still staring at the ground. "I haven't tried to turn it over in nine, ten years. I figure there's some things better left alone. You know what I mean?"

"Uh, guess so. Is that something you thought about getting rid of?"

"Well, yes and no. I figure if they want it, they'll come and get it, you know?"

"You mean it's not yours?" asked Melvina's father, annoyed.

"It's mine. It's just...I don't know...what with the neutrons and all. I'm not sure whether I ought to go out in that field."

"Neutrons?" asked Melvina's father, now clearly exasperated.

The farmer sniffed. "You know, the takeoff. Landed damn quiet, but you never heard anything like it taking off."

"Pardon?"

"The takeoff! The spaceship! *You* know. Little purply-colored guys no bigger than her there." The farmer paused to peer closely at Melvina, as if suddenly unsure whether or not she might just be a little purple around the gills.

"Yeah, well," said Melvina's father, his manner changed as though he were not really hearing this man at all, "I was mostly interested in the truck. I thought you might want to get it out of there, maybe even sell it. You know, parts, that kind of thing."

Melvina was all ears, staring at the farmer, enrapt. She had never heard a man talk this way, and the talk drew her like a magnet, opened her ears to the adult conversation she would usually ignore and endure.

"Yeah," said the farmer, "that first time they came near startled me to death. Never seen anything like it. 'Course, by the third or fourth time, it almost felt like friends comin' over."

"Well, it's been nice talking to you," Melvina's father said, taking a step back toward the truck, stopped by another fit of coughing.

"It's only recently they've been coming in disguise, right up the road, looking just about like anybody else," said the farmer,

16

shooting another look at Melvina.

Melvina's father reached for the door of the truck, gesturing at her to go around and get in her side. "If you ever do decide to chuck that old junker, you let me know," he croaked. "I'll probably be back this way some time again."

"And the thing is," the farmer was saying, talking as if Melvina's father were still in front of him, "I don't know what they want. It worries me. Maybe they're having second thoughts. Maybe they want to get rid of—all evidence of their visits. You know, *all* evidence. Or maybe they're mad about that time Ellie wouldn't let 'em in the house. Maybe they've even decided to prepare—clean us off the earth so they can colonize. I don't know. It worries me. What do you keep coming back like this for? Why play these games with me? I *know* who you are. I *know*. I'm no fool. Wait!"

But by this time Melvina's father was backing down that driveway just about as fast as anyone ever had, and with a bump and a slam they were out on the paved road and gone.

Melvina's mind was racing. She looked at her hands, searching for any trace of purple, worrying about that poor old farmer, out there all alone with *those* things banging on the door at night. She looked up at her father, who was driving faster than usual, hands grasping the steering wheel tightly.

"Daddy?" asked Melvina.

"Crazy old coot," said her father at the road in front of them.

"Did he really see them?" asked Melvina.

"No such thing!" exploded her father.

But for Melvina, the power of the farmer's words was stronger than her father's denial. She wanted to believe her father, but the passion, the fire in the farmer's eyes had burned the idea into her. "No bigger than her there," he had said, and that was what had tipped the scales. It was as though his eyes had bored through her, had seen some terrible secret even Melvina didn't know.

For a while after that, at night sometimes, she would kneel by her window in the darkness, checking to make sure there was nothing, and no one, outside.

• • •

The reason you have to know about the farmer and the spacemen is so you can understand why the color of Paul Newman's eyes was so important to Melvina. That may sound as crazy as spaceships in the back forty, but it is not.

17

There is one more thing you need to understand, and that is American preadolescent sex rites, as practiced in places like Tradewater Crossing, Kentucky.

It may seem tacky to bring it up, but even though it is not talked about much, we all know. It is hotly denied and just as ardently practiced. All that time that *Dick, Jane, and Sally* is fed to little Tradewater girls; all that time they are weaned on *The Waltons* and virtuously defended heroines who scream, trip, twist an ankle, and become utterly incapacitated at the sound of a fart; all that time some patriotic Tradewater male is plotting the execution of his key role in her development.

Sometimes it is a friend of the family. Sometimes an uncle, a brother, even Dad—sometimes everybody together. It is rarely that ubiquitous and much maligned creep in the bushes, but almost anyone else will do. The lucky girls make it to courting age unscathed—in which case a date, a teacher, hell, even the village parson will do nicely.

The only rule of the game seems to be to derive maximum pleasure from the humiliation of an unwilling female participant. Now, this may constitute some sort of rite of passage, like public defloration in less advanced tribes or clitoridectomies—it often enough has similar consequences for the unwitting girl's future self-image and sexual enjoyment—but whatever it is, it occurs as frequently as if it were a prerequisite for female citizenship. Draft for boys, rape or molestation for girls. Blue booties and pink ones.

While it may save our feelings not to talk about it, it does not save our daughters' sanity not to have any idea what they are in for. In Melvina's case, what happened was so foreign to her experience of the world previously, so utterly contrary to everything her loving family had taught her, that Melvina was at a complete loss to understand why some friend of her brother Lester would drop by when everyone else was out and greet her by throwing her to the floor, slapping her across the face, and struggling to get her underwear off.

In addition to the pain and outrage, Melvina was frightened and very confused. Mom, before she had gone into the hospital, had called John a *"nice* boy." Dad had always slapped him on the back and taken him out to see his latest rusted acquisition. Hell, John was Lester's best friend! It made no sense to her. No sense that in her own home she should be so vulnerable. No sense that this could be happening. And she had only a vague idea as to what really *was* happening.

That's when Melvina, for the first time in years, thought of the spacemen. Could he be one? Could she be one? Maybe that was why he was doing this terrible thing to her. Maybe they had been looking for her and her father for years: maybe they, too, had become "evidence" of the spacemen's visits. Maybe it had something to do with invading the earth, colonizing it. Spacemen. It made the most sense to her at the time, and so Melvina clung to the thought, clung to it while she yelled and struggled and finally slipped out from under him. He chased her upstairs and was surprised to find her standing in the doorway of Lester's bedroom, pointing her brother's twelve-gauge shotgun at him.

"Aw, c'mon now, Mel," John said, taking a step down the stairs. "Put that thing down."

"You can't fool me," said Melvina, shaking, blood on her blouse, all of eleven years old. "*You're* not John."

John ran a nervous tongue over his lips, tried to clear his throat. "I'm John. You know me. Come on, we were just having fun. We—goddammit, give me that!" He was yelling, starting up the stairs again.

Melvina closed her eyes and pulled the trigger.

• • •

Melvina never tried to explain to her brother Lester why she had been ranting about spacemen when he came back and found her in the hallway, still clutching the gun. It was too embarrassing and still too real. For weeks Melvina fought feelings of unreality and fear. She even feared Lester and her father.

The two men were never able to find words to talk about why John had hurt her. Later on, Melvina figured it out. She came to understand that there were no spacemen involved, but it took time for her to give up that crazy idea completely. So many bad things happened after that. She felt like the farmer, waiting for the end of the world.

Her mother never came home from the hospital. She was transferred to the State Psychiatric Institute, where for more than three years, especially after their father died, Melvina and Lester went to visit each weekend. It got harder and harder to go, until finally they could not even tell each other it meant anything to her that they were there.

It was so much, so awful—all seeming to flow from that mo-

19

ment when John pushed her down, knocked her world on its ear. Melvina walked through it like a puppet, with stiff, jerky movements that did not feel genuine. She had periods of incredible anxiety in which she would brood about the farmer's fears, knowing it was crazy, unable to fend off an overwhelming feeling of doom. In school someone read, "This is the way the world ends...," and Melvina thought, "Sort of."

It was many months later, after the worst was over, when Melvina's parents had succumbed to their slow and inexorable diseases, that she finally realized the world was not ending, at least not like the farmer thought. It was at a Paul Newman movie Lester took her to see, somewhere in the middle of *Butch Cassidy and the Sundance Kid*, that Melvina found herself struck by the color of Newman's eyes. It was the first time, since that day in the living room, she felt something was beautiful.

All at once Melvina Skittle experienced an earthshaking moment of monumental insight. It was as though the screen before her opened up, and the sky behind it as well. She felt in that instant as though she possessed the wisdom of ages, suitable for carving in stone. All at once it occurred to her that no one could bear to destroy a world that contained something as beautiful as Paul Newman's eyes. The spacemen did not matter. Everything was going to be all right.

Melvina was laughing and crying, shaking her concerned brother, wishing only that she could make him understand this wonderful thing. It never occurred to her that it might sound silly, no sensible reason for giving her allegiance back to the world of the living, for daring to trust again, for daring to feel.

All she knew was that even if there were spacemen investigating our planet, observing our casual cruelties, our run-of-the-mill atrocities, there would be things about us that would stay their judgmental purple paws. Maybe it would be the blue of Paul Newman's eyes that would make them decide to rope off the planet and preserve it as a park.

Of course, it is just as possible that it would be Melvina's smile, the smile Sal encountered on the sleeping girl's face when she came into the living room the next morning, *that* smile, that would melt the hearts of the spacemen. Melvina was no great beauty. Her face could never have launched a thousand ships. Not even one. But it is possible, just possible, that smile of hers could have sunk a few.

3

QxBPch—and Mate

Huge windows faced west, filling the room with warmth and light. Melvina woke by lazy stages, rolling around in the sheets, alternately basking in the sun and sliding into the coolness beneath the covers. She had no idea where she was, and it felt good. She had no desire to open her eyes, disturb the neon etchings dancing on the inside of her lids. Feeling immensely peaceful, she fell back to sleep.

When Melvina woke a second time, she went through the series of sensations again, scarcely aware they were familiar. She thought, *It's almost as good as being on the road.* Later she would tell Sal, "It's the only time you're ever really free. The only time nobody in the whole world—maybe even you—knows exactly where you are. All the strings are cut. It's just you and the moment, just being alive."

Sal would say, "I never realized a good sense of direction was a roadblock to self-actualization." But even that would not spoil it. Nothing could. For the first time Melvina could remember, she felt young and alive and utterly free.

"Well, here I am," announced Melvina to the room at large. Finding a bathrobe on the foot of the couch, she wrapped herself in it and ran to the windows. "Amazing," she proclaimed as she looked out over the city. "My head!" she exclaimed as she decided, abruptly, to sit down. "From beer?" she wondered out loud. "Did I drink anything else?" She thought about it for a moment and gave up. "What a night," she grinned, gently cradling her headache in her hands.

When she had composed herself, she wondered where Sal was. She noticed it was two o'clock. "I don't even remember sleeping," she said, "I must have been awfully tired." *Good*, she thought, *no dreams.*

She wandered around Sal's living room, taking it in. It was a spacious, airy room, the spare furnishings of a quality she had rarely seen. There were many books, few plants or knickknacks,

21

the major ornamentation existing in the muted tones of the finely finished wood of chairs and tables and shelves. A single, pastoral print interrupted the white, high walls, and Melvina, standing in front of it, realized it was not especially meant to draw the eye. She turned away, disturbed, deciding the decor lay somewhere between Cautious and Routinely Well-to-Do.

There was a letter on a table near the kitchen, the small writing evidencing a fastidious hand. Melvina read:

Salutations Young Stranger,

Damned near had heart failure this a.m. on entering room. Am not used to tripping over the nude and barely nubile before I've had my morning coffee. In future, please utilize sleepwear provided.

"Fearless Leader called bright and early to issue marching orders. (The phone ringing while I showered did not interrupt your slumber.) Mine were to confiscate and launder your hirsutulous ensemble. (Done.) Also to provide some means of covering you in the interim. (Note pile of tasteful clothing on couch. Don't complain. People who wear argyle socks with old sneakers have no right to complain about anything.) Your orders are to sally forth, collect supplies, and render dinner for four. If you require a cookbook, there are several around here somewhere. Finding them could keep you busy for hours. Also, Ramona wished me to mention that she is not, repeat, not a vegetarian. Nor am I. And I hate *tofu.*

Grades are due tomorrow, so I won't be the first one back. I've provided keys for your use. Don't forget or lose them. Use them! I don't know whether one locks one's doors in Kentucky, but one damned well better in Philadelphia.

By the way, is that fuzzy thing of yours alive? It didn't look it this morning, but then I'm not certain whether or not it's supposed to be. One more thing: What is your name? Ramona told me but I forgot.

Remember, please, that such as it is, this is my home. Do treat it gently, and, if you have any social diseases, don't sit on the toilet seat.—S.

Melvina stared at the sheet of paper. She started at the top and read it again. She frowned, wrinkled her chin, and folded the paper lengthwise, turning each half back. "No," she said. She unfolded it and folded the top down. "That's right," she smiled, remembering. In a flash she made a passable airplane out of the note and sailed it across the apartment. It did a loop-de-loop upward almost to the ceiling and then plunged down, sticking itself nose-first in a hanging fern. Melvina saluted.

"Dadavi?" she called, turning toward the couch. She rummaged among the sheets. "There you are. Of course you're alive. Do you know what 'tofu' is?"

Dadavi only purred, a tiny sound she amplified by nuzzling Melvina's ear. She was a scrawny white Persian, mostly fur, long for a kitten and endowed with small paws and face. From a distance of three feet, she looked like the tacky accessory to a flamboyant wardrobe.

"Can you believe that?" asked Melvina. "Dead? First Julie thinks you're a boa, then Ramona goes, 'Oh! Ermine!' You'd think they never saw a *cat* before...." Muttering, Melvina found Sal's dictionary and looked up 'tofu.' "See? I told you there was no such thing." She flipped back toward the v's. "Hm, so I guess they just eat meat and—bread. Weird."

Melvina found a scrap of paper, wrote, *'Tofu' isn't even in your dictionary!* and filed it between the appropriate pages.

• • •

"You know," said Ramona, "you didn't have to come all the way down to let me in. There's a button that opens the door."

"I pushed it," said Melvina defensively. "It didn't work."

"You have to hold it until the person gets the door open—I'll show you."

Melvina fairly flew up the stairs ahead of Ramona. She had Sal's door open with a flourish by the time Ramona got there.

"Show off," said Ramona. She paused in the doorway to sniff the aromas of Melvina's cooking, stepped forward to throw down her purse and briefcase, and stretched out in an armchair.

Melvina closed the door and leaned against it, staring at Ramona. She was shocked. To a young woman to whom the concept of matching accessories was utterly foreign, to a girl who had grown up in a world where mother-aged women were worn down and used up, Ramona looked like a vision out of a women's magazine. Every inch the proper professional. *More than that,* thought Melvina, *she looks like a Great Lady.* Gray-eyed Athena in tasteful leather pumps.

Ramona had always possessed the ability to look utterly at ease, in any getup, in any situation. She always looked as though she knew Exactly What Was Going On. The lithe movements of a gazelle in slow motion, the look of slightly weary wisdom, the ability to look any person or predicament squarely in the eye—it is no wonder that few rounds were ever won with her.

Melvina gaped. Finally she managed to ask, "What do you do for a living?"

"Me?" asked Ramona, opening her eyes and looking at Melvina, "I administer women's programs at Bartholow Memorial." She scowled. "Loads of fun."

"Is that a hospital?"

"Yes. Let's not talk about it. How are *you?*" Ramona stood up, gave Melvina a critical once-over. "You must have been a tired little bear. You look immensely better, even more huggable. You mind?" inquired Ramona, spreading her arms.

Melvina grinned. They hugged. She wished she could stay like that, inhaling Ramona's tweeds, forever. Ramona pushed her back, looked her in the eye. "You look much less rumpled. Younger. Are you sure you're twenty-one?"

"Almost twenty-two," nodded Melvina. "You want to see what I made?"

"Sure," said Ramona, kicking off her shoes, padding into the kitchen behind Melvina. "Smells good. By the way, polyester becomes you."

Melvina turned from the stove and made a face. "Sal has a weird sense of humor, if that's what you call it. I couldn't find my clothes anywhere."

Ramona smirked and changed the subject. "What's this? Pot roast?"

"Yeah, that's the main course. I made chicken as a side dish. Over here I've got a loaf of wheat bread and this round bread the guy said was Russian."

"Interesting. You've got enough here to feed an army. No vegetables?"

Melvina looked puzzled. "I put some broccoli and potatoes on for me...."

"Well, put on some more for everyone else," said Ramona, lifting a lid.

"I thought...." began Melvina.

"What?"

"Nothing. It's just that Sal left me a note...."

"Yeah?"

"It wasn't a very nice note."

"Where is it?"

24

Melvina pointed through the doorway at the hanging fern.

Ramona laughed. "Good for you."

"Ramona, what's a vegetarian?"

"Someone who doesn't eat meat. Why?"

"Oh," said Melvina, thinking.

"What's the matter?"

"Nothing. I think I got it all straightened out."

"Are you a vegetarian?"

"I don't think so."

"Neither am I. What's the problem?"

"Really, it's okay."

"Good. Hey, I'll bet Sal's got some wine in the fridge. You want to relax after your labors? It'll be a while before Sal and Julie get here."

Melvina agreed and a few minutes later they were settled in chairs in front of the living room windows. There was a tension in the air Melvina did not find relaxing. After an uncomfortable pause, Ramona said, "So, here we are."

Melvina gave her a suspicious look. "Why do I feel like I'm in for the third degree?"

"Probably," said Ramona, smiling over the top of her glass, "because you are."

"Uh-uh," said Melvina, shaking her head, "I told you everything last night."

"Sure about that?" asked Ramona, flashing one of her more winning smiles.

"Positive."

"Aren't your parents going to be worried about you?"

"Nope," said Melvina with finality.

"Won't your Uncle Lester be worried about you—or the car?"

"Huh? Oh, yeah. He'll be okay.... How'd you know my uncle's name was Lester?"

"You said it last night."

Melvina thought for a moment. "No, I didn't."

Ramona shrugged. "I guess I saw Uncle Lester's name on those credit cards you obligingly flashed around."

Melvina frowned at her glass. "Why do I get this feeling we're playing chess?"

"Because we are." Ramona set her glass down. "Let's not, okay? I'll lay my cards on the table." She leaned forward, elbows on knees. "I like you, Melvina. I hardly know you, but I'm concerned about you. You worry me." She chewed her lip thought-

25

fully. "From the moment I laid eyes on you, I felt there was something you were trying to hide." She paused, hurrying on when Melvina began to speak. "You said you came here to look for a friend, but I get the feeling you came here running away from something, or somebody. I'm scared for you, and I guess that's why I'm prying." She pressed her lips together and inclined her head. "There, that's *my* confession." She sat back. "Now, how about you?"

Melvina looked from her glass to a corner of the room above and behind Ramona. She said nothing for a while. When at last her eyes met Ramona's, she sighed. "Really, I've told you everything that's important. My family knows I can take care of myself. They know I'll take care of the car. There's no problem. Really."

"No one back in Tradewater Crossing going to be tearing their hair out worrying about you?"

"No. Really." Melvina paused, her eyes narrowing. "Tradewater Crossing? How'd you...."

"Saw it on your license when you opened your wallet." Ramona tapped her temple. "Photographic memory. Want me to recite your uncle's MasterCharge number?"

Melvina smirked. "You do numbers, too? That's impressive."

"Now, now," said Ramona, "let's be nice." She rose and stood in front of the windows. "Okay, Melvina. I guess we'll call a truce. I'll just have to trust you." She threw a smile over her shoulder at Melvina and added, glancing down at the window sill, "Oh, look who's here, Dadadee."

"Dadavi. That's Togolese for 'little sister.'"

Ramona raised one eyebrow. "They speak much 'Togolese' in Tradewater Crossing?"

Melvina smiled. "No, my social studies teacher was in the Peace Corps. That was his nickname for me." She fiddled with her wine glass. "Hey, you got any ideas about finding Laura?"

"Oh, yes, Laura, our lady of mystery. Well, she's not in the phone book, and when I called information, they didn't say the number was unlisted. They said they had no listing for a Laura or L. Maynard."

"So you mean she has no phone?"

"Not in her name. Then I was trying to think of ways to track her. Do you know what school she went to?"

"Nope. Just that it was in Philadelphia."

"Hmm. Colleges don't give out much info on alumnae. There's

only one other thing I thought of...."

"Yeah?"

"Well, I have a friend who collects things, sort of. The woman is a bit of a pack rat, if you know what I mean, never throws anything out. She has old phone books, women's newspapers, Lord knows what. I thought that maybe, if we could pick up Laura's trail while she was in college, when you're sure she was here, we'd get somewhere."

Melvina nodded. "That sounds good."

"We can go after supper—I already gave her a call. And even if we don't find anything, seeing her place is worth the visit. Really. It ought to be in the guidebooks."

"Sounds interesting," said Melvina, picking up a book from the window sill.

"What have you got?"

"It's a photograph album I found when I was looking for Sal's cookbooks. I think I found you in here."

Ramona grimaced. "Let me see that. So! While I've been checking up on you, you've been digging through my sordid past!"

Melvina grinned. "Turnabout's fair play. Is this you?"

"Oh, yes," said Ramona, looking over Melvina's shoulder. "Wait a minute," she added, going for her purse. She dug out a pair of half glasses and took the book. "Ah, let's see, here we are. Yes, that's me. Not bad."

"You haven't changed much."

"Oh yes I have. I thought I could do anything back then."

"Is that Sal?"

"Yup, she's the one who hasn't changed—we couldn't have been much older than you when that was taken. There's Carla, she's the friend who died recently." Ramona shook her head. "And let's see, there's the woman we're going to see tonight, Arlene. She looks different now—of course, she was a lot older to start with. Oh, look, that's May. You remember her? She's the one who let you in last night. She's like a fine wine, just keeps getting better with age. I've always wondered what she saw in Bets—not that I don't like Bets. It's just...."

"Want to see my favorite?" Melvina flipped to a shot of Sal and Ramona. Sal was perched, precariously it seemed, on a railing. Ramona was grinning at her, hands in the pockets of her white coat. It had been a breezy day, and it left the two of them looking wind-blown and joyous.

27

"Yeah, that's a nice picture. I have a copy. That was taken right here in Philly."

"Isn't that like a lab coat you're wearing?"

"Yup. See? I worked at a hospital, even then."

"Huh," said Melvina. "What did you do?"

"As little as possible. Hey, you want to go way back? I think somewhere, among Sal's childhood pictures, she's got one of me. Here it is. I used to tell her she could put the one of her and her nanny on the page opposite me. You know, rich brat, poor brat."

Melvina stared at the picture. There was Ramona, barely recognizable, little more than a baby, seated on a rickety back stoop, grubby and grinning. On the opposite page stood Sal, five or six years old, a shy skinny girl in a party dress. The shrubs around her were well-manicured and just behind her stood a dark-skinned woman, beaming proudly. Sal looked frightened, and one of her hands reached uncertainly towards the woman's skirt.

"Well, at least you looked happier."

"I probably was," said Ramona, gazing at the pictures. "Poor Sal went through a long line of nursemaids and nannies. She was her favorite, I think. I remember she died when we were in college."

"I feel like I know you both a lot better after looking at that," said Melvina, closing the album.

"Maybe so," said Ramona, taking off her glasses. "Don't have any revealing pictures you'd like to share?"

"Not a one," said Melvina, setting the photo album aside.

"Why is it," mused Ramona, "I have this feeling you won the chess game?"

"Search me," said Melvina with a shrug and a smile.

• • •

"I don't think I can move," said Julie, rising and making her way to an armchair. "Between being up all night and eating this much, I don't feel like I'll ever move again."

"Don't get too comfortable," Ramona told her. "As soon as this table's cleared, we're going over to Mary and Arlene's."

"And me without my hard hat," moaned Julie. "I can see the headline now: *Overstuffed Woman Explodes Under Weight of Junk Avalanche*. What a way to go! Have a heart, Ramona."

Ramona spun around, her hands full of dishes. "What! And betray our sacred trust? Never. Neither wind nor snow nor—

how does that go?"

"Nor pet-owning citizens," suggested Sal, "with or without Pooper-Scoopers."

Ramona fixed her eyes skeptically on Sal. "Is that really part of the Post Office motto?"

"Definitely," said Sal, reaching for a serving dish. "By the way, before you go charging off into the night—are you aware that you haven't allowed me to get a single, teensy-weensy word in edgewise?"

"Not really, but I'll give it my fullest consideration," said Ramona as she breezed into the kitchen.

Sal put down her stack of dishes and pressed the back of one hand to her forehead. "In case anyone has been wondering how to operationally define the word 'impossible....'"

"And that about does it," announced Ramona, swooping back into the room and grabbing Sal's pile of dishes. "God bless the inventor of the concept 'soak.' Anyone need to use the girls' room before we go?"

"Go now," Julie urged Melvina. "You'll never *find* it at Mary and Arlene's."

"You must be exaggerating," said Melvina, shaking her head.

"If you can't believe a journalist, who can you believe?" asked Sal.

Julie turned to face Sal. "Was that a dig?" she demanded. "Just for the record, was that or was that not a dig?"

Ramona cleared her throat. "Ladies. Let us not quibble when there are missions to be accomplished, damsels to be distressed, lost loves to be located...."

"*I'm* not going," said Sal.

"Oh, yes you are," Julie informed her, giving her a helpful shove in the direction of the door.

"Ladies," intoned Ramona a second time. With only minor scuffling and a few more futile refusals, everyone was rounded up and herded out the door.

4

The Junk Lady's Apprentice

Mary was a genial woman in her late sixties. With her cheeks so pink and her hair pulled back into plaits that wound around the crown of her head, she looked the picture of an Alpine granny. Warmly, she invited them in and inquired about the evening's weather. After a few pleasantries she suggested that she summon Arlene.

"ARLENE!" she bellowed up the stairs, startling Melvina, "Company!" Mary turned back to her guests, folding her hands over her midriff and once again assuming her grandmotherly mien.

From somewhere upstairs came an answering "Who's it?"

Mary surveyed her charges. "Oh, RAMONA! SAL! (You're Julie, right?) JULIE! And, uh, oh, yes, the LITTLE SKITTLE! (Just teasing, dear.)"

"Right down!" came the reply.

Melvina leaned toward Julie and whispered, "This isn't at all like you said it would be."

"This is *Mary's* part of the house," answered Julie, *sotto voce.*

"What's this?" asked Mary, turning toward them.

"Oh, Melvina thought she'd see Arlene's stuff as soon as we came through the door."

Mary smiled at Melvina. "It's only due to unflagging effort on my part that you don't.... No, this is where I live. Arlene has the top two floors. Of course, Arlene eats and sleeps down here with me—if she's good."

"What do you mean?" asked Melvina. Just then, a stumble was heard at the top of the stairs. There was a curse and then the door on the landing flew open. Arlene, and a beach ball, came bouncing down the stairs.

"Back! Back!" shouted Mary in a voice that seemed unnecessarily harsh.

"I didn't *ask* it to come," protested Arlene, shooting an angry look at the beach ball, now nestled in Melvina's arms. "But *look* at it, will you?" commanded Arlene with a flourish, "Holds air as good as ever. I told you it would."

Mary lowered her head and stretched out a pointing arm. "*Now.* I mean it. Beach balls or bunnies, there's not much difference as far as you're concerned. It'll *breed*, I know it will.... Take it back!"

Arlene retrieved the beach ball from Melvina, who was caught momentarily reliving a picnic with her family at Fowler's Pond when she was four years old. "Huh?" exclaimed Melvina as the ball was snatched away.

"C'mon," grumbled Arlene, "we're being exiled."

"Mary," suggested Sal, "why don't we have a cup of tea down here while Melvina gets the grand tour?"

"Yeah," said Julie, "why don't you guys give us a yell when you're ready to get down to work?"

"No appreciation for objects d'art anymore," muttered Arlene.

"Now, Arlene," began Ramona, ever the conciliator, "you'll have more room to move around with us down here. And anyway, you know you'd just as soon show her around yourself."

Arlene turned doleful eyes on Melvina. "Yeah," she decided. She gestured to Melvina and lumbered up the stairs.

Looking at her size and girth, Melvina was not surprised Arlene lumbered. *The surprising thing,* thought Melvina, *was how she skipped down those stairs.* Such light steps! Such a big woman! Melvina ruminated on it as she followed her upstairs.

Arlene was Mary's age, Melvina guessed, an old woman who cared little about her appearance. She wore immense baggy pants, belted with rope, and a man's flannel shirt, once probably red. Her features were not petite. Her ears stuck out from under a straw-like mass of white and yellow and brown hair, and her dark eyes peeked out from under bushy white brows and heavy lids. Her hands, usually hidden in her pockets, were tremendous and clumsy looking. Her fingers were stubby, the knuckles the size of walnuts, swollen and shiny and probably painful.

"Well," rumbled Arlene in her low voice, "what do you want to see first?" Arlene pushed her glasses up her nose and peered down at Melvina. "You like music?"

"Sure," shrugged Melvina.

"Got some instruments." Arlene reached up to pull the string on an overhead bulb and trudged down the hallway.

Melvina was shocked. The hallway itself was narrowed by stacks of things on either side to the point where it appeared that the lurching sway of Arlene's broad shoulders presaged a cave-in. There were stacks of printed material: sheet music, bundled newspapers, esoteric journals. There were chairs that appeared to be suspended, somehow, from the ceiling. Hanging upside-down like that, unmatched chairs of every description, they did not look like furniture at all, more like wooden portals through which she must pass. There were odd items stuffed here and there: a hair dryer, a small leather suitcase, the broken toy of some long-ago child.

From floor to ceiling on either side, pressing in on her, Melvina was confronted with a generous array of all the kinds of junk she had ever seen discarded. Especially with Arlene filling up the space ahead, the hallway, depending on whether one tended toward claustrophobia or claustrophilia, felt very much like either a coffin or a womb. Melvina shuddered.

"Here we go," said Arlene almost cheerfully, turning on the light in a little room at the end of the hall. "You play?"

Melvina sighed with relief as she entered the slightly less crowded room. "Me? The guitar a little, but not very well."

"I got a few guitars over here. This one's pretty much broken," Arlene waved the two halves of a guitar, joined only by its strings. "Here's one that's kinda cute. Half-sized. Oh, yeah, here's my prize. Look at that, will you. That's a—Spanish, archtop, f-hole guitar. Just a mail-order thing, but listen to the sound." Arlene strummed it once. Somewhere beyond the pain of its tunelessness, Melvina thought she detected a pretty nice tone. "Amazing," said Arlene, shaking her head. "They must of made it that nice by accident.... Let's see. Oh, look at this." Arlene dragged out a beat-up case. "Now when I got this, I thought it was just a cheap old horn. Hell, it was *gray*, not even brass looking. But when I went to polish it up...." Arlene opened the case with a grand gesture.

"Wow! Is that *silver*? A silver trumpet?"

"Yup, it's a jazz trumpet. A beauty, ain't she? Can you blow? No? Well, listen to this." Arlene raised the horn and warmed the mouthpiece with her lips. After a false start she launched into a melody, a love song. The tune was vaguely familiar to Melvina, some sort of quasi-Oriental Broadway air.

The old woman was red-faced, her cheeks puffed out grotesquely, but Melvina found herself mesmerized, transported by the clear, sweet sound. Each note hung in the air with an aching melancholy that echoed through the upstairs, sad and beautiful.

When it was over, Melvina stayed as she was, mouth open. She strained to hear the last, dying notes. Finally, she shook her head. "I've never heard anything like it."

Arlene nodded in agreement.

From downstairs, far away, a shout drifted up: "Not the damned trumpet!"

"Some people," grumbled Arlene. The spell was broken. Arlene shoved the trumpet in its case, talking as she did. "Yeah, well, I got a cornet or two, a coupla trombones. Over there's a violin. Somebody borrowed the flute, that's a snare drum but the bottom is out of it. Oh, yes," she added, lighting up, "and this here's the bouzouki."

"Bazooka?" asked Melvina in alarm.

"No, it's a Greek instrument." Arlene pulled it out of a Naugahyde bag. "A little like a mandolin or a—what's that Russian thing?—a balalaika."

"What's this?"

"Well, I think someone carved all this out so they could inlay the front, you know, like with mother of pearl? Only they never finished it."

"That could be beautiful."

"Uh-huh." Arlene ran her fingertips over the carved wood. "The world's full of things that could be beautiful. Me, I figure that I'll either fix it up or fix it, or hang onto it till someone comes along who can."

"So, you mean you're sort of a caretaker for all this?"

Arlene hesitated, "Sort of. It's a little like a museum, too. Come here, " Arlene snapped off the light and shuffled down the hallway, turning in at another room. "See this? You know what this is?"

"An awl?"

"No, it's an ice pick. See the handle here, see where the finish is worn away and the wood is sort of—well, see the color, and the smoothness?"

"Yeah," said Melvina, turning it around in her hands.

"Well, that part, the way it is, that's just from years and years of *use*, of sweat. It's like the finish of their labor...." Arlene paused, looking at it, "And that's all we have left of them. Most people in this world, they never make a movie, or paint a picture, or write a book. They never get buildings named after them. They come and they go." Arlene looked at Melvina. "That's all they leave behind, all you can know them by," Arlene broke

33

off, and a look of unspeakable sadness crossed her face. "And then someone else comes along and throws it all away."

Melvina wanted to say something, to break the silence that fell over the room. "So you mean it's kind of like—archaeology—only you don't wait for things to be buried?"

"Well, yeah," said Arlene, smiling. She turned to leave the room, then turned back, "That was my mother's—and her mother's before her."

Melvina stayed behind for a moment, looking at the ice pick, before she followed Arlene.

"You want to see the upstairs?"

Melvina nodded and they climbed another flight of stairs. This time, Arlene's step was brisk. *She's in her element*, thought Melvina, smiling and shaking her head. She could feel herself struggling to hang onto the disdain, even distaste, she had felt at first toward Arlene, but she was losing ground fast. A part of her had already fallen under the old woman's spell.

Melvina could see it reflected in Arlene's face when she turned at the top of the stairs. Her heavy features were animated, she was grinning. "Want to see my workroom?"

Melvina nodded and followed her into a medium-sized room that looked nearly as crowded as the others they had passed. There was a cluttered desk in an alcove near the cupola window. For the first time Melvina noticed that most of the windows were made of leaded glass. This particular window had blue glass trim all the way around the central clear portion. The sash above had stained glass in several colors that formed a kind of abstract star.

"That's really neat," said Melvina, pointing.

"Yeah, some of it we did ourselves." Arlene winked happily.

"You mean you and Mary? I didn't think she came up here."

"Oh, sure," said Arlene. "She spends almost as much time here as I do."

"You wouldn't think so, the way she was downstairs."

"That's nothing.... It's partly like a game. And partly," Arlene shrugged, "she means it." Arlene began rummaging around her desk as she talked. "She left a few times. Then she came back. This last time we decided she needed a place of her own. You know, so she could get away a little. So she could have things nice. And not just the stuff," Arlene gestured. "Sometimes I can be just as bad. I get ranting and raving—I get worked up." Arlene shrugged again. "It works this way."

Melvina looked around the room. There were all kinds of projects at various stages of incompletion. Near the door stood a chair with its seat half caned. Over by the desk was a table with a large number of small parts arrayed on it. Whatever it was, it was in too many pieces to be identifiable. There was a bookcase that was done but not painted, a cart with one wheel off, a lamp in the middle of being rewired. High up along one wall, kites of different colors and designs were hung.

Arlene looked up from what she was doing. "Ever fly a kite?"

Melvina nodded.

"Ever make a kite?"

Melvina considered. "Not really—but today I made a paper airplane."

Arlene nodded, "Close enough. Sooner or later, everyone should make something that flies."

Melvina raised one eyebrow. "What do you mean?"

Arlene looked up and dropped her shoulders. "Oh, I don't know. Next best thing to flying yourself —I mean really flying, like birds. None of this airplane stuff."

"Hm," said Melvina, knitting her eyebrows, "like the guy in the story? The one who made wings?"

"Yeah, kinda." Arlene smiled.

"I remember. Icarus flew too near the sun and his wings melted."

Arlene's eyes blazed. "Stupid story! They made out like it was because he was stupid."

Melvina took a step back and shook her head cautiously. "Wasn't it because he didn't listen to his father?"

"Same difference," snorted Arlene. "I mean, if you imagine it, if you really imagine it was you, can't you understand why he got so close?"

Melvina answered warily, like a student taking an oral exam. "Because he got so wrapped up in it, he forgot what he was doing?"

Arlene bobbed her head up and down energetically. "I mean, *imagine* it. There you are, soaring above the clouds, banking into the breezes," Arlene straightened her arms down and out, closed her eyes dreamily, "the sun warming your back, the whole world beneath you—I'll bet even the fall was glorious." Arlene threw back her head when she said it, her face looking, momentarily, like the handsome younger woman in the photograph Ramona had pointed out.

"I guess you're right," said Melvina, gazing uncertainly at the kites.

"Watching things fly, trying to *control* things that fly," Arlene chuckled to herself, "has always been one of mankind's biggest vicarious thrills.... Kites go *way* back. Not a bad thing. I think making a kite is good for the soul, an act of faith. Hell, 'Go fly a kite' shouldn't be an insult. Ought to be the national motto: 'In God We Trust—Go Fly a Kite.'"

Melvina laughed.

"Don't laugh. I'm serious. If flying wasn't important, it'd be free." Arlene paused, her face working. Then she began again, speaking very carefully. "What I mean to say is that it's like, well—did you know that in medieval times there were all these rules about who could use what kind of falcon to hunt with? Peasants were only allowed to hunt with kestrels." Arlene shook her head sadly. "Hunt! A kestrel's only about the size of a robin, maybe a little bigger. So here's the poorest people, the hungriest ones, and they can only go hunting with a bird too small to catch anything bigger than an insect, maybe a wee little rodent." Arlene measured out a tiny space with her thumb and forefinger in front of one eye. "So there you are." Arlene turned back to the desk.

Melvina just stood there, very confused, looking from the kites to Arlene and back. She tried to think of something to say and could not.

After a few minutes Arlene spoke again. "But you know, the kestrel isn't such a bad bird. It's quick, it's agile. It has to make up in speed and agility what it lacks in size and power." Arlene paused and smiled at Melvina. "Kind of like you and me." She winked. "Once upon a time I thought the kestrel was like a good symbol for the poor, you know? Look, let me show you. I made a coupla these." Arlene searched through a drawer and brought out a tiny silver bird. "Here, let me get you a magnifying glass. Bring the lamp over. See?"

Melvina peered through the glass at the little bird, amazed. It was less than five eighths of an inch long, but each detail had been carefully worked into it. "Wow, how'd you do that?"

"It took me a *long* time," Arlene said proudly. "I couldn't do it anymore—not with these hands. I even did some of it under a microscope, low power.... Did you see my microscope?"

"Nope," said Melvina, still examining the kestrel.

Arlene was fidgeting around the room all of a sudden, awkward once again. "You really like that?"

"It's beautiful," said Melvina, leaning closer to the magnifying glass. "I can't believe someone could do this."

"Hey," said Arlene, "you gonna be staying around here? I mean, are you gonna be in Philly for awhile?"

"Don't know," said Melvina, looking up from the bird.

"I was just thinking I might be able to teach you. I mean, there're things I can't do anymore, but *you* could learn."

The Junk Lady's Apprentice, thought Melvina, trying to keep her face impassive, *the crazy old lady's helper.* She thought of her father, remembered standing beside him when he talked to the farmer. Part of her moved forward, part of her moved back. But then she saw the kites on the wall, the light in Arlene's eyes, the silver kestrel lying on the table—and, numbly, she heard herself saying, "That would be neat."

They were both quiet, suddenly shy. Melvina bent to peer through the magnifying glass again.

"Hey, would you like to have that?" blurted Arlene. "I don't think my idea's ever going to catch on, I mean...."

Melvina looked up and they smiled at each other.

"Let me find a piece of string," said Arlene, disappearing through the doorway. "It's got a loop to be a necklace."

When Arlene left the room, Melvina sat still for a moment, staring straight ahead at the colored glass of the window. Then she began digging through her pockets, pulling things out and setting them on the desk.

"What's this?" asked Arlene when she returned.

"Oh," said Melvina casually, "I have a collection, too. Only I carry mine around with me." She paused to pick a jackknife out of her pile. "Here. This is a well-worn tool."

Arlene looked at Melvina.

"Well, you're giving *me* something," said Melvina, turning the jackknife over in her hand. "And anyway, this is a good home for it."

"Is it yours?"

"No," said Melvina, "it was my father's." She set it down on the desk.

Arlene picked up the knife and handed Melvina some wiry thread. "Can you get this through the loop?"

"Yeah, I think so," said Melvina, bending to the task. She glanced up. "By the way, thank you."

Arlene smiled down at her feet. "Go fly a kite."

"Oh, here's some more," said Arlene, burrowing through a pile in one corner of the cramped room.

"Great," said Julie, who was picking through a musty pile of old newspapers, nose delicately averted.

"...And tell her I've found some old student directories," Ramona was saying to Melvina. "Basically, just tell her to get her ass up here."

Melvina shook her head and trotted out of the room, threading through hallways and downstairs with a sureness she would never have believed possible only a few hours before. She found Mary and Sal where she had left them, still seated at the kitchen table. She hesitated and then came forward. "Boy," she exclaimed cheerfully, "it's a lot easier to walk around down here."

"Uh-huh," acknowledged Sal, lighting a cigarette.

"I'm sorry," said Mary, "I was just about to go up and help."

"Well, actually," Melvina began slowly, pointing at Sal, "this is the one I was sent to fetch."

"No thanks," exhaled Sal, picking up her tea cup.

"Ramona wants to know why you won't help."

"Hey," said Sal to Mary, "if you really are going up there—you suppose we could find a little shot of something to throw in this before you go?"

Melvina cut off Mary's reply. "Look, at least tell me why you won't help. Ramona'll want to know."

Sal sat back in her chair and sighed out her next puff of smoke. "Just tell her that I think this whole Easter egg hunt is useless, foolish, and ill-conceived."

"Uh-huh," said Melvina.

"Oh, come on," interceded Mary. "It'll be fun."

"No, it won't," said Sal, shaking her head. "It's just a waste of time and energy."

"How do you know?" demanded Melvina.

"Because," replied Sal nonchalantly, "as I tried to tell Ramona all through dinner, *I know* where Laura Maynard is."

5

Second Thoughts

The Cadillac glided over Philadelphia's potholed streets, its ride deceptively smooth. Inside, Ramona sat in front, half turned, keeping a constant verbal barrage aimed at Sal, who sat across from Julie in the back. Sal swatted at Ramona's insults and imprecations with an imperious hand, a self-satisfied smile playing around her mouth. She waited for the brief moments Ramona conceded to breath to languidly defend herself.

Well, thought Julie, *at least Sal's having fun. She's got Ramona all to herself, and here I am, stuck in the peanut gallery.* She sighed, playing with the window button. *That's not Sal's fault. It is her fault she refuses to acknowledge my existence. It's her fault that when I ask her, 'How come getting close to Ramona is just a little easier than getting to the moon?' she won't answer me, won't tell me what's going on with that woman. But this, this is Ramona's doing, or undoing, I don't know. When I walk out tonight, that's it, and I feel awful, and Ramona's going to feel awful, and....* Julie squeezed her eyes shut, pressed a knuckle hard against her lips as she turned toward the window. *I just can't go through this. We've been such good friends, I won't let her ruin that.*

Julie sniffed and looked toward Melvina. "Hey, Mel," she called over the cross fire.

Melvina glanced at Julie in the rearview mirror as she stopped the car at a red light. She turned around. "You feeling okay?" she asked.

Julie shrugged with her mouth and shoulders, "Would you take me straight home? I'm beat."

Ramona paused in mid-tirade, "You all right?"

"Yeah, I just need to catch up with myself."

Ramona reached back to pat her knee, gave directions to Melvina, and returned to her argument with Sal. Julie turned away toward the window, chin pressed into her hand. She was not angry, she just felt sad. *Ramona's getting the big surprise.* She shook her head. *Her problem is that she's always too involved with what's going on to notice what's going on. Right now, it's Sal. This week, it's Melvina. But it's always something. I didn't see that before. Hell, when we were just friends, I probably was the distraction on more than one occasion. I didn't understand. I just saw the beautiful, tragic Ramona, hopping from bed to bed, never quite understood.*

Julie turned to look at Sal. She stared boldly, enjoying Sal's slight discomfort, minimal awareness. *And there's the bitch who holds the key. She and Carla were the only ones who really knew her way back, who seem to know her well. Carla's gone, and that one, she's got some kind of invisible string attached to Ramona, a dainty little chain she likes to yank once in a while.*

Julie looked away. *It's sad, it's really a pity. But I'm not going to do it. I've got a career that's going great guns, a little girl coming home from college for the summer, and I'm not going to put myself in a strait jacket over their folie à deux.*

Julie glanced out the window as the car turned, recognizing her street. She gathered up her jacket and purse. She felt a sudden urgency about getting out of the car, a need to get away before her resolution weakened.

"Is this it?" asked Melvina, pulling up to the curb. Ramona nodded.

"Well, good night," smiled Julie, steeling herself. "Good luck," she said to Melvina, "I hope you find your friend." She hesitated on the curb. "I'm really sorry to be running out on you this way," she said to Ramona.

"That's okay," said Ramona, squeezing her hand, "I just hope you feel better."

"I will," said Julie, turning away, "I hope so."

A Simple Matter of Persuasion

Melvina turned her chair backwards and sat astride it, her hands clasping the sides, her chin resting on top. "So Laura Maynard's in New York," she said thoughtfully, staring off into a corner of the kitchen.

"Well, at least we know where she is," sighed Ramona, pausing to pour a cup of tea. "Even if all our labors tonight *were* for naught." She shot a look at Sal, who was sitting across from Melvina, swizzling her drink with a lazy forefinger.

"Oh, no," said Melvina, sitting up straight, "You two start in again and I'm gonna go sleep in the car."

"I don't think you could sleep in *that* car," observed Sal, still playing with her drink. She glanced over at Ramona, "I never would have believed an automobile could be that loud with the engine turned off."

Melvina stuck out her tongue at Sal, who was not looking. "Now girls," remonstrated Ramona, who was. She set her cup on the table and sat down. "You've certainly had your fun with us tonight, haven't you, Sal?"

Sal chuckled. "It *was* pretty funny."

Ramona did her best imitation of a Bets growl.

Sal laughed. "I predict that in the future my desire to speak will be treated much less cavalierly." She raised her glass to Ramona. "Of course," she added, setting the glass down, "I also predict that, in my lifetime at least, I will *never* hear the end of this."

"Never," agreed Ramona, dunking her tea bag.

"What amazes me," said Melvina, "is that she was your student and you didn't even remember her."

Sal smiled indulgently. "Where did you say you took college courses, Melvina? Was that Raccoon Community College?" Sal paused but rode on over Melvina's answer. "Doesn't matter. It's different in a large university. Introductory psych courses are *huge*. I honestly don't remember more than three or four from

41

the whole mess of them—and that's only because some, unlike Laura, took other courses with me."

"Ah, but you remember Sue What's-Her-Name, don't you?" Ramona asked slyly.

Sal shook her head. "Please don't remind me."

"You never know," continued Ramona. "She was a student around the same time as Laura Maynard.... In fact, she's living in New York City, too. Maybe you ought to give her a call, Sal. She might be able to help."

"No!" intoned Sal, the word sounding like an agonized moo.

"Oh, come on," implored Ramona playfully.

"Wait a minute," interrupted Melvina. "Who's this Sue? Do you really think she might know Laura?"

"It's rather improbable," pronounced Sal. "Ramona's just teasing me."

"Why?" asked Melvina, looking from one to the other. "Uh, did you have an affair or something?"

"Oh, I like that," smiled Ramona at Sal, "sounds so, I don't know, 'an affair.'"

"No," said Sal. "Maybe we had an 'or something,' but we did *not* have an affair!"

Ramona noticed Melvina's look of bewilderment. "Sue was one of Sal's students, that's all. She was a lesbian, a very ardent feminist. Sal, on the other hand, is a bit of a closet case—not *all* of us are out at our jobs...." Ramona paused for a superior toss of her head. "Anywho, one night, guess who runs into whom down at Peaks? I thought Sal was going to have a coronary...."

"And I thought the place was undergraduate-proof," muttered Sal.

"Sue was thrilled to see ol' Sal. She went on and on..."

"And on," added Sal.

"...About role models and lesbian herstory and...."

"Why 'women' should be spelled with two *y*s...."

"Yeah, like that. Anyway, Sue was thrilled and Sal was mortified, and after that, Sue regarded Sal as her very favorite teacher. She took *all* her courses...." Ramona fluttered her eyelashes at Sal. "And pranced all over the department being ever so 'out' and 'gay pride' and all that, and Sal lived in constant terror that Ms. Radical Lesbian Feminist..."

"That's 'Ralf,' for short...."

"...Was going to blow Sal's cover."

"I threw a big party when Ral...er, Susan...graduated," commented Sal wistfully.

"And *everybody* who was *anybody* was there," added Ramona in her best highfalutin tone.

"Except, of course, Sue," Melvina surmised.

"You got it."

"Hey, does she still keep in touch with you?" asked Ramona.

"Yes," groaned Sal.

"You know, it might be worth giving her a call," suggested Melvina. Sal made a face. "I wouldn't mind meeting someone who could strike fear into the hard heart of Sal Deevers."

"Rotten kid," observed Sal to Ramona.

"So, how'd you happen to check up on Laura, anyway?" asked Melvina after a pause. "I didn't think you were interested."

"Oh, I'm not," said Sal, turning to face her. "However, there comes a point in grading papers and finals, when *any* diversion is a blessing. I was stretching my legs, so I flipped through my files." She shrugged. "When I found her in *there,* that surprised me, so I made a few calls. The alumni office gave me her address."

"However," added Ramona, "once again the phone company hasn't been any help, so...."

"So I guess you'll just have to hop in your, uh, unique little jalopy, and go looking for her," Sal grinned. "So sorry to see you go, it's been...."

"Enough," said Ramona, "or I invite Sue for the weekend."

Melvina was looking at the table, a frown wrinkling her mouth into her chin. "Look, I know I was just kind of—dumped on you when you were—well, not terribly up on what was happening. I'm really sorry about that. You've been a real sport to put up with me."

"Mel, I didn't...," began Sal.

"No, really, it's okay.... And I do want to go to New York. I think it's a lot easier to look for someone when you're right there." Melvina stood up from the table and stretched. "In fact, if I'm planning an early start tomorrow, I better get some sleep. Thank you—both of you. Everyone's been really nice to me." Melvina gave Ramona a hug, patted Sal's shoulder, and turned to leave the room. "Oh, yeah," she added, turning back, "when you see Arlene, will you thank her for me?"

"Sure," said Ramona, looking after Melvina from under lowered brows. There was silence for a moment as they listened to Melvina greet Dadavi, scoop her up in her arms, and pad off to

43

the bathroom. Ramona gave Sal's shoulder a shove, "*Now* look what you've done."

• • •

"Well, it may be fifteen-two and fifteen-four and the rest-don't-score, but I believe that puts me over," said Sal, laying down her cards and moving her peg. She shook her head, "Tea and cribbage in the middle of the night? I don't know what's gotten into you, Ramona. Are you ever planning to go home?"

Ramona threw her cards face down in disgust, got up and tiptoed to the kitchen door, then crept back. "I wanted to talk to you. I was just waiting to make sure you-know-who is sound asleep."

"Oh, no," said Sal, resting her forehead in her hand, "not more scheming and running around."

"Nothing of the kind," snorted Ramona. "It's just that I'm really worried about that kid. I hate the idea of sending her off into the wild blue yonder like this."

Sal shrugged. "She managed to fly in from the wild blue yonder okay."

"You don't understand," said Ramona dejectedly.

"Sure I do. Look, why don't I give her Sue's address and phone number? She'd be glad to help her out."

"That's not what I mean." Ramona frowned. "That's not it at all. First of all, we don't know a damned thing about her."

"Sure we do," said Sal matter-of-factly, shuffling the cards. "She's a charmer and a car thief. What more do you need to know?"

"Come on. For one thing, I'm not sure I believe what she told us. I can't prove it, but I don't think it'll wash. I got a listing for her Uncle Lester from Information and I tried it all day without getting an answer."

"So, he works."

"All the time? I don't know, something isn't right."

"What do you suppose?" asked Sal, leaning close. "You think she shot him?"

"Cut it out!" barked Ramona, pushing Sal away.

"Come off it, Ramona. You don't have to bend yourself out of shape over every homeless puppy that comes along, do you?"

Ramona shook her head. "It's not like that, Sal. It's not like that at all. I just get this feeling—like she's a bomb, all wound up and ready to explode...." She broke off, shook her head again. "Don't you feel it?"

44

Sal raised her eyebrows noncommittally. "Maybe a little moody. I don't know. What is it you want to do, anyway?"

Ramona paused for a moment, then started in like a football coach about to give the game plan for the second half, "Well, I thought...."

"Oh, no," said Sal. "I can feel it coming. Shit. I thought for a moment you were genuinely concerned about...."

"Sh! I *am*."

"Then why is it I get this feeling your idea involves me?"

Ramona looked down at the table.

"Ramona, what is it?"

"Look, Sal. It's...I hate to just cut her loose, that's all. I can tell she's going to go, no matter what we say, but I thought, I thought...." Sal's eyes bored into her. "Well, you're not teaching this summer. You haven't planned any trips or anything. I just thought it wouldn't hurt if you set aside a couple of days...."

"Jesus Christ, Ramona. Do you realize how absurd that is? Do you? You want me to pick up and take off with that—child? Just drop everything and climb into that—car of hers, or *somebody's*...."

"Come on, Sal. It wouldn't be so bad. You're always talking about taking trips and you never do. It'd just be a couple of days, and you'd get out and maybe see some old friends and, hell, I think it'd do you a world of good."

"Really? You think it'd be just lovely? Then why don't *you* go off on her treasure hunt? Huh? How come *you're* not volunteering for this little expedition? Couldn't you use a few days of sun and fun with some little nymphet young enough to be your goddamned *daughter*? Come off it, Ramona. It's ridiculous and you know it."

"No, it isn't. It's just different, that's all. Does it really upset you that much? A little impulsiveness, a little spontaneity? You spend every winter making meticulous plans for trips you never take. Not that you can't afford to. Not that you can't get any time off. No. You just can't stand to budge from your misery, can you?"

"That's enough," said Sal impatiently.

"Yeah? Did the doctor hit a nerve? You don't like that, do you? You'd rather sit around here, and drink, and feel sorry for yourself...."

"That's enough! Stop bullying me. You're not going to coerce me into any of your crazy ideas."

45

"Oh, yeah?"

Sal said nothing, just set the playing cards aside and folded her hands on the table.

Ramona jumped up and began to pace back and forth across the kitchen. After a few turns she said, "Sal, I really hate to have to do this." She moved to stand behind Sal's chair. *"But, if you don't agree to go to New York with Melvina, I may have to pull out all the stops, I may have to get really nasty."*

Sal craned her head up and around to look at Ramona.

"That's right, Sal. If you don't go to New York with Melvina Skittle in that—thing of hers, that horrid car, I'm going to have to destroy you."

"What the hell are you talking about?"

"Don't swear, Sal, it's unladylike." Ramona shook her head. "It's obvious. What's the worst thing that anyone could ever do to little-Miss-Pluperfect-you? Think about it, Sal. Imagine someone picking up the phone, even this one here, and calling the chairman of your esteemed department, even right now, in the middle of the night...."

"That's absurd," scoffed Sal, "and you don't even know his number."

"Oh, yeah? You wanna bet on that? Don't try to avoid it—*face* it, Sal. Yes, someone could call up that condescending old fart who heads your department—the one who tried to pick me up at your faculty party three years ago—someone could just wake him up in the middle of the night and...tell him the awful truth about you."

Sal was shaking her head, laughing into her lap. "Oh, come on, Ramona."

"Don't deny it, Sal. Just imagine, *if they knew.* That's right, what if they found out that you're not the uptight little old maid they've been *led to believe* you are? What if they found out the real, the horrible facts. The *truth,* Sal. The truth that, yes, their very own Miss Brooks, their beloved, harmless old spinster chum, is, in fact—can I even bear to utter it?—yes, Sal, a leather-clad, teeth-gnashing, whip-carrying Lesbian Butchess!"

Sal laughed out loud. "You've outdone yourself, Ramona, you really have. I wish we had this on tape."

"Oh, yeah?" exclaimed Ramona, leaping away from the chair, crouching to whisper into Sal's ear. "You don't think I'm serious, *do you?"*

"Come off it. This is all very entertaining, but it's silly as hell.

46

I mean, for one thing, whether I choose to flaunt my preferences or not, I'm a tenured faculty member. Furthermore, it's included in the University's nondiscrimination statement."

"That's nothing!" Ramona stood up, shaking her head. "You don't understand, do you? You don't know what happens when a bunch of academics gets a hold of this kind of hot skivvy. You think they'll shrug it off, take it in stride, deal with it in some sort of enlightened manner? *NO!* Just imagine it, Sal: They'll book *The Killing of Sister George* for the next departmental colloquium, and ask *you* to comment on the social significance of cigar-butt-eating rituals among lesbian couples. They'll choose *The Children's Hour* as this year's faculty Christmas play—and ask you to play both leads. Oh, yes, and you'll get lots of Christmas presents from your colleagues: six different editions of *The Well of Loneliness,* a gift certificate good for one crew cut at Don's House of Barbering, four confessions of preadolescent same-sex sex-play, three invitations from male colleagues to discover that you are, after all, a *real* woman, two unhappily married female colleagues begging to play 'Test Drive a Lesbian,' *and*—last but certainly not least—a copy of *The Cunt Coloring Book* and a box of sixty-four red crayons!" Ramona paused to catch her breath.

Sal was shaking her head, sputtering and chortling to herself. "Sixty-four red crayons, huh? Not bad, Ramona, not bad at all."

"So," said Ramona, back in her chair, her elbows on her knees, "you'll do it, right?"

Sal shook her head. "Nope. You can threaten and cajole me all night, and it's not going to change my mind."

Ramona jumped up from the table, turned toward the stove, and began playing with the knobs. She was silent for a minute and then sighed. "You're right. I can't coerce you into anything." She sighed again. "I never *have* coerced you into anything. Either you're incoercible, or I'm not very good at it." Ramona paused. Her hands grasped the sides of the stove. "I don't know what to do."

"Come on," said Sal, turning towards her. "You're making a big deal out of this."

Ramona did not answer right away. Her words, when she uttered them, sounded forced, despairing. "It *is* a big deal. I've never felt something so strongly—and I feel so helpless."

Sal drummed her fingers on the table. "Look, you're a very

47

sensitive, caring person, and I think that's wonderful. But Melvina's not a child. She got herself all the way up here under her own steam. She can take care of herself, Ramona. I'm not her mother. You're not her mother. She's already got one mother, and that's enough."

Ramona was shaking her head. "I don't know how to explain it. I just feel it. All I've got to go on is something inside me. But I tell you, dammit, if I could just grab the time and go, if the accreditation and the review weren't *both* blowing into Bartholow next week...."

Sal nestled her chin in her palms. "I don't like to see you this anxious, justified or not."

Ramona sat down. "I know it's asking a lot...."

"It is," said Sal, frowning.

"I'm sorry," said Ramona, looking at the table.

They were both quiet for a while. "Funny," remarked Sal, "we never do ask much of each other."

"Yeah, I guess you're right." They fell silent for another moment.

"Shit," said Sal.

"What is it?"

"You know what it is."

Ramona nodded.

Sal stood up. "I better get to bed then."

"Thanks, Sal."

"Shit. You going to come by in the morning?"

"Yeah, I can do that. I'll take a few hours off."

"Okay." Sal rubbed her eyes. "Dammit, I just don't want you sitting here for the next week tearing your hair out."

"I know," said Ramona humbly.

"I know I'm going to hate myself for this."

"I'm sorry, Sal, really."

"Christ, don't be sorry. Will you lock up when you leave?"

"Yeah," said Ramona, sitting at the table. She could hear Sal opening and closing her bedroom door, the sounds of her moving around. Ramona leaned back in her chair and stretched her legs. She plucked a cigarette from Sal's pack, lit it, and inhaled deeply, luxuriating in her illicit indulgence. She stretched out even more in the chair, tilting it onto its back legs, and caught sight of herself in the shiny chrome of Sal's toaster. Her distorted face looked tired to her, even old. She drew another drag from the cigarette and grinned at herself in the toaster, "Nope, not bad at all."

48

7

Dan'l Boone and the Bigot Go to New York

There was a faint hissing sound, like water boiling off a pan. Over that Melvina could hear a hard-edged bubbling, punctuated by pops and snaps. Then there was a tinny, irregular noise—a light, varied scraping of metal against metal. Melvina rolled over and inhaled deeply. Bacon. She listened to the tinny rattle and diagnosed scrambled eggs. *Poor Les,* she thought, *the lengths he goes to get me out of bed in the morning.* She smiled to herself as she reached for the clock on the bedside table, groping with her eyes closed.

A thought came to her suddenly: *No, that's not Les. Les can't get out of bed anymore.* Melvina snatched back her hand as though from a flame. She rolled onto her belly and pulled her arms under her, burying her face in the pillow. It was worst when it snuck up on her like that.

An image was forming in her mind, rolling closer like a slow zoom. It was a piece of a black convertible top, torn and flapped back carelessly. A dark stain was becoming clearer, then a liquid puddle congealing around tiny granular lumps and a swatch of hair, pressed against the material as if it had grown there. The image was coming toward her, getting larger. It was so eerie, isolated like that, just a ragged piece of a picture. A voice suddenly boomed over her shoulder, "We thought he was—gone. Thought it for sure." Melvina pulled her hands out from under her, brought them up to cover her ears.

At her own touch she startled, felt cool fingers, realized she was awake. She chuckled to herself, shaking her head as she pushed herself up. *I better make us some breakfast,* she thought. Only when she opened her eyes did she realize she was not at home.

• • •

"Face it, Deevers," Sal muttered to herself, "you're losing ground." She paused to contemplate the scrambled eggs, bounce them around the skillet with a fork. "How do you like that? Rubber eggs." Sal smiled. "*Oeufs brouilles* they ain't. On the other hand, I'd say they constitute an authentic *ouevre de* short order cook—hell, that's probably how she likes 'em." Sal turned down the heat and wandered over to the refrigerator, fork in hand. "Tomato juice!" she exclaimed, taking out the can. "Opener?" she inquired of the silverware drawer. She poured juice into three tall glasses, leaving one half full. "Salt and pepper?" she asked the glasses, "a twist of lemon?" She chuckled as she garnished them. Finally, with a furtive look in either direction Sal opened a cupboard and took out a fifth of vodka. Swiftly, she spun off the cap. "Are you ready for this?" she asked the half-full glass of tomato juice as she filled it to the brim.

"*NOOOO!*"

Sal jumped, nearly dropping the vodka. With a shaking hand she shoved the bottle onto the nearest shelf and tore into the living room. "What the...?"

Melvina was sitting on the edge of the couch, her arms bracing her, her head hanging down.

"Melvina? Are you all right?"

Melvina raised a drained and pasty face, her eyes peering out at Sal from within bruised circles, a single tear clinging to her chin.

"Jesus, what happened to you?" asked Sal, swooping over to grab her arm.

Melvina worked on a grin, a gesture that provided in intention what it lacked in execution. "I woke up," she said gamely, her voice thin.

"Well," said Sal, regaining her composure, "I'm sure we all feel that way, but really...."

"No, no," said Melvina, her color beginning to return. She waved a hand. "It's okay, really.... I think Dadavi bit me."

"What?" Sal looked down at the kitten, crouched quietly on the pillow with her paws folded under her. "Stuffed animals don't bite," she decided.

Melvina laughed. "Hey, is that breakfast I smell?"

"Huh? Oh, yeah."

"Wow, that's really nice of you," said Melvina, touching Sal's arm. "Here I thought you were glad to be getting rid of me, and you go to all this trouble."

"Shame, isn't it," commented Sal distractedly as she remembered the bottle in the kitchen.

There was a sound at the door. "Is that Ramona?" asked Melvina, struggling to her feet.

"Probably," said Sal with alarm. She hoisted Melvina up, shoved her in the general direction of the front door, and trotted back to the kitchen. The traitorous cap of the vodka bottle was lying in full view on the counter. Sal's hand closed around it.

"What have we here?" boomed Ramona, striding into the kitchen like an Amazon warrior. "Breakfast? How thoughtful! Shall I take things to the table? Where are we going to eat?"

"Oh," blurted Sal, one closed fist hanging casually at her side, "wouldn't it be nicer to eat out there in the sunshine?"

"Fine," said Ramona, clattering plates and glasses.

Sal moved toward the cupboard, poised to work quickly as soon as Ramona left the room. She just managed to get the cap on the bottle before Ramona and Melvina returned.

"There," said Sal, her heart thundering, "I think that's everything." She breathed a sigh of relief she refused to analyze as she followed the others out and sat down.

"Here," said Ramona to Melvina, "you get first dibs on the eggs. You're looking a little peaked this morning."

"She says her cat bit her," remarked Sal, recovered, spreading butter on her toast.

"Oh, really?" commented Ramona, reaching for her glass of tomato juice.

Sal's hand froze in mid-reach toward the butter dish when she saw the glass in Ramona's hand.

"Well," began Ramona, pausing to take a hearty swallow. "My God," she spluttered, gagging, "What the hell's *in* this?"

It took a long time, but finally, bravely, Sal lifted her eyes to meet Ramona's across the table. Neither said another word about it.

• • •

"Now," said Ramona, pulling several shopping bags closer to the armchair and gesturing for Sal and Melvina to sit down, "I know I got here a little later than I said, but I figured someone had to outfit you two for this expedition."

"Oh, no," said Sal, rolling her eyes.

"What'd you get?" chirped Melvina, leaning forward.

"Well, first of all, I got a few things for you, our un-luggaged friend. You can't wear those clothes forever, especially if Sal's going to permit herself to be seen with you."

"I guess so," agreed Melvina, looking uncertainly at Sal.

"So-o-o, I got a few changes of clothes. Little things, you

51

know, like underwear? Let's see, here's a pair of corduroys, and a few shirts. And here's a jacket."

"Jesus Christ, Ramona," interjected Sal.

"I know, it's just that it could still get cold, and you *are* headed north...."

"I wasn't talking about the jacket. Although you're right, New York can't be more than one, two hundred miles from the Arctic Circle."

"Come on," said Ramona. "Look, Mel, this one's reversible, see? You can be plaid if you feel plaid, or solid if you want to."

"That's really nice," said Melvina, "but you shouldn't...."

"Unlike some people," said Ramona with a look toward Sal, "I do remember what it's like to be young and impoverished. I mean, I was never young, impoverished, and in possession of a twenty-thousand dollar car, but then...."

"An *ugly* twenty-thousand dollar car," added Sal. "I don't know how you expect me to get into that...."

"Don't say another word, Sal, I've got just the thing." Ramona burrowed in a shopping bag. Sal groaned. "Aha! Here it is, Sal, just what you need for this trip."

Sal turned to Melvina. "She always does this. She always has to get me something bizarre and insist I take it with me."

"No! This isn't bizarre. This is *essential*. You said you're worried about someone seeing you riding around in Mel's car. You said you thought you'd die of embarrassment. Well, what could make you feel more at home than—a pith helmet!"

"This is absurd," muttered Sal, shaking her head. "How did I ever get myself into this?"

"What is it?" asked Melvina.

"It's a safari hat. Isn't it great? Look at it, Sal. It'll go with the leopard skin seat covers."

"*Nothing* goes with the leopard skin seat covers. Even the *car* doesn't go with the leopard skin seat covers."

"But *this* will."

"This is silly," said Sal to the ceiling.

"Life is silly, Sal. It's time you got used to that."

"The fact of this trip is just becoming real to me," remarked Sal sadly.

"Oh, you don't understand. It's all psychology. If you ride down the street in a vehicle that strange, people will stare at you. But if you just carry it a little further, dare to be a little crazier, people will figure you know what you're doing—they'll defer to your eccentricity."

"Sure," said Sal.

"Really?" asked Melvina.

"Absolutely," stated Ramona.

• • •

The cassette was coming to an end. Melvina pushed a button that moved the back of the driver's seat to a position more nearly perpendicular to the ground. She sighed. It was a beautiful day for driving, sunny and clear, yet not too warm. It was all too easy to be lulled into a reverie by the warm sun and the unbroken highway. Melvina leaned over and flipped on the CB. The screamer was still going at it, tying up the airwaves with squeals and cackles. A disgruntled male voice broke in momentarily, barked, "Will someone please pluck that chicken?" Melvina smiled and glanced over at Sal, who was scowling at the radio. Melvina switched it off, cancelled the cruise control, and pulled out smoothly to pass a slow-moving car.

There was a scratching noise in the cat box behind the seat and then Dadavi emerged, hopping into Sal's lap and proceeding to give herself an end-to-end bath. Watching Sal out of the corner of her eye, Melvina thought she saw the kitten receive a surreptitious caress. She grinned as she reached over to switch the cassette back on. A country instrumental began, driven by a catchy backbeat. Sal turned her head toward the window.

Melvina made a face and wished Sal had let her put the top down. She was not sure bringing her was such a good idea.

"Kind of quiet, aren't you?" asked Melvina.

Sal did not turn. "Just enjoying a quiet sulk."

"Why'd you come, anyway?"

"Don't ask me. I'm not sure I could tell you."

Melvina did not reply. She wondered how difficult people always managed to find their way into other people's beautiful days. "Look, since you're here, why don't we make the best of it, huh? Is there anything I can do to make you feel better? Would you rather drive?"

"This? No, thank you. Your driving may be—exciting, but I think I'd rather the suicide seat to the wheel."

Melvina nodded wearily.

"On the other hand, I really wouldn't mind if you threw that tape out the window."

"You don't like it? Why didn't you say something before?"

"Before? I didn't mind it the first time. In fact the second time could be chalked up as a kind of sociological experience, but the third, and now, the fourth...."

"Good driving music," grumbled Melvina, ejecting the tape.

"Thank you. I was on the verge of submerging myself totally in the Country Experience, whipping your poor cat into a rough semblance of a Dan'l Boone hat...."

"Okay, that's enough. I took it out. Listen, I've got the feeling you don't like me very much. I wondered about that before, but...."

Sal was quiet for a moment, then resumed her former tone. "Me? Not like you? I who adore the very toes you step on?"

"Very funny. Come on, why don't you just say what you really think?"

"What I really think? Or what I'd really think if, in fact, I didn't like you?"

"Whatever," said Melvina.

"All right. Let's see. Let's suppose that I didn't like you. Let's assume, hypothetically of course, that I hated your guts. Let's see, why would that be? Would it have anything to do with the way you breezed into town and wrought havoc in the lives of everyone you've touched? Could it have anything to do with the puerile and cloying manner in which you hang on my good-hearted, if foolhardy, friend Ramona? Do you suppose it'd have anything to do with your generally manipulative and dishonest manner of dealing with others?"

"I think that's enough," mumbled Melvina.

"So do I."

Melvina shot a look at Sal. "I don't think I'm such a bad person. I don't think I'm dishonest and I don't think I'm manipulative. I'm sorry if I've messed anything up for anyone, but I certainly didn't know, and didn't mean to do anything like that."

"Uh-huh," said Sal disinterestedly.

"Look, I'm sorry you don't want to be here. But *I* never asked you. I never even hinted. I know it sure as hell wasn't your idea, and I'm sorry Ramona talked you into it. I wish she didn't."

"What you mean is, you wish Ramona had come instead."

"Maybe I do! So what?"

Sal paused, continuing in a softer tone. "So, I don't know which is worse. Watching her tolerate your adolescent infatuation, or watching her sniff around after that dark horse darling of American journalism."

54

Melvina shook her head. "You ever been thrown out of a moving car? Jesus, where do you get off talking like that? First of all, I don't have any sort of 'adolescent infatuation,' whatever the hell that is. Secondly, Julie is a friend of mine, and I don't like that remark you made. Sometimes, Sal, I think you're a goddamned bigot."

Sal shook her head ruefully, laughed to herself, "A bigot, huh? You think *I'm* a bigot. Ten minutes, two days out of the sticks and you think you know enough to decide who's a bigot? Well, let me set you straight: you're right, I'm a bigot. I'm the worst, the best bigot you're ever going to see. And you know why? Because I don't climb up on my high horse and go around preaching some sort of bullshit liberalism at everyone. All I know is myself. I know exactly where my bigotry begins, and exactly where it ends. I make no bones about it, I tell no lies—to myself or anyone else. And that's something. Because I'll tell you: there's no one in this country, not one person, who isn't a bigot. White, black, it makes no difference. We all get it just the same, from the first goddamned moment we fall out of the womb. Hell, if the stones had ears, they'd be bigots, too. About color, about religion, about sexual preference and sexual positions. So don't you get up on your little soap box and start in on me."

Melvina was staring straight ahead at the road, her hands clenching the steering wheel. A cord in her neck looked ready to pop, but she did not say a word.

"Look," said Sal after a few minutes. "Look, I'm sorry. You're right, I'm wrong. Julie's a fine person. It's not her, it's—I'm just upset this morning. Nothing to do with you, it's something that happened at the apartment."

Melvina caught her eye. "Upset 'cause Ramona caught you at the old coo coo ca-choo?" Melvina made a crude gesture with her right hand, the fingers splayed out and bent, the thumb jerked toward her lips. Sal winced visibly. "I didn't miss that. And I haven't missed how you are with Ramona, either. I may not know as many big words as you, but I hope you don't forget that there's a big difference between being ignorant and being stupid."

Sal frowned, mumbled, "You could have fooled me."

"Watch it," warned Melvina. "We can be nasty or we can be nice. I think the choice is up to us."

55

• • •

A half hour later, Sal spoke. "You ready for a truce?"

"Yup," said Melvina, nonchalantly putting her tape back into the player.

"Well," said Sal, suppressing a little annoyance, "you just missed the exit for the Holland Tunnel."

"I know. I didn't want a tunnel."

"Why not?"

"Well, this is the first time I've ever been to New York. This is a big moment for me. I want to go over a bridge, I want to yell hello to everyone in New York, I want to yell hello to Peter Nero...."

"Who's Peter Nero?"

"He's a piano player. I heard him play 'Porgy and Bess' on a record—it made me cry. He lives in New York. He was in a movie called *Sunday in New York*."

"Oh. Is that the same Peter Nero who conducts the Philadelphia Pops?"

Melvina shrugged. "Maybe he commutes."

"He'll never hear you."

"Of course he'll hear me. I mean, it's not every day you ride in triumph over the George Washington Bridge, take New York by storm. He'll know. It's the thought that counts."

"Sure. Maybe he'll just happen to be hanging off the bridge by his thumbs, and he'll hear you and it'll make his day."

"Oh, come on. Don't be a spoilsport. Isn't there anyone you want to yell hello to?"

"Offhand? Let me consult my address book."

They were silent until Melvina stopped the car in line for the toll booth.

"Well, thought of anyone yet?" asked Melvina, flipping aside levers over the sun visors.

"Not really. I suppose you could yell hello to Kate Millett for Ramona."

"Who's Kate Millett?" asked Melvina, pushing a button on the dash.

"She's—oh, it doesn't matter. Even Ramona's entitled to a crush now and then. Hey, what are you doing?"

"The top," said Melvina, grinning, "is going *down*."

"Please, Melvina, not that. I don't want to drive around New York in this thing with the top down. We'll get killed. I'll be embarrassed. Dadavi will be blown away by the wind."

"Uh-uh," said Melvina, reaching in the back seat. "Just put on your pith helmet and try to think of someone to yell hello to."

"Oh, come on, Mel."

"Nope. Hang onto Dadavi. Here we go. Got a person?"

"Oh," said Sal, disgruntled, "if you must. Andy Warhol."

"Who's he?"

"The only person I can think of who'd be utterly indifferent to inclusion in such a bizarre ritual."

"Okay," shrugged Melvina, paying her toll and accelerating the car. "Look at that!"

"Look at what? The Palisades?"

"Whatever. Just everything. I mean, I can't believe it. We're actually going to New York. Wa-hoo! How ya doin' Peter Nero! Come on, Sal, you can help."

"No I can't, I've got to hang onto my helmet."

"Stop ducking down like that. Let go of Dadavi. She'll be okay—she's used to this. We're right in the middle of the bridge. Hello, New York! Hi, Peter Nero! Hello, Kate Millett!"

Sal braced herself in her seat, feeling unreal as they sped along beneath a bright sky, high above the gray river. She gaped at the high towers of the bridge, cartwheeling over her head; she closed her eyes just as they reached the other side, plunged downward into a dark tunnel, heard the echo of Melvina's final shout, "How ya doin' Mr. Warhol-ee-ol-ee-ol!"

8

Lowdown in Uptown

As Melvina came down the block, she tried to catch Sal's eye. No luck. Sal was gazing fixedly at the other side of the street. Melvina sighed and lowered her chin until it pressed against her chest. She slapped her feet down on the pavement, examining her shoes as she walked.

She was dizzy from craning to look at the buildings they had passed. The skyscrapers played tricks with a small-town girl's sense of height and distance: if she stood two streets from Pelmer's drugstore back home, it looked the same size as some of these monsters viewed from a mile away. Melvina shook her head, trying to clear it. *Right now,* she thought, *Laura feels about as close as Pelmer's.* By the time Melvina reached the car, she found herself wondering idly whether Laura really existed—or whether she was just the comforting fantasy of a troubled mind.

Melvina opened the door of the Cadillac and climbed in.

"What's the matter? No one home?"

"Worse," said Melvina, starting the car, "someone was."

"Look," said Sal, glancing nervously across the street, "we'll have to plot strategy on the move. Let's get this thing in gear."

"What's the hurry?" Melvina was leisurely sliding the shift into reverse.

"I told you before, you don't dally around fire hydrants. He said we'd better be gone by the time he came back."

"Cop?"

"Uh-huh." Sal looked over her shoulder as they pulled out.

"I think you're overreacting." Melvina stopped at the corner, frowned down the cross streets. "Where now? What do we do?"

Sal sank back in her seat. "What happened? Who was there?"

"Not Laura. Some girl talked to me over the intercom."

"Are you sure you buzzed the right place?"

"Oh, yeah. The girl recognized her name. She said Laura moved out a couple of months before she moved in. She didn't

58

know her personally and the other roommates weren't there. She did say she thought Laura works for a publisher."

"Right," nodded Sal. "That's what the alumni office told me."

"Where do you suppose she moved this time? Seattle?"

Sal gave Melvina an almost sympathetic look. "Come on. People move all the time in the city. Maybe she got a raise, had a fight with a roomie, moved in with a friend—who knows?" Melvina stared grimly at the dashboard. A horn honked. "First of all, you're holding up traffic—and secondly, I don't go in for role reversal. *I'm* the cynic around here."

Melvina flexed the corners of her mouth momentarily and drove through the intersection.

"That's better. Now listen, this calls for regrouping, a new plan of attack." Sal wrinkled her forehead. "I've got a friend in publishing.... She might help us get a line on Laura. As I understand it, those people switch jobs more often than Dadavi falls asleep."

Melvina looked at Sal hopefully and reached out to stroke the cat curled up between them. She scooped up the unprotesting creature and perched her on her shoulder. "So, what's the game plan?"

"Well, next phone booth you see, stop and let me out. I'll make a few calls, see if I can find us someplace to stay."

Melvina nodded. When she stopped the car, she asked, "How long is this going to take?" Sal shrugged as she climbed out. "Well, where am I supposed to park?" Melvina called after her.

"Just drive around the block." Sal turned and smiled. "And try not to look conspicuous."

"Drive around the block?" yelped Melvina. "I don't know these streets, one-way here and dead-end there and—I may never find you again!"

Sal rolled her eyes up and to one side, thought about it, and smirked. "I could never be that lucky," she remarked as she turned toward the phone.

Melvina sighed and put the car in gear. The afternoon was still sunny, although the blue sky looked hazy through the airborne effluvia of the city. The shadows were just beginning to lengthen, and it amazed her that she could drive down one street, all sunshine and warmth, and then turn a corner onto a street completely shadowed by tall buildings. She tried to wrap her mind around the idea that the entire population of Tradewater Crossing could easily be stuffed into just a few floors of one of these huge structures, but she had to give it up. It was like trying to imagine the speed of light.

As Melvina feared, driving 'around the block' was no simple matter. She traveled ten blocks to get back where she started, and the first time she tried, her mistakes cost her an extra four blocks. The trip was fascinating, filled with bustling impresarios and sauntering lovers, old men bent over checkerboards and young kids vaulting hydrants. There were the purposeful strides of those between destinations and the studied casual stillness of those loitering with no place to go. She caught the self-absorbed gaze of a teetering wino, the quick suspicious glance from under the babushka of an old woman, her face a mask of intricate lines. She caught, too, the sultry, defiant stare of a young man, lounging on a corner, his dark eyes burning from under hooded lids, every muscle and feature of his magnificent body straining against the thin cloth that covered it.

By the time Melvina circled twice around the streets, her eyes and imagination were filled to their limits. What at first delighted or dazzled or startled her, now pushed itself against eyes that ached, a mind that longed for a quiet, dark place in which to digest it all. Melvina pulled over by Sal and honked.

Impatiently, Sal waved her on, and Melvina thought that if a car could trudge, hers would be doing it. On her third circuit of the area she saw a small troop of children making their way home from music lessons, lugging all manner of instruments. In *her* hometown they would have been carrying clarinets or flutes if they were girls, trumpets or trombones or even a sousaphone if they were boys. But here in this strange world the instrument cases were like none she had ever seen. Were they cellos? Saxophones? And what could that one be? Melvina felt a kind of embarrassment that here she was, twice as old as some of them, and she had no idea what was in the cases they were carrying. *I guess I don't know much,* she thought. She smiled sadly. *And most of what I do know isn't worth knowing.*

She passed the strange young man on the corner once again, and as she slowed to turn, she thought she saw him wink at her. She looked away, confused, ashamed. *Maybe it's the car,* she thought, glancing back in the rearview mirror in time to see him uncross his folded arms, turn to speak to a well-dressed man who walked up to him.

When she pulled up by Sal this time, Sal, still on the phone, motioned her to wait. Melvina drummed her fingers on the steering wheel. Hearing a car honk behind her, she tried out a gesture she had seen another driver use. The car's engine gunned as it pulled out to pass her. The driver gestured at her with his middle finger. Melvina shrugged and wondered what the gesture she had used meant.

Sal hung up the phone and got into the car. "Okay, where's our map?"

"Where are we going?"

"Well, *you're* going to stay with Sue White—remember, she used to be my student? And I'm...."

"Wait a minute. Is that the one you call Ralph?"

"Uh-huh. Lovely girl. I'm sure you'll have a much better time with her than with me and a bunch of old reprobates."

"But how come we're not going to the same place?"

"Calm down. Liz and Kate—Liz is the one who can get us a line on the publishing house—well, they don't really have room for both of us. New York apartments aren't very big, and anyway, we haven't seen each other in a long time. I figured you'd just as soon stay clear of the reunion. So-o, I gave Susan a call, asked her if she'd mind putting you up, showing you the town...."

"You mean putting up with me, don't you?"

"Oh, come on. This is going to be fun."

"For who? I mean, what's going on here? Are you just trying to get rid of me?" Sal smiled and patted Melvina's knee, started to speak and then thought better of it. "Well?" demanded Melvina. "I mean, first you and Ramona spend half an hour telling me what a weird person this Sue is, and then you decide, on the spur of the moment, to dump me off on her. Is this a joke?"

Sal sat back. "Why, Melvina Skittle, I do believe you're feeling a little—scared?" Sal cocked an eyebrow, brought her face closer to Melvina's. "Is New York a little overwhelming, small-town girl?"

Melvina stared at the steering wheel. "Yeah, it is. And the idea of you taking off. And this business about this woman. I don't know her! I mean...."

Sal shook her head. "I'm afraid there's a little confusion here. Ramona and I were just carrying on. There's nothing wrong with Susan. She's a perfectly nice human being. We were just joking about her political views, that's all. Honest. She's only got *one* head."

Melvina said nothing.

Sal sighed. "Listen, you don't understand. This is the day and age of the lesbian feminist. Me, *I'm* the dinosaur. Hell, even Ramona's more up on things than I am. You don't understand. We grew up in a different world. Most homosexuals were too busy feeling like freaks to—to do much more than try to find a little love in a hard world, try not to feel too ashamed." She looked away. Melvina was silent.

"So many of the people I knew—we were desperate for self-respect, but it never occurred to us to demand it. I think the gay movement is great, a wonderful thing. There's only a couple of things that bother me. One is that when I hear the RALFs, excuse me, the radical lesbian feminists, going on, I always get this weird feeling. Like they're from another planet. I mean, I once heard this gal arguing that for her, saving the whales was as integral a part of her definition of a lesbian feminist as anything else. Saving the whales? Jesus, I can't even save myself. It's like they have to tie everything in the universe into one big ball, you know what I mean? After a while, it starts to sound like some sort of elaborate, gigantic rationalization. Like if they spend all their time quibbling over what new causes to include, what P.C. practices to dictate, they won't have to notice that they're lesbians, you know what I mean?" Sal looked at Melvina.

"What's 'pee-see?'"

"'Politically Correct,' can you believe that?" Sal shook her head. "I met another woman at a party, she told me that her identification as a lesbian had nothing to do with her sexual preference. That's right, she said that given her feminist consciousness and the values to which men in our society have been acculturated, she was politically impelled to adopt a lesbian position."

Melvina looked puzzled.

Sal nodded. "I'm not making this up. Can you believe that?" Sal laughed. "I'm afraid I was a little under the weather at the time...."

Melvina smirked. "An unusual thing, I'm sure."

"Well, I said to her, 'Do your politics require that you have orgasms with women or only that you fake them?'" Sal laughed again.

"I think you've lost me," said Melvina.

"Forget it. I don't know. It's just that the pendulum swings, it always does. One week the *Village Voice* gets into leather, and every C.P.A. from here to Hoboken climbs into chains. Then the next week—Don't you see? Everybody's yelling, 'Come out, come out, wherever you are!' Only that's *this* week. Where will they be when all hell breaks loose, when all those pretend liberals get tired of gay lib? Hmm? There'll just be the same old crowd, the old dykes with all their distastefully incorrect political attitudes, the same old scapegoats who, if you ask 'em why they're dykes will just look at their shoes and tell you that, well, women turn them on.... You know what I mean?"

"I guess so." Melvina hunched cautiously over the steering wheel. "Uh, what does this have to do with Sue?"

"Nothing, I guess. I just wanted to present my position before she gets ahold of you."

"If you're so worried about her poisoning my mind, why are you leaving me with her?"

Sal shrugged. "You miss the point."

Melvina glanced over at Sal, found herself looking for a telltale bulge in Sal's jacket, a flask, a pint bottle of something. "You're a little less coherent than when you got out to make the phone calls."

Sal shrugged again. "Tired."

"I know what you mean. Where are we going?"

"Oh, yes, make a right up there."

Melvina said nothing. She felt annoyed with Sal, with Laura, with Sue—whoever she was—possibly with the entire city of New York. She felt again the need for a dark corner, some safe place where she could digest the experiences of the last two days, get used to the idea she was not going to find Laura right away, get used to the idea she was going to stay with some strange person named Sue.

Sal lit a cigarette. "Let me explain it another way."

Melvina kept her eyes on the road and waved Sal away with one hand.

"No, this is much more straightforward. There are just two kinds of lesbian feminists you have to watch out for: RALFs and DRELFs. RALFs aren't too bad. They figure that lesbianism would be fine if they could just get the sex out of homosexuality. They're trying, in collectives and communes all over the country, to change homosexuality into homobanality. See? They're just a little top-heavy, intellectualizing. And they're annoying because they're against everything I believe in."

Melvina held back for a few moments and then sighed. "Okay, I give up. What's that?"

"Easy: smoking, sex, meat-eating, and elitism."

63

"Uh-huh." Melvina shook her head, "I had to ask, didn't I?"

"DRELFs, on the other hand, they frighten me," continued Sal. "DRELFs—that stands for *Dread* Lesbian Feminists—are another thing altogether. They have absolutely no sense of humor. They are utterly serious, totally political animals. And I'll tell you something. A politician who isn't in it for the money is the most deadly creature on earth."

"Of course," replied Melvina numbly.

"I'll even bet," mused Sal, "that it was the right-wing counterpart of a DRELF that thought up the neutron bomb. Had to be.... People get grossed out by S & M, but I'll tell you, you take the sex out of S & M, and what you get is an extremist, right or left. Doesn't matter. *They* scare the hell out of me...."

Melvina hunched further over the steering wheel, listening to Sal go on about RALFs and DRELFs and hoping that this person Sue just would not be home when they got there.

• • •

Melvina was not much experienced in such matters, but the building they entered seemed very plush. "Is this where she lives?" she asked incredulously while they waited for the concierge to phone upstairs.

"She's taking care of her parents' apartment. They're off on a trip," muttered Sal with annoyance, turning her attention to the man at the desk.

Melvina stepped back and looked around. It was not a new building, but whoever had refurbished it had kept all the old grandeur intact. The marble had the burnish and slight hollowing that comes with age. The high mirrors and full chandelier were lovely but quaint, somehow, remnants of a craftsmanship rarely affordable anymore. Melvina nudged Sal. "This isn't a hotel?"

"No," said Sal, directing Melvina toward the elevator.

Melvina was quiet on the way up, suddenly aware of her jeans and sneakers, chiding herself for feeling cowed by the wealth and politics of someone she had not even met.

"Hey," said Sal, squeezing her arm, "it's not so bad. Really. I promise you, Liz will help us track her down. You'll have a chance for a little R & R, and then we'll go see Laura."

Melvina nodded, tried to smile. Idly, she wondered if she could sneak off and spend the night in the car.

The woman who opened the door did not match the lobby. She

was barefoot and wore a T-shirt that proclaimed 'Women's Music!' from under a baggy pair of overalls. Her face looked haggard. Her hair was close-cropped and nondescript. Her most remarkable feature was the very blue, almost luminous, eyes, which burned out of her pale face. "Dr. Deevers!" she exclaimed, hugging a surprised and stiff Sal.

"Uh, Sal," said Sal.

"That's right. And you must be Melvina?" Melvina received an apprizing clasp of the shoulders. "Well, come in. What have we here?" she asked, taking the shopping bag Melvina proffered in confusion.

"Uh, a cat box."

"Oh?" inquired Sue, looking puzzled, peering into the bag.

"This goes with it," blurted Melvina, reaching inside the jacket Ramona had given her and surrendering Dadavi. "Is it okay?"

Sue smiled and cuddled the kitten. "Well, I'm supposed to be allergic to cats, but I won't tell if you won't."

"I'm sorry," said Melvina, examining her shoes.

"No, really, it's all right. It's a joke, kind of. My sister always wanted a kitten and my mother told her we couldn't get one because I was allergic." Sue laughed and shook her head. "How was I supposed to know? It wasn't till I moved out on my own that I ever got close enough to a cat to find out I wasn't."

Sal laughed. Melvina furrowed her eyebrows. "You mean you weren't?"

Sal elbowed her. "You'll have to forgive Melvina. I think she's a little overwhelmed by our whirlwind trip."

Sue patted Melvina's shoulder sympathetically and suggested they sit down.

"No, look, thanks," said Sal, turning toward the door, "but I told Liz I'd meet her for a late lunch. I hate to just drop in and run like this, but I'll be back tomorrow afternoon or the next morning, depending on how our sleuthing goes."

"Great. You'll keep us posted?"

"Sure. Well, bye Mel. Take good care of her, Sue." And just like that, Sal was gone.

"Whew," said Melvina. "I feel like *Around the World in Eighty Days.*"

"I know, that's how I always get sick. I get involved in too much, all at once, run around like a wind-up toy, and then...." she paused to make a noise like a motor running down, "crash."

Melvina chuckled. "Sounds like me. Only I don't get sick.

Just bitchy and confused."

"I was going to offer you tea, or soup. On the other hand," Sue cocked her head to one side, "you look like what you really want is to lie down for a bit."

Melvina smiled gratefully. "That'd be terrific."

"Okay, why don't you lie down on the couch and I'll get you an afghan. Did you pass on tea or would you like some now?"

"How about after I wake up? Hey, this is really nice of you. I mean, you look like you've been sick and all, and I...."

Sue shook her head. "It's a relief to stop playing invalid. Now I get to play hostess instead. The only hard part's going to be letting you take a nap without talking your ear off. I've been cooped up here for quite awhile, and," she shrugged self-deprecatingly, "I don't usually get the chance to meet a friend of Dr....Sal's. I must admit, I'm bursting with questions."

Melvina laughed. "Well, thanks."

Sue wrinkled her nose and waved Melvina off toward the living room.

Melvina felt all at once the weariness she carried. Stretching out on the couch was a tremendous relief. When Sue came in with a blanket, Melvina managed a lazy smile. She wanted to make a joke about the carpet, but she was already half-asleep. Her last thought as she snuggled down happily under the covering was that, of the frequent surprises in this world, some at least were nicer than she expected.

9

Deep Muscle Massage

When Melvina woke, the last rays of the afternoon sun were sliding off her feet. The couch was set along one wall of the living room, at a right angle to the windows. Across the room, sitting cross-legged in an upholstered chair was Sue, bathed in a pool of light from a floor lamp that arched above her. Melvina ran her hands over her eyes and propped her head on her arm, watching Sue read.

The chair seemed to be carpeted with books and papers. Under it all sat Sue, two pencils stuck behind one ear, perusing a book with a ferocity Melvina had never before witnessed. Her brows were furrowed, and across her face paraded a series of expressions too numerous for Melvina to catalogue. Often Sue would rest the book more heavily against her leg, reaching out with her left hand, which held a third pencil, to make notations on the pages of the book itself. Her writing ranged from quick hard slashes to thoughtful checks, from what might be pensive questions to what looked more like outraged exclamations.

Melvina sighed and grinned, feeling truly edified. Here was the way to read a book! Read a book? No, more like do battle with it, bring to it all the gusto and passion the author had lovingly poured into her work. It had never occurred to Melvina to read a book that way, but rolling onto her back and interlacing her fingers behind her head, she resolved that this was something she must learn.

"Oh, you're awake!" exclaimed Sue, looking up as befuddled as if it were she who had just awoke. In her instant of confusion, Sue dropped her pencil and began rooting around in the cushions as she added, "Just a few minutes and I'll be done."

Melvina rolled onto her side, propping herself on her elbow. She chuckled, feeling both protective and fond of Sue, wanting to needle her just a little. "Lose your pencil?"

"Yeah," Sue looked up, flashed that apologetic smile once again, "don't worry, it's in here somewhere. I'll find it."

67

A pile of loose papers, jostled by her knee, fluttered to the floor.

Melvina grinned. "Wouldn't it be easier to use one of the others?" She flicked the top of her own ear with her free hand.

"Huh? Oh!" Sue felt the pencils behind her ear, rolled her eyes and shook her head. "Clever, huh?"

"Clever to have spares," observed Melvina gallantly.

"Yeah, well, Pat always says that if I ever lose anything, like a two-by-four, I should check behind my ears."

"Pat?" inquired Melvina.

"My lover." Sue went back to her book, leaving Melvina feeling mildly chagrined—and wondering why.

Melvina got up, stretched, and asked where the bathroom was. By the time she got back Sue was collecting her books.

"See? All done. While you've been sleeping, I've been busy. I knocked off another chapter of that dreadful book, and even immortalized you in pencil."

"Me, in pencil?"

"Yeah, let's see, where did I put you?" Sue went back to her pile of papers and picked through the stack. "Here you are...now don't laugh. My attempts at drawing are rather, uh, impressionistic." She handed Melvina a page torn out of a notebook, where in bold line and delicate shading, Melvina lay in repose, an angelic face amid a wild tangle of afghan and curls.

Melvina smiled. "Not bad. I couldn't do that well." Melvina considered the drawing. "In fact, I think you've improved on the basic design."

Sue peered over her shoulder at the sketch and then shook her head. "Nope. Not really. When you sleep you toss and turn, but sometimes you settle down into a truly beatific slumber. When I saw that little cat-smile of yours, I just couldn't resist. Shoved Postman aside and started gawking and doodling."

Melvina could feel her ears redden. She was glad Sue stood behind her where her embarrassment could not be seen. "Nice," said Melvina gruffly, shoving the picture over her shoulder.

Sue laughed lightly as she turned and walked into the kitchen. "You take compliments well. It figures that any friend of Deevers...."

Melvina was not sure whether or not she liked the comparison. "It's nice we have *something* in common," she called after her.

"I didn't mean that negatively," said Sue when Melvina

joined her in the kitchen. "I hold Sal in the highest regard. That 331 course was almost a religious experience for me." She looked to Melvina for some kind of comment.

"I, well, I've never heard her lecture."

"Oh? I thought you knew her from the university."

Melvina shook her head. "We're just friends."

Sue digested this for a moment. "Good, well you can give me all the inside dope. I've always wondered what she's really like. I mean, she's kind of a private person—I only met her once outside school."

"Really?"

"Yeah, one night this friend and I decided to tour the bars." Sue laughed and shook her head, settling her chin on her hand. "We called it our 'sociological survey.' We hit as many as we could. What a trip! We finally closed an after hours club, sloshed to the gills. It was a truly memorable experience. Anyway, we went to this one place, 'Polyester City,' you know, mostly older women. They frown on what they called the 'flannel shirt and hiking boots set.' Us," Sue paused to give Melvina an inclusive pat on the shoulder. Melvina nodded, remembering Bets and the dress code, feeling at the same time mildly traitorous. "Anyway, we got there, looked around, had a drink. It was pretty dead for a Saturday night, and we were about to leave, when *guess* who I saw off at one end of the bar, lurking in the shadows...."

"Sal."

"Yup, she was so well hidden you'd have thought she was travelling incognito, but once we spotted her we had to say 'hi.'"

Melvina smiled, remembering another version of the story.

"She was with this beautiful woman, who was very nice, made us feel right at home...."

Melvina smirked, imagining Ramona's delight, Sal's discomfort.

"What *was* her name? You might have met her—tall, dark hair, long. Probably late thirties, maybe forty—oh, yes, and these really amazing gray eyes, look right through you...."

"That was Ramona."

"Right, that was her name."

"Only she's Sal's age. And her hair's shorter now."

"Really? Well, I guess with the light in there. Is she...?"

"No," said Melvina, "they're just friends."

"Huh, I remember for weeks after that we couldn't get over Dr. Deever's 'friend.' I mean, you have to understand, running into our prof in a women's bar was quite the coup. We'd wondered about Deevers, but Ramona really floored us. We kept saying, 'And here we thought Deevers was so *sedate*....'"

Melvina laughed. "The secret life of college professors."

"Yeah, I mean that was a big deal. You know, I was just coming out then, and it was really nice to think—oh, you know, role models and all that."

"Yeah, I know." It made Melvina feel funny to hear the whole thing from the other side, to realize there was more than one side to the story. She compared her first impressions of Sal with Sue's and wondered at how different they were. "So tell me," she asked thoughtfully, "what's Sal like as a teacher?"

"Wonderful," said Sue as she opened the refrigerator. She took out a tureen of gazpacho. "She's an excellent teacher. That's half of what was so great about finding out she was gay. I learned so *much* from her. She's tough, but she's...well, she teaches you to ask the right questions. I mean, she doesn't publish much anymore, but she's the kind of teacher who turns out really good researchers." Sue ladled the soup into bowls. "She comes on very critical, analytical. She can be funny as hell. I always got the feeling she really had to love what she was doing to do it so well. You know what I mean?"

Melvina nodded, spooning her soup.

"Of course, it figures. You know what they say about being twice as good to get half as far."

Melvina, who did not, nodded agreeably. She was still trying to reconcile her Sal with Ramona's Sal with this very different Sal that Sue had known. She decided she was hungry and gave up.

• • •

"What do you want to do now?"

They were back in the living room: Melvina standing by the windows, watching the streetlights wink on here and there in the distance; Sue in her arm chair, knees drawn up to her chin.

"Hey, Earth to Melvina."

Melvina turned around reluctantly, her hands in her pockets. She worried in some vague way about missing the lights going on.

"You in there?"

"Oh, sure, I...."

"It's okay by me. It's just Sal sort of recruited me to take you around, show you the sights."

70

Melvina shook her head uncertainly. "You sure you're up to it? You look tired."

"Yeah, you're right. This is the most excitement I've had for quite some time."

"Listen, it'd be okay with me if we waited till tomorrow."

Sue smiled. "That's nice of you—but I want you to know I'm not as frail as you think. Why...."

"No, it's nothing like that," Melvina hurried to say. "Look. Two days ago I was just pulling into Philadelphia. Two days before that I was in Kentucky.... I've been an awful lot of places and met an awful lot of people and done an awful lot of things in such a short time. I don't mind a breather. Really."

"Kentucky, huh? I *thought* I detected a slight accent, but here all this time I was thinking, 'South Philly for sure.'"

Melvina peered closely at Sue, straining through the twilight to ferret out how serious she was. There was silence for a few moments. "I, uh...." Melvina began.

Sue spluttered into laughter, like an overfilled balloon giving in to the limits of elasticity. "I'm sorry, that's terrible. You'll have to forgive me. It's just...." Sue was having trouble getting her words out, still carrying on like a hyena.

Melvina, concerned, rushed forward to pound her on the back, switch on a lamp so she could better take stock of the situation. Satisfied that Sue was merely silly, she stood back, arms crossed, and smiled indulgently. "You mean my accent's just a little bit obvious."

Sue nodded, still laughing. She finally got control of herself. "You're a good sport, Mel, I'm sorry. It's just, you know how it is. You don't know somebody, and you're trying to be so *nice,* so *polite*...." Sue started giggling again, held up a hand to signal she was trying to stop. "I—I'm laughing at me, really. I mean, ever since you walked in the door I've been dying to ask you where you acquired that lovely drawl. It's just ridiculous, isn't it? Here we are, two perfectly nice people, and we're tiptoeing around each other like we were live hand grenades."

Melvina got Sue's point and had to smile. "Yeah, I guess you're right. We're being too polite to get to know each other."

Sue nodded vigorously, quelling her outburst. "I mean, here neither one of us, I think, wants to go anywhere tonight, and we can't even say so. You keep telling me why I don't want to go, and I...."

Melvina chuckled. "We're a pair, huh?"

71

"Enough," announced Sue, trying to get out of her chair. Melvina grabbed her under the arms and gave her a helpful yank. "From now on I promise to be more sincere. Maybe less polite, but more sincere." Melvina stuck out her hand to shake on it. Sue saluted. Both laughed. "That's better. Okay, now, what do you want to do?"

"I dunno. Hang around, chew the fat, chomp down some more of that soup of yours...."

"Sounds good. How about some music? What do you like?"

"Oh, anything. I specially like a nice round of country music, mountain music. It's not all *Your Cheatin' Heart*, you know." Sue nodded. "Of course, when my parents got married, my brother Lester told me, they hired this band for the reception everyone said played a really nice version of *Your Cheatin' Heart*. Only thing nobody told them was that *everything* they played sounded like *Your Cheatin' Heart*. Even the bridal waltz. Les said my Mom didn't think that was funny at all."

Sue smiled as she flipped through a stack of records. "Sounds like your brother was there."

"He was. I mean, Lester's my half-brother. My Mom was Lester's stepmother."

"Oh."

"Les and Mom were real close. I mean, Les was only seven when his Mom died. He was nine when his Dad, my Dad, married my Mom. He was very attached to her."

"Was?"

Melvina did not say anything for a moment. Sue paused with a record held delicately between her hands. "My Mom's—dead," Melvina said quietly. She looked at her feet, embarrassed. "I never like to tell people that. They never know quite how to react, and then *I* feel funny."

Sue made a sympathetic face and tossed her eyebrows up. "It's silly for you to feel embarrassed just because other people don't know how to deal with it. I mean, I can understand their reaction. We live in a society that keeps death as far away from us as possible. You know what I mean?"

Melvina nodded. The look on her face was almost grateful.

"And for someone like me, it is hard to imagine. My parents aren't separated or divorced, neither one's died. I don't really know what that would be like."

"Yeah, I see what you mean."

"Not to change the subject, but I think you'll really like this

72

one. Let's see if I can get the needle in the right place. It's kind of neat." Sue lowered the tone arm with a practiced eye. She grinned at Melvina. "How do you like that aim?"

"Great."

"So, what does your Dad do for a living?"

Melvina gave a short laugh and kicked the carpet. "Here we go again."

"Huh?"

"Well, Sue," said Melvina in a deliberately casual voice, "my father was a miner. And he was quite a few years older than my Mom to begin with. Therefore it shouldn't come as too much of a surprise to find out that he died, too."

Sue just looked at Melvina.

"See? Got you. Listen, it's really not as bad as it sounds. I always knew my father was, well, I always knew he had health problems. I was kind'a ready for that." Melvina gave up trying to look at Sue. "I mean, I loved him, he was a good person, but I always knew he was a sick old man."

"What about your mother?" Sue asked quietly.

Melvina took a breath. "She had cancer. In her brain. It took her a long time to..., and they put her in a state hospital, a mental hospital. I don't think there were three people outside the family who ever understood that she wasn't just crazy."

"That's awful," said Sue.

"Well, there are a lot of stupid people in the world, that's all. I think it was worse because she was an outsider. And the other thing, I guess—I don't really know because I was pretty little when it started—was at first, before they knew what was going on, you know, before it was diagnosed. Well, she started acting a little strange, I guess, and, well, you know."

Sue nodded.

Melvina turned around and walked to the window. "Anyway, you can see what I mean about talking about it. I feel kind of apologetic..."

"Why?"

"I don't know. It all sounds so dismal...."

"Look, you've manage to live with it. Why should you feel sorry because someone else asks to hear about it?"

Melvina turned around. "I guess so," she said, shrugging. "It just makes me feel like the—death of the party."

Sue got up from the floor and crossed the room to Melvina. "I feel like giving you a hug."

Melvina accepted the embrace with her hands in her pockets. She smiled. "That's nice."

"So, tell me, is Lester your only brother?"

"Lester's the youngest of my father's first bunch of kids. He's got an older sister and brother."

"What about the second bunch?"

Melvina grinned. "I'm the second bunch. How about you?"

"Two sisters. One older, one younger. We're thick as thieves."

"Yeah, Les and I have always been real close. The other two haven't lived at home since I can remember—they're a lot older." Melvina smiled, rocking back on her heels. "This is some carpet you got here. You ever lose anybody in it?"

"You're changing the subject," observed Sue.

"Uh-huh. I think we've talked enough about me."

"Well, the carpet *is* lovely. I suggest you take off your shoes and walk around on it—or your clothes and roll around—whichever you please, but I wasn't done cross-examining you."

"Oh, really?" Melvina used one foot to pry off the sneaker on the other.

"Yeah, I was going to ask you what your brother Lester does."

"Not much," answered Melvina crisply, dangling her free sneaker from her toes and winging it across the room. She started in on the other one. "And if you don't stop asking me questions, I'm gonna take off more than my sneakers and embarrass you to death."

"Oh, come on," Sue gave her a jovial prod, "tell me about him. Don't get coy on me now."

Melvina winged the other sneaker onto the couch, narrowly missing Dadavi, who woke up, raised her head to look around, and decided it was time to move. Melvina apologized to the cat, cast her arms out wide, Christ-like, and did a most impressive unbroken forward fall onto the rug.

"Are you all right?" In a flash Sue was on her knees next to the prostrate Melvina, who chortled and rolled over.

"How'd you like that, convincing, huh?"

"Amazing," Sue said flatly, frowning, "Where'd you learn that?"

"When we were kids Lester and I were always trying to figure out how stunt men did all those crazy things. Only problem was, we didn't know about those big air mattresses and breakaway furniture and all that. We're lucky we never—broke anything."

74

"You two must have been a barrel of laughs," said Sue sternly, sitting back on her heels.

"Fun, fun, fun," said Melvina, rolling onto her stomach. Then, soberly, "We had some good times." She buried her face in the carpet and began kicking her arms and legs in mock tantrum. "Now will you *puh-leeze* stop asking me all these questions?"

"Okay, okay," conceded Sue, laughing in spite of herself. "You seem wound up like a spring. Maybe what you need is a good backrub."

Melvina stopped flailing her limbs abruptly, turning her face toward Sue as she did so. "You do backrubs?"

"Oh, sure. Backrub's my middle name, didn't you know?"

"Susan Backrub White," said Melvina with feigned pensiveness, rolling the *r*.

"You game?"

"Sure," shrugged Melvina. "Now?"

"Why not?"

"Okay." Melvina made herself comfortable on the rug.

"Let me put another record on."

Melvina watched Sue fuss with the stereo, pausing on her way back to stroke Dadavi.

"Nice cat you have," she said, kneeling next to Melvina and placing her hands experimentally on her shoulders. She then pulled Melvina's shirt up and ran her hands over her back. "Not bad," she announced, "but the bra's got to go. Shirt, too."

Melvina tried to look at Sue out of the corner of her eye as she fiddled with the buttons beneath her. She felt suddenly shy and tried to take her shirt off without moving off the floor.

"Here, let me help. This is kind of like undressing a Barbie doll." Sue tossed the bra onto the couch, and Melvina made a grab for the shirt, pulling it underneath her.

"Rug's scratchy."

"Okay. Hm, pull your pants down a little?"

"What?"

"They cover your lower back."

They cover my ass, thought Melvina, trying to catch a glimpse of Sue's expression. "Is this how they do backrubs in New York?" grumbled Melvina aloud.

Sue chuckled. "Yup, it's called the 'New York Method.'"

Melvina pressed her arms to her sides and waited with all the anticipation of a prisoner on death row.

"You're stiff as a board." Sue shook Melvina by the shoulders.

75

"Let go, will you?"

The inviting warmth of Sue's hands on her back made Melvina even more uncomfortable. "Uh, I am," she lied.

"No you're not."

Melvina resisted for a while longer before she had an inspiration. "Hey," she began, raising her voice over what seemed to her to be the volume of Sue's not altogether gentle ministrations, "would you call yourself a, uh, lesbian feminist. A radical lesbian feminist?"

Sue made faces at the unyielding hardness of Melvina's muscles while she digested her question. "I think that would be fairly accurate," she replied. "Why do you ask?"

"No reason." Melvina contemplated the fact of Sue's lover Pat and recalled Sal's discourses on the asexual inclinations of certain lesbian feminists. Relaxing, she decided that, after all, it was safe to enjoy her backrub.

"That's better!" exclaimed Sue. "I didn't realize my politics were that important to you."

Melvina grunted, feeling the warmth spread from Sue's hands to her back.

"You've got quite a knot in your right shoulder."

"That's the one Dadavi likes to sit on."

"I doubt that's it. Feels like you've been carrying around a lot more than Dadavi." Melvina said nothing. "How long have you had her, anyway?"

"Few months," mumbled Melvina dreamily.

"Is she full-grown?"

"I guess so. When I took her to the vet he said she was around six months. She hasn't grown much of any since. He said she might have been clipped by a car—that or she was shocky from malnutrition."

"Really? She looks pretty healthy now."

"Yeah, but she's kind of a space cadet, you know?"

"Uh-huh. Bring your arm around like this."

Melvina yelped as Sue brought her arm behind her and began kneading under her shoulder blade. She tried to pull her arm back from where it was, but Sue had the leverage. "What are you trying to do?"

"Don't worry. It's called deep muscle massage. It'll do you a world of good."

Melvina gave up. She let Sue prod and nudge and knead her into a pleasant state of semi-awareness. After a while Sue went back to a vigorous rubdown, working her way all around Melvina's back, her upper arms, the sides of her back. Sue's hands never left her. They wore down her resistance until a flow of warmth spread from Melvina's back all through her. It was almost uncomfortably pleasurable.

"Let me try those shoulders again."

Melvina hummed her assent.

"Wait a sec. I need to change my position." Sue swung a leg over Melvina and crouched over her, working on her shoulders and neck.

Sue's closeness had an almost electrifying effect on the unwary Melvina. What had felt warm and relaxed was becoming all at once warm and liquid, a kind of hot and cold running shivers that stood all the little hairs down Melvina's back on end. "I, uh," said Melvina, trying to push herself off the floor.

"Uh-uh," said Sue, who had the better position, pushing her gently but firmly back down, "I'm not through yet."

"But," said Melvina, who felt an honorable sense of urgency to move away from what felt so good and so dangerous.

"It's all right. I'll let you know when I'm done."

Melvina swallowed hard and considered chewing on the carpet. She was beginning to feel weak and rubbery, near melting into the rug. She pulled her hands underneath her chest and made fists of them.

"You're starting to get tense again," noted Sue cheerfully.

"No kidding," mumbled Melvina into the carpet.

"What was that?"

"Nothing."

"Why don't we talk? It might help you to take your mind off your muscles and relax."

"Fat chance," mumbled Melvina, gritting her teeth. She was beginning to wonder where all this was going to lead. Every square inch of her skin felt sensitive and alive, every muscle poised between ecstatic tautness and delirious weakness. Everything inside felt like it was heating up and melting down, seeming to flow toward one or two particular parts of her. "Erg," said Melvina. She worried that she would just implode, right there, underneath the well-intentioned and unknowing hands of Sue White. Would she lose control and turn into some kind of savage sex maniac like she had read about in the scandal sheets?

"So," asked Sue casually, "how long you been out?"

Melvina groaned.

"Pardon me?"

"Awhile," croaked Melvina.

"Are you uncomfortable?"

"No, I'm okay. I guess I'm just not used to that deep massage stuff."

"Oh. Me, I love a backrub. Any kind of massage. I told Pat that if I ever wrote my autobiography I'd have to entitle it *It Began with a Backrub: My Life as a Lesbian*."

"Heh-heh," managed Melvina feebly, glad that Pat was not there to see them.

There was silence for a few minutes while Sue massaged and Melvina endured. "I need a little better leverage for these shoulders," Sue informed her, perching herself on top of Melvina.

Melvina's eyes opened wide, her hands shot out from under her and clutched the carpet. It was too much. Sue's strong hands on her shoulders, the weight of her on Melvina's buttocks moving her rhythmically back and forth. Melvina felt her nipples harden, brushing lightly against the rug. Involuntarily, her back arched a little, and she began to wonder whether she was about to commit a carnal sin with the carpet.

"So," suggested Sue lightly, "tell me about your brother Lester."

Melvina tried to answer her from between clenched teeth. Her first effort came out as a whimper. Then she managed, "What are you, a glutton for punishment?"

Sue gave Melvina a playful tap on the back of the head. "I just want to get to *know* you."

"Uh-huh," replied Melvina.

"Come *on*."

Melvina could feel her breath coming harder now. She decided that talking had to be more decorous than panting. "Okay," she said breathlessly, *"My Brother Lester*, by Melvina Skittle. My brother Lester—is a real swell guy. He always took care of me, looked out for me, especially after my parents...." She trailed off. "Anyway, he had all these big ideas, about how bright I was, how he was gonna get up the money to send me to college. He was really proud of me." Melvina felt a tear in the corner of her eye, wondered idly whether it was sorrow or frustration. She decided it was too dangerous to think about. "Only it didn't work out that way."

"What do you mean?"

"Well, he had an accident." She paused, only to rush on. "You

78

ever hear the expression 'a ton of bricks?' Well, that's kind of what happened. He was out of work, and driving around to different places, you know, looking, and, well, there was this truck and this place where they were building something, you know, and...." She broke off suddenly, remembering the convertible top, the blood. Tears filled her eyes. Sue stopped massaging her, paused with her warm hands pressed gently against her back.

Melvina's voice was very quiet. "The poor guy. It took them awhile to dig him out." She sighed. "His neck was broken. Paralyzed." Sue climbed off Melvina, sat beside her on the floor, one hand still on her back. Melvina felt her tears overflow and sobbed, unsure whether it was for Lester or for the exquisite agony of the backrub, now ended.

"That's terrible," said Sue.

"Yeah, it was," said Melvina bitterly. "There we were. No job, no insurance. Me still in high school. Lester...." She broke off again.

"Could you sue?"

"Sure. We sued. It was their fault. The load wasn't handled right, the equipment was defective, poor maintenance. Oh, yeah, we had them, the whole nine yards."

"So?"

"Big company, little people. Do you know how long those things drag on?"

Sue nodded.

"Lester wouldn't let me leave school. The idea almost killed him. So I went, and I worked. The church ran bake sales for us. We got by."

There was a pause. "Sal said something about a Cadillac, an Uncle Lester?"

"Oh yeah, him." Melvina smiled bitterly. "Lester was named after him."

"Did he help out?"

"Precious little."

"So, what happened?"

Melvina looked at the carpet, shrugged. "I took care of Lester. It wasn't so bad. Broke his heart about college, though. He wanted me out of that town. Typical. I feel bad about him, lying there. He worries about me.... Anywho, the lawsuit finally got settled, a few months ago. Lotsa money. And Les decided it was about time I took a break, got away from it all. He'd been trying to get me to take a breather for years. So-o-o, here I am."

"Here you are," said Sue quietly, running her fingers through Melvina's curls. It felt good to Melvina. She felt embarrassed for her tears, sorry for her brother, and wistful about the frustrated passion, now ebbing from her body. "I'm glad you told me," Sue said.

Melvina shrugged, her face pressed into the carpet.

"I really respect you, you know," Sue added. "You've been through a lot."

Melvina shrugged again, feeling very old, very tired. She focused her attention on the gentle touch of Sue's hand on her head, and before she realized it was happening, she fell asleep.

10

Streetlight Ballet

Melvina woke suddenly, momentarily puzzled as to why she had been sleeping on the floor. The afghan was over her, wool tickling her back, and whatever she had been dreaming must have been pleasant since she found, to her consternation, that she was aroused. She lifted her head gingerly, feeling the texture of the carpet embossed on her cheek, and wondered what time it was.

"Well," said Sue's voice, "I've got to give it to you and Dadavi—you sleep more than any two creatures I've ever met. In fact, you sleep like you haven't slept in years."

Melvina looked up to see Sue curled in her chair, a wine glass in one hand, a book resting carelessly on her lap. "Maybe I haven't. I didn't realize—how long have I...?"

"An hour or so. Are you sure you aren't part cat?"

Melvina smiled and rolled over under the afghan. She sat up with her back to Sue and put on her shirt. It was not until she did so that she noticed how wonderfully fluid the movement was. "Wow. You give a mean backrub." She got up and faced Sue, arching her back appreciatively.

Sue raised her glass, bowing her head to the praise. "See? I told you, I'm expert in these matters. You want a little? It's good for the blood."

Melvina nodded. "So," she called after Sue as she went out to get the wine, "Our Lady of Anemia will drink a little wine and pass up a good, red steak?"

"Bleah," said Sue as she returned from the kitchen.

Melvina took the wine glass and sat on the floor. Sue dropped down in front of her chair, leaning back against it.

"I *am* getting better. Look at how long I rubbed your back."

Melvina nodded. "Thanks again. By the way, I'm sorry...."

Sue leaned forward and pressed her fingertips against Melvina's mouth. "That's enough. You apologize too much." Sue started to move away, but instead slid her hand toward Melvina's neck. Melvina's heart skipped a beat. "Hey, what is this? I couldn't help but notice it."

"Oh," said Melvina unsteadily, glancing down, "that's something a friend gave me."

"Do you mind?" Sue leaned forward to peer at the kestrel, holding it toward the light of the reading lamp. Melvina was pulled forward by the string around her neck. "How beautiful!"

"Yeah," said Melvina. She swallowed hard, too close to Sue for comfort. "My—my friend made it. She's—very talented."

"So detailed! It looks like a tiny eagle."

"No, it's a, it's a kestrel."

"Well," said Sue, releasing the kestrel and Melvina, "it really is lovely. We'll have to get a chain for it tomorrow. On a string you'll lose that for sure."

Melvina sat back, almost dizzy. She agreed with Sue, unaware of what she was agreeing with or to, thinking only that Sue was certainly a beautiful woman, Melvina a cad. She found herself unable to take her eyes off the smooth curve of Sue's neck, her delicate chin, her—Melvina forced her eyes away, drummed her fingers casually on one knee. She felt dangerously close to making a fool of herself. But even as she tried to restrain her feelings, the warmth and scent of Sue, so close only moments ago, returned to torment her.

Melvina realized Sue was speaking, had been for some time.

"I said, 'How long since you saw your friend Laura?'"

"Oh," said Melvina, glad to pick up the drift of the conversation so easily, "years and years."

"Really?" Sue sat back against the chair. "Would you like some more wine?"

Melvina looked down at her glass and saw it was empty. "My goodness," she exclaimed, hoping the wine could account for the surge of feeling inside her. "No, I think that's enough for me."

"You sure? I was going to have just a little more."

"No, really, that's okay. I better not. You go ahead." Sue rose to take their glasses to the kitchen. Melvina sighed as she left the room. She decided she had better get up and walk around.

Melvina paced back and forth, shaking the cobwebs from her head, trying to shake Sue. She felt constrained by the small size of the apartment, and wished she could step out into the cool night air. She stood by the window, gazing out at the city. She watched traffic lights change silently in the distance, a ballet of sequence and color parading down the avenue.

"Hey, you okay?" It was Sue, standing close to her.

"Yeah," said Melvina slowly. "I just like to watch the lights. Listen, it must be late. You don't have to stay up, you know. You can go to bed."

Sue patted Melvina's shoulder affectionately and turned away. When Melvina heard the reading lamp click off, she focused her attention again on the distant lights.

A few moments passed before Melvina heard Sue's breathing near her. She startled. "I thought you...."

"No, I just thought you could see better with the lamp off." Sue rested her chin on Melvina's shoulder, steadied herself by holding Melvina's upper arms lightly. They stood together for awhile, looking out into the night. Sue's nearness started all those strange reactions in Melvina once again, but at the same time she felt very comfortable, very safe. When Sue leaned against her like that, it made Melvina feel strong and capable, protecting and protected. She reached up and patted Sue's hand.

They stood that way a moment longer, and then Sue reached around Melvina and gave her a warm hug. "The lights are beautiful, aren't they?"

Melvina nodded, shoving her hands in her pockets.

Sue stayed as she was, her arms encircling Melvina. "This is nice," she said, and then they said nothing for a long time.

Sue's body slowly relaxed until they were pressed tightly together. Melvina sighed and shifted her weight. Sue let go of Melvina's arms and slowly began to rub them, a movement so light at first as to be almost imperceptible. Little by little, as with gentle waves lapping against the side of a boat, Melvina became aware of Sue's caresses.

"Feels good," said Melvina, who reflected lazily on the idea that there was an awful lot of room for warmth and affection in a simple, nonsexual relationship. Melvina leaned back against Sue just a little, beginning to feel sleepy and relaxed.

She felt Sue's warm breath in her ear, the gentle motion of Sue's hands, moving ever so slowly along her arms, ever so lightly onto her belly—Melvina's eyes opened wide. Her first instinct was to stiffen, arch precipitately away from the electrifying change in her reaction to Sue's touch. She realized that to do so would knock them both off balance, topple them over, and so she forced herself to remain as she was—torn, melting, looking desperately toward the unseeing lights in the distance.

Sue's hands moved over Melvina's abdomen in tentative circles, lightly at first and then more boldly. Melvina held her breath, overwhelmed by the flood of feelings coursing through her, transfixed at the center of the whirlpool, helpless before the sweet twisting sensation somewhere in her belly. She could not believe this was happening to her.

With increasing certainty, Sue's hands traveled over her, flattening out to stroke the outside of Melvina's thighs, curving to trace the lines of her body, cupping tenderly to caress her breasts. "Oh my God," gasped Melvina, stumbling forward.

"What is it?" asked Sue quietly, catching and steadying her.

Melvina pressed herself against Sue, terrified that the touching would stop, terrified that it would continue. "I, I...." she said, her voice unsteady. She swallowed hard. Sue reached up to stroke Melvina's brow, trace the line of her cheek. "I, uh, I don't want to sound stupid," blurted Melvina.

"It's all right," came the soft voice, vibrating warmly next to Melvina's ear.

"It's just I, well, is this like, uh, are you, uh...." Melvina felt Sue's lips brush her shoulder, felt the warmth of a passionate kiss that was almost painful on the side of her neck. "Jesus, I mean—are you seducing me? Is this, does this...."

Melvina heard something behind her that sounded like a chuckle. Her face reddened. For a moment she feared she had just made a complete ass of herself. Sue nuzzled her ear. "I guess you could call it that."

Melvina relaxed for a moment, relieved. Sue stepped back from Melvina, grasped her shoulders, gently turned her to face her. "But wait a minute," said Melvina as Sue began to pull her closer. She felt frightened, all at once, and her mind raced, looking for something to say.

Sue felt Melvina stiffen and stood back. She pursed her lips, put her head to one side. With one hand she reached out to touch the side of Melvina's face reassuringly, said, "Is it all right?"

"I—uh, what about Pat?" asked Melvina triumphantly, relieved to have found something coherent to say.

Sue smiled, looped one of Melvina's curls around her finger. "We have an open relationship," she said.

"What does that mean?"

Sue shook her head as she pulled Melvina toward her. "That means it's okay," she said, dropping her chin, resting her forehead against Melvina's and her arms on her shoulders. "Is something wrong?"

"No," said Melvina quickly. "It's just...," she began more slowly.

"Yes?" inquired Sue, stroking her back.

Melvina felt overwhelmed and confused. She knew she was stalling, she was not sure why. "Well, Sal said," she began, turning her head to one side.

Sue put one finger beside Melvina's chin, turned her face back to look at her. "*What* did Sal say?" her voice was gentle but direct.

Melvina dropped her eyes, smiled nervously. She was beginning to feel very foolish. "Uh, she said that, uh," Melvina sighed. "She said that certain feminists—radical, uh—were trying to take the, uh, sex out of homosexuality, or something like that." Melvina shook her head and looked at the floor. She worried that her stalling had just managed to destroy whatever chance was left that Sue would touch her again.

"Oh," said Sue, resting her chin momentarily on top of Melvina's lowered head. "Well," she said brightly, "I guess you've got a choice."

Melvina looked up at Sue sideways.

"We can stand here and debate the issue..."

Melvina's heart fell.

"...Or," said Sue quietly, taking her hand, "you can come find out for yourself."

11

In Which One of Our Heroines Falls into a Bed

Melvina dreamt she was in a large, dark room filled with books. They were not on shelves as in a library but scattered about in bunches and piles Melvina kept stumbling over and knocking into further disarray. The light was so dim she could not see the titles. She found her way by groping boldly in front of her, hoping she would find what she was looking for—and know it when she found it.

• • •

Melvina was sitting at a table by a boarded window. The table was high and the light was poor. There seemed to be stacks of telephone books in front of her. *Let's see,* she thought, *Laura Maynard.* She looked under the *L*s. *Labido, no...L'Alba, no...Lame, Lane—Lois Lane—no...Laurel, Lauren, Lester, no— this isn't right, not even close.* Then she remembered that was not the way to look it up. *That's right, her last name.* She picked up another book and flipped through the *M*s. *Manhattan, Malaysia, Mexico...What's going on here? This can't be right....*

"Mmm, that's nice."

Melvina opened her eyes. It was still dark. She was lying half off the couch, her left hand under Sue's shoulder, her cheek resting on her stomach.

"Go ahead, go on," murmured Sue. "Do what you were doing."

"I was asleep," said Melvina, confused.

"Sure you were."

"I was! I was dreaming."

"Well, then, go back to sleep," suggested Sue, picking up Melvina's hand and putting it back where it had been a moment ago.

• • •

It was just beginning to get light in Sue's living room when Melvina next woke. "What is it?" she asked.

"You're on the floor again," said Sue, tugging on her arm.

"Again?"

"Never mind. Look, this opens up into a bed."

"That's too much bother."

"No, it isn't.... Or listen, if you want we can go into the bedroom."

"Isn't that your parents' bedroom?"

"Yeah."

"I'll help you pull out the couch."

• • •

"I hate to admit this," said Sue, who was lying on her back with one arm around Melvina, "but I think I'm ready for a nap."

"That's okay," said Melvina, drawing a sheet over them.

"This is decadent, you know. I'm beginning to understand why you sleep so much."

The phone rang.

"Shit."

"Forget it."

"No," said Sue, trying to sit up, "I ought to answer it."

"Nope," said Melvina, throwing her upper body across Sue's, "if you've got the energy for that, I can think of lots better things to do."

"Come on," said Sue halfheartedly.

"Forget it," said Melvina. "If you ignore it long enough, it'll go away."

• • •

"What time is it?"

"I don't know. It's getting pretty dark."

"I'll get up and check the clock."

"No, you don't. I'm not letting you go, even for a second."

Sue laughed. "I've noticed that. You know, I'm having a lovely time," she laughed again, "but there are moments when I wonder about you."

"What do you mean?"

"I don't know. Has someone kept you locked up, or what?"

Melvina peered at Sue through the deepening shadows. She *thought* Sue was joking, but sometimes she was not sure. "It's at least half your fault."

Sue laughed. "Guilty. I just never thought I was that endlessly fascinating."

"Well, maybe you are."

• • •

The telephone rang.

87

"Let me get it. Come on, Mel, it could be Sal."

"Tell her to go fly her own kite," mumbled Melvina.

"Well I will if you'll let me answer the phone."

Melvina shifted her position just a little. Sue groaned. "How do you ever expect me to get this right if you won't let me practice?" grumbled Melvina.

"Right," sighed Sue.

• • •

"Whoa, you've got a whole tray there!"

"Well, I'm famished, aren't you?"

"And wine? You just want to get me drunk so you can have your way with me."

"That was *last* night." They laughed.

"Mm, you worried about crumbs in the bed?" asked Melvina, sitting cross-legged, one hand cupped fastidiously under her cracker and cheese.

"It'll give Dadavi something to munch on," Sue paused to set the kitten in her lap and turned to plump the pillows behind her. "That poor cat hasn't even touched the food we gave her."

"She doesn't eat much," mumbled Melvina, her mouth full. "She's small."

"Eat much, hell, she doesn't *do* much. Is she always like this?" Melvina nodded. "I keep rolling on her."

Melvina shrugged. "She likes to be near you—like me."

Sue tossed her head. "I guess women from Kentucky have wonderful taste."

"You could say that," said Melvina slyly.

Sue stroked Dadavi thoughtfully. "So, were you out back home? Does Lester know?"

"Yeah. He was pretty cool about it."

"Really?"

"Um, it came up once, by accident. I used to go down to the drug store and get him all these magazines. You know, I'd just clean out the shelves. He couldn't go out or anything, so...." Melvina paused to take a bite of her cracker. "We used to look at them together. You know, *Popular Mechanics, Car and Driver, Playboy,* like that...."

"You bought him *PLAYBOY?*"

"Well, actually, I usually got *Penthouse.*"

"That's pretty weird, don't you think? I mean, did he ask you to get those...."

"He didn't *ask* me to get him anything. It's just he gets down a lot, you know? He gets depressed, just lying there like that? I mean, Jesus, he was only twenty-five when it happened." Sue was trying to be understanding, Melvina could tell, but it made her angry Sue seemed to disapprove, somehow, of something as ordinary as *Playboy*. They were silent for a moment. "I remember I showed him this swell article in *FuturScience* about how—ten, maybe fifteen, years from now—they're gonna be able to hook someone like him up to computers, you know, hook his brain to the computer and the computer to his muscles so he'll be able to do everything again, just like he used to...." Melvina trailed off, looking immensely sad.

"It's okay," said Sue, patting Melvina's shoulder. "I understand. I mean, your brother's in a pretty rotten situation and all. It's just—well, I don't really think now's the time to go into it. Tell me what happened."

Melvina rested her elbow on her knee and her forehead on her hand. "Well, anyway. He and I were looking through this—magazine, that's all. And I turned the page, and there were some pictures, I don't know, I just didn't expect them. They sort of took me by surprise. And I, well, I kind of whistled."

Sue laughed. "So what happened then? What did Lester do?"

Melvina smiled a sad little smile. "He just shook his head and said, 'Well, what d'you know?'"

"That was it?"

"That was it. End of conversation. We never talked about it again." Melvina shrugged. "I can't explain it. After the accident, when I was taking care of him, we got really close. I mean, we'd always gotten along, he was always really great to me...but it was different. I mean, I took care of *him*, you know? He needed me. It was like he learned to really trust me, and—like for the first time he saw me as a person, not just his little sister." Melvina paused, looking for words. "We got really close. Like we knew each other inside out, like we didn't even have to *say* anything. You know what I mean?"

Sue nodded. She rested her hand on Melvina's knee, tracing little patterns with one finger. "It must have been hard for you to take this trip."

"What do you mean?"

"Oh, leaving Lester. You really miss him, don't you?"

Slowly, Melvina turned to face Sue. She met her eyes. The look on Melvina's face startled Sue and frightened her. Rage. That was what it was—pure, unvarnished rage. Melvina's hands were clenched into fists, her shoulders hardened and squared. Her voice, when it came, was low in pitch but squeezed out of her lungs with a force that made it hiss: *"Why do you always have to talk about Lester?"*

Sue sat back involuntarily, snatching her hand away from Melvina's knee. She felt the hairs on her neck prickle and stand up. For a moment she dared not speak. When she did, she spoke very carefully, "I don't know what I said, Mel, but I'm sorry. I didn't mean to upset you." She waited, holding her breath.

Melvina's eyes did not move, did not flinch. They converged ferociously on a point just behind Sue, and as Sue watched, the focus slowly shifted, almost imperceptibly, to an imagined point still farther away. Melvina's eyes were glassy.

"Melvina!" said Sue sharply. "Can you hear me?"

Melvina continued to sit as she was for another moment and then, in a delayed reaction, shook her head briskly. She sat looking down at the bed, her head hanging dejectedly, her breathing loud and fast. "I'm sorry," she mumbled.

Sue crossed one arm over her chest, rested the elbow of her other arm on top. Her fingers played absentmindedly around the corners of her mouth. Her brow furrowed. She waited. "Melvina," she finally asked, her voice quiet, "can I hold you?"

Melvina nodded, tumbling gratefully into Sue's arms. Sue gathered her up, tucking Melvina's head under her chin, and held her for a long time. Sue's mind was racing, generating a slew of questions she dared not ask, answers she dared not consider. The motions of comfort were heartfelt, but strangely automatic, preoccupied as she was. She caught herself, finally, staring blankly into a dark corner of the room. She glanced down and noticed that her hand, stroking Melvina's curls, was trembling.

• • •

The phone was ringing. Sue struggled to disentangle herself from Melvina and blunder out of bed toward the phone. Melvina was not sure whether she was dreaming or not. "It's okay," Sue said to her, "I'll be right back." Melvina clutched her pillow and fell asleep.

• • •

"What's that?" Melvina was half awake.

"The door buzzer. I'll get it." Sue was out of bed, throwing on a robe before Melvina understood her words.

"The door buzzer?" exclaimed Melvina, sitting bolt upright in bed, taking in all at once Sue's retreating figure, shimmering in the sunshine. "Who the hell...?"

"Who knows?" called Sue over her shoulder, maddeningly cheerful. "Could be a friend dropping by, maybe my parents back already..." Melvina's eyes opened wide. "...Hell, maybe Pat's flown in unexpectedly... but it's probably Sal."

With each of the possibilities Sue suggested, Melvina's nascent feeling of panic grew. She pictured anonymous friends of Sue's, strolling casually into their impromptu boudoir, chuckling at hayseed Melvina, naked on the sofa bed. She imagined Sue's parents—elegantly turned out, youngish, one of those improbably gorgeous couples out of an ad for an imported liqueur—striding unsuspectingly into their very own living room only to discover their daughter with a—gasp, shudder—lesbian (mother strikes a photogenic pose of horror, father smites his virile bosom with one perfectly manicured hand).

Worse yet, what if the caller were—Melvina clutched the bed sheet to her chest—Sue's lover Pat? Melvina pictured herself, naked and helpless, pitched through the seventh story living room window by an understandably enraged and appropriately gigantic (but brilliant and lovely, Melvina was sure of that) woman. Pat would stand, stricken, among the shards of glass that littered the rug (gulp, *that* living room rug), her arms dangling at her sides, her mighty head bowed. "How—how *could* you?" she would ask Sue before, horrified at herself and her lover's betrayal, throwing herself out the very opening she had created using poor Melvina's body.

Melvina struggled to swallow and failed. She could hear Sue by now, fumbling with the locks on the apartment door. Melvina shook her head numbly. *Or what,* she thought, *if it's Sal?* Without another thought, in expectation of only the inescapable prospect of unendurable embarrassment, Melvina dove under the covers, aiming for the side of the bed nearest the wall. Half by accident and half from a well-honed instinct for survival, she landed between the sheets where they wrapped around the side of the mattress. Being small and lean, she fit snugly between the mattress and the wall, creating only a minor wrinkle in the disarray of the bedclothes.

"Oh, hi," Sue was saying, "come on in. Yeah, I think she's awake. In the living room."

What am I doing here? This is crazy, thought Melvina. But at the same moment she was carefully monitoring her breathing,

91

counseling herself to take slow, inaudible breaths.

"Where did you say she was?"

"In the living room. I.... She was here a minute ago. She must be in the bathroom."

"That's okay. There's no rush."

"Have you had breakfast?"

"And lunch. It's almost two."

"Oh, I...."

Sal laughed. "That's quite all right. You two must have been having quite a time.... Close any bars? You were never here when I called."

"Oh, I'm sorry. How are your friends?"

"I had a very nice time."

"You look a lot more relaxed."

"I am. It's good to get away. Everyone's been telling me I needed a break."

"Well, they were right. Now, what was that you were telling me over the phone?"

"I *thought* you were only half awake.... Liz got ahold of some folks over at the publishing house where Laura was working. It seems she left the job *and* the city..."

"Really?"

"...To get married." There was a pause in the conversation.

Melvina felt a peculiar sensation in the pit of her stomach, a pang rather like the slight twisting of a screwdriver with its blade jammed into her. A moment passed before she wondered at the pause in the conversation between Sal and Sue, sensed a nonverbal significance or communication she could only guess. She felt the urge to scramble forth from her hiding place, pelt Sal with questions, know all of what was going on. She realized she was trapped by the bizarre nature of her actions, and she wondered how the hell she was going to find a graceful way to extricate herself.

"Oh," said Sue's voice, "did Melvina know she was married?"

Melvina could hear the shrug in Sal's reply, "She should have guessed."

"So, where's she living?"

"Somewhere near Boston. The woman who'd know is on vacation for a week. Liz's friend knew that the husband's working over on the eastern end of Connecticut in some sort of defense plant. An engineer or something."

"Hm. So he commutes from Boston?"

"I guess so.... Hey, you know, Melvina's taking a long time in the bathroom, and she's awfully *quiet*."

Melvina could hear the soft padding of Sue's feet and then her voice from a little distance. "Sal? She's not in here. Melvina?" Another moment passed. "And she's not in here, either. Will you take a look in the kitchen?"

There were the sounds of both of them moving around the apartment. They regrouped in the living room. Melvina felt the rest of the sheets and blankets being thrown back on top of her. "Well, what do you know? I leave her here for just *two* days, and you go and lose her. I know she's small, Sue, but *really*...."

"Come on, Sal, I'm not sure this is so funny. Where could she be? She was right here when you buzzed. Let's see, I got up, she said 'Who's that,' I—I *know* she was here. There's only one way out of the apartment, we checked all the rooms...."

"Look, don't worry about it. She has to be around here somewhere."

"But...where? I...could she have passed out somewhere?"

"Wouldn't we have *noticed* her, lying around?"

"Well, where could she be?"

"Take it easy."

"It's just, last night, she got so upset...."

"About what?"

"Well, I don't know. It was just so sudden, she...."

"What happened?"

"It had something to do with her brother. We were talking and—but then she *seemed* okay. I...."

"Look. She has to be here somewhere. If you're really that worried, why don't we take a good look around? You take the bedroom closets, I'll check the kitchen cabinets. Be sure to look under the bed and behind the door."

Melvina heard the sounds of searching again.

"Now, now," Sal's voice was comforting Sue, "don't be upset. Maybe she slipped past us somehow, ran down to the garage to the car."

"Why would she do that?"

"Who knows—maybe she wanted to get a change of clothes or something."

Melvina felt horrible. She wished they would stay out of the living room long enough for her to climb out of her hiding place. The strain of holding herself in so awkward a position was beginning to take its toll, and she could feel herself starting to slide down the wall, pulling out the sheets from under the mattress a little at a time.

"Look, I'll only be a minute. I'm going to throw on some clothes." Melvina heard the bathroom door close.

"Be sure to check the tub!" Sal called through the door, chuckling. Melvina heard another door open and close and then everything was silent.

This is it, thought Melvina, straining her ears against the quiet, *now or never.* Ever so cautiously, she began working her way through the covers, pulling her torso up a little so she could peek out. She scanned as much of the room as she could see. *Good,* she thought. Sal was not in Sue's reading chair, was not anywhere by the windows. She pulled herself up a little more, boldly poking her head and shoulders out from under the covers. *Whew,* she thought.

Behind her head, where the hallway opened into the living room, Melvina heard a sound like a match being lit. *Oh, shit,* thought Melvina, pressing her forehead against the cool of the sheets.

"Take your time, Sue," came Sal's voice. "I *told* you she'd turn up."

Melvina groaned. She lifted her head and twisted around to see Sal standing at the foot of the sofabed, lighting a cigarette. Sal seemed utterly composed, completely unsurprised. The crease in her tan slacks was perfect. Her skin looked dark next to the crisp white of her sports shirt. Her sunglasses reflected back only the flame of the match she held.

Melvina could feel her face becoming redder and redder.

"So," said Sal, flicking the match toward a potted plant by the stereo. The match went out and landed exactly where she had aimed it.

"I don't think Sue's going to appreciate you smoking," said Melvina, trying to reclaim some portion of her dignity.

Sal ignored her remark. "Well, I'm not even going to ask what you're doing there," she began, taking a long drag on the cigarette. "I'll assume that it's—ah—a little too kinky for my refined intellect to comprehend and let it go at that."

Melvina did not feel like Sal would ever let it go. She was reminded of the night at Arlene's, of Sal's obvious enjoyment of the ruckus she had started. Melvina remembered that Sue could emerge from the bathroom at any moment and felt an urgent need to get out of the situation before it got any worse. "Look," she began, half in explanation, half in desperate appeal, "I don't have any clothes on."

Sal craned her head to one side in cool appraisal. "You're right about that. What do you know."

"Could you...?" urged Melvina in quiet supplication.

"What?" said Sal in a stage whisper. "Could this be our very own little Melvina, the nymph-who-knows-no-shame, embarrassed at her own nakedness, enveloped in a kind of, shall we say, *apres-la-pomme* modesty?"

Melvina grimaced.

"Would you like me to turn my back?"

Melvina nodded.

"Leave the room?"

"Yeah," said Melvina gratefully.

"Am I really *embarrassing* you?"

Melvina nodded her head vigorously.

"Well, in *that* case," said Sal cheerfully, strolling over to the reading chair across from the bed and stretching her lanky frame out comfortably in it. "There," she said with satisfaction.

Melvina looked toward the hallway with dread. "You're trying to humiliate me," she hissed.

"Correction," said Sal casually, taking another deep drag on her cigarette and exhaling slowly, "I'm succeeding." Sal paused. "And it couldn't happen to a nicer person—scaring poor Sue like that," she added in mock reproof. She reflected a moment. "Of course, it looks like scaring her was the least of it," Sal gazed pointedly at the rumpled bed. She shook her head. "How could I have done this to poor Sue, bringing you here like that...."

Melvina took a deep breath and pulled savagely at one of the sheets, trying to free it from the other bedclothes, starting to toss it over one shoulder. The strength of her action, however, pulled loose the supports of her own precarious position, and, cursing, Melvina fell down behind the bed.

Sal laughed in spite of herself. "Could you use some help?" she inquired chivalrously.

Melvina's reply, muffled by the sheets, was still decipherably obscene.

• • •

They were standing between the kitchen and the apartment door. Sue's hands were fretting nervously around Melvina's face and collar, wanting to touch her and yet feeling oddly constrained by Sal's presence. "I *did* want to talk to you before you

95

left," Sue said, her brows knit, her face a study of caring and concern.

"I know," said Melvina, dropping her gaze.

"Hey, it's okay, it's just...." Sue's hand darted to the opening of Melvina's shirt. "Oh, I almost forgot."

"What?"

"Well," her voice grew quieter, "we didn't get a chance to get you that chain. I thought—wait a minute." Sue turned and trotted toward the bedroom.

Melvina glanced at Sal, who was leaning against the kitchen counter, her attention absorbed in scratching Dadavi's chin.

"Here we go," said Sue, coming back into the foyer. "Let me see that."

Melvina bowed her head and let Sue remove the string from around her neck. Sal looked up suddenly, putting her head to one side in an effort to see what Sue was holding.

"It's Melvina's little bird," said Sue in explanation, resting the necklace on the counter near Sal while she undid the knot. "I wanted to get her a chain so she wouldn't lose it."

"Let me see that," said Sal abruptly, in a hard voice that startled both Sue and Melvina. Sal fingered the kestrel, holding it carefully at a presbyopic distance. Sue continued to work at the knot in the string, her eyes on Sal. "Huh," said Sal finally, dropping it on the counter. She shot a look at Melvina. "It figures. And here all this time I thought she was busy up there showing you her garbage."

Melvina pulled in her chin giving Sal a surprised and puzzled look. Even as she decided she had no idea what Sal could mean, she had a vague sense that her kestrel was not the first she had seen. She sorted through the least focused of her memories of her time in Philadelphia, haunted by a sense of having glimpsed a tiny flash of silver at the throat of one of the women. Not Sal. Not Arlene, she would have noticed it when they were talking about the kestrel. Who could it have been? Mary? Ramona? Julie? She had no idea. Bets? May? She shook her head, unsure whether she was misremembering a crucifix or just making up something that had never been.

"Well, it's fitting," said Sal, turning away, her tone bitter.

Melvina and Sue looked at each other. "There," said Sue warmly, as if she could cancel out Sal's comment.

"Are you sure you...?"

Sue nodded, reaching around Melvina to clasp the chain, "I

can get another. I like your bird, I don't want you to lose it."

Sal scooped up Dadavi. "Don't mind me," she grumbled, ambling toward the door. "I'll get the elevator."

As soon as Sal turned the corner, Sue threw her arms around Melvina and hugged her hard. "What do you suppose that was all about?" she whispered in Melvina's ear.

Melvina shrugged and squeezed Sue against her. "Who knows," she murmured, "she gets weird sometimes. Poor you. Stuck with all the weirdos."

"No, no, no," said Sue, pulling back, taking Melvina's face in her hands, "Listen, I don't want to get you mad or anything, but I do want to say something. Last night...."

Melvina tried to look away.

Sue held her face more firmly, looking directly into Melvina's eyes. "Listen to me. I thought about it most of the night. I don't know *exactly* what's going on, but—I've gotten to know you, and I feel something here," she touched her chest. "I can feel it. I mean, I don't want to sound like an idiot. But I hope maybe you'll, you know, keep in touch, maybe we can get together again, talk...."

Words failed, and they just hugged and nodded and moved reassuring hands against receptive backs.

"I'm not going to be here much longer," said Sue, "but you can always reach me through my parents."

Melvina made a face.

"All right, then. I'll let Sal know where I'll be, okay?"

Melvina nodded and gazed wistfully at Sue. "I...," she began and then gave it up and just kissed her, amazed at the way the hardness of her passion could melt into such tenderness.

Sal could be heard down the hallway, clearing her throat.

Sue and Melvina stepped back from one another. "Well," said Sue, trying for a casual tone.

"Thank you," began Melvina.

Sue waved the words away. "I just hope you find your friend," she said, then paused. "I also hope you come back."

Melvina nodded. She gathered her jacket and the bag with the cat box in it, daring not to look back until she had reached Sal and the elevator.

12

NY to CT in Six Nasty Comments

"Do you still want to go on with this?"

Melvina made a face at the road in front of her. It was an impatient face, a what-kind-of-stupid-question-is-that? face. "Yes," she said in a bored, emphatic manner, as though she had already answered the question a dozen times before. "What I'd like to know," she went on in a tone not much gentler, "is where the hell we're going and what it is you think we're going to do till that friend of Laura's gets back from vacation."

Sal sighed, her eyes inscrutable behind dark glasses. "Look, I didn't mean to tear you away from anything. I felt kind of bad in the first place, leaving you there like that...."

"Hah," interjected Melvina.

Sal made a clucking noise. "Testy, aren't we? I figure if we're going to have to wait a week while some friend of Laura's goes to a wedding in Florida...."

"Weddings," muttered Melvina darkly.

"It's an occupational hazard, my dear." Sal turned back in her seat, pulled a cigarette pack out of her coat. "In fact," she added airily, "I was rooting for yours." She paused to hunch over the match she had lit. With the cigarette still unlit, the match went out. She tossed it into the ashtray, "Could you roll up that window for a minute?"

Melvina made a deprecatory noise as she started to reach for the window control.

"I wasn't raised lighting these things on street corners."

"Give me that." Melvina snatched the cigarette out of Sal's hand. Keeping one hand on the wheel, she lit the cigarette with exaggerated ease. "I was," she said, handing it to Sal.

"Will wonders never cease?" Sal leaned back in her seat. "And here I thought *Sesame Street* was supposed to keep the preschool set out of mischief."

Melvina shook her head. "Next time, try the lighter."

Sal said nothing.

"Did it ever cross your mind that maybe you're just a wee bit ageist?"

Sal reacted with hyperbolic surprise. "Oh, no, our sweet little Melvina, taken over by the pod people! Can it be? Is it true? Did that nasty ol' Sue whisper feminist nothings in your ear while getting you all het up?"

"That's bugging the hell out of you, isn't it?" asked Melvina with some satisfaction.

"Well," said Sal flatly, "it seems as though, when you're not acting like one of those bereaved little monkeys in the Harlow experiments, you're strutting around feeling so pleased with yourself I could gag."

Melvina smiled and tsked sympathetically. "You're hopeless, Sal.... Where do I get off this thing, anyway?"

"Brewster. Then we take Eighty-four East."

"Who are these people?"

"Bob and Hank. They've got a place out in Ridgewater. Real nice, out in the country. I'm sure you'll like it." Melvina looked skeptical. "Really. Listen, it wouldn't be fair to impose on our respective hostesses for over a week. Bob and Hank have plenty of room. When they heard we were up here, they insisted we visit."

"Great. You know sometimes I think you don't care about finding Laura at all. Sometimes I feel like you just decided to take a nice little trip and visit all your friends."

"So, what's wrong with that? Maybe I'd be more torn up about this Laura thing if I had even the vaguest idea why you're so hellbent on finding her. I mean, I don't even know the woman, I hardly know you, and here I am on this Easter egg hunt. What do you expect?"

Melvina shrugged.

"It's not like Liz isn't still going to be chasing around on this thing. We came up with some other ideas on how to get her address, and if she finds out anything...."

"Sure."

Sal frowned. "You know I *did* have a theory about why you were looking for this Laura."

"Really?"

"Yeah. I thought it was a case of terminal lust that drove you to go searching for the one woman in Kentucky you'd ever encountered who you thought, you know...."

Melvina gave Sal a dirty look.

"Well, it was an idea. Kinky, but possible. I'd have thought that your little—close encounter of the third kind, you know, with Sue—combined with this business about your Laura being married..., but that hasn't made you any less eager to find her."

"You have a one-track mind, Sal," said Melvina wearily. "She's just a real good friend, and it's just important to me that I talk to her."

"Sure. After all this time, out of the blue. For no particular reason." Melvina did not say anything. She glanced toward the exit sign and into the rearview mirror and flicked on her turn signal. Sal shook her head. "Okay, ignore me. It's just that in my experience, most of the 'great' mysteries turn out to be a thick layer of hype over a nasty little core of the simplest motives."

Melvina glanced at Sal with interest and then looked back at the road, the expression on her face suggesting she was absorbed in thought. "Hm," she said finally. "I guess," she went on slowly, "that's like that little mystery about why you never answered Ramona's note.... Although maybe the real mystery is why she'd even care after all these years."

"What are you talking about?"

"Nothing," said Melvina as she guided the car around the curve. "I was under the impression that you two were lovers and it didn't work out. But it was a long time ago, I guess you wouldn't remember."

Melvina's driving required her to keep her eyes on the road for the next few minutes. When she finally looked at Sal and saw the expression on her face, she realized how wrong she was.

13

The Good Kite Ramona

After Sunday's rain the skies had cleared completely, and now the unobstructed sun beat down from a vault of Kodachrome blue. Sal was in her element. By ten thirty she had staked out a lawn chair near the pool, stripped down to a surprisingly minimal swimsuit, and resplendent with oil, had abandoned herself to ultraviolet absorption.

Dadavi attempted to climb up into what lap was available.

"Hank!" called Sal, holding the cat away from her with glistening hands, "Melvina! Anyone!"

Melvina appeared on the patio, sized up the situation, and strode over to reclaim her cat. "Sorry about that."

"Hm," replied Sal, adjusting her sunglasses and lapsing back into solar meditation.

Melvina stood by Sal's chaise lounge for a moment, adjusting Dadavi on her shoulder and gawking at this revelation of Sal's anatomy.

"Can I help you?" Sal inquired unexpectedly, raising her head and peering over her dark glasses.

"Huh? Oh, no."

"You're in my light," elaborated Sal pointedly.

"Oh, I'm sorry," stammered Melvina, retreating a few paces and seating herself on the grass. She gazed at Sal, her eyes taking in the fine cheek bones, the strong chin, the delicate hollows above her collar bones. She watched Sal's rhythmic breathing, the way her breasts came up to press against the fabric that covered them, the nipples taut—Melvina gave her head a shake. *What the hell am I doing?* she thought, while her gaze traced the arch of Sal's diaphragm, lingered over the sensual rise of her belly with each breath, the hollows that appeared near her hips each time she exhaled. *I've gone around the bend,* she decided. She tried to imagine what Sal, sharp-tongued Sal, never at a loss for words, would say if she were to notice Melvina staring, but instead Melvina found herself wondering how Sal would look without the bathing suit, how her dark skin would feel against—

"Here, catch this." It was Hank, loping past Melvina, tossing her his towel. Hardly breaking his stride, he dove into the pool.

Sal heard the splash and went so far as to lift her head for a moment, aim a languid wave at Hank's swimming figure. This accomplished, she reverted to her former state of oblivion.

Looking at Sal, Melvina sighed. *This isn't the way it's supposed to be.* Melvina had always regarded her sexual desires, when she admitted them, in much the same way she thought of the postcard her oldest brother sent her from California.

When George had first been stationed there, he sent Melvina a 3-D picture postcard of the Enchanted Castle at Disneyland. She was barely old enough to read the message on the back, and the words, whatever they said, were quickly forgotten. But the picture of the castle, shimmering and changing colors as the card was tilted back and forth, had remained vivid in Melvina's memory.

It became a secret place in Melvina's heart, a magical world of her dominion. She shook her head to remember how she had longed to go to California and see this place, this land of dreams. She had known it would not be like she imagined, but still she held onto the feeling that there was some part of her, some need, that would be fulfilled once and for all, if only she could lay eyes on the place.

Sex, or intimacy, or feeling loved—whatever it was Melvina craved—had always seemed much the same to her. The first morning she awoke in Ridgewater she felt sore from her love-making with Sue, but she also felt relaxed, even sated. She had thought, rather proudly, that now not only did she know an awful lot more about her body and feelings and sex in general, but she would be forever free from the driving, miserable rage of passions she had so long tried to ignore.

Melvina noticed that while she was thinking this, her eyes had been riveted by the sight of one stray hair, peeking out from the top of the bottom piece of Sal's swimsuit. It was just one dark hair, a curl that beckoned to her like the coy crook of a finger, like the movement of Sue's hand as she had gestured to Melvina to climb into the freshly made bed.

Melvina looked away. She watched the smooth, powerful motions of Hank's arms as he swam up and down the pool. She appreciated, in a detached aesthetic manner, the definition of the muscles in his back, the lean hardness of his thighs. She felt not at all the voyeur as she admired his physique, smiling at her own preconceptions of how a gay man should look and act. *Well,* she thought, *I know a lot more than when I left home. Hell, I know a lot more about some things than most of the people in the State of Kentucky.* Melvina stretched her shoulders upward, keeping a steadying hand on Dadavi. She thrilled to the warmth of the sun on her back, playing over her shoulder blades like a gentle caress. It made her think of Sue. She missed her already.

"Do you miss her, too?" she asked Dadavi, holding the cat out in front of her as she laid back on the grass. "Sure you do," she decided, cuddling her against her face and neck.

"I wonder if we'll ever see her again," Melvina mumbled into Dadavi's scruff. A sharp feeling stabbed her, an ache, an echo of loss. She wrapped both arms over the cat's tiny body and hugged her, unprotesting, to her breast. *I have no right,* thought Melvina, and stopped, afraid to think, afraid that in not saying "I love you" she had told a kind of lie.

Melvina made a growly noise and rolled onto her stomach, propping herself on her elbows to protect Dadavi from her weight. "So, what d'you think?" she asked the cat, who was struggling to turn over. Melvina cast a sidelong look at Sal.

It seemed to her that Sal, still basking in the sun, just now so alluring, was quite the conundrum. There she lay, next door to naked, utterly unaware, entirely at ease. To Melvina she felt as near as the moon. Melvina wondered at her self-possession, her isolation, that intense quality of inaccessibility she radiated.

Melvina felt certain Sal would never have hidden in a sofa bed, never would have allowed herself to be embarrassed as she had been. Melvina sighed. There were so many things she did not understand. There was Sue who could love her so wonderfully—and have this other lover, Pat. There was Melvina, pretty well smitten with Sue, who could be excited by this aloof, arrogant woman who had to be nearly fifty. *Fifty! Oh, my God,* thought Melvina. And, finally, there was the sixty-thousand-dollar question about Sal and Ramona, how obvious it was they cared deeply for one another, how puzzling that there seemed so long-standing and unquestioned an estrangement between them. *And it's killing Sal,* reflected Melvina. Sal who only seemed to relax and come alive here, away from Ramona.

"Goddamned soap opera," muttered Melvina at the lawn in front of her. She frowned and scrambled to her feet, clutching

103

Dadavi.

"Got my towel?" called Hank, climbing out of the pool.

Melvina bent to pluck it off the ground and toss it to him. She turned toward the house.

"Where're you going?" he asked, trotting after her.

"I don't know," she shrugged.

"Well, how about coming with me? I have to go into town. Funny, how I always end up knocking off work to run errands on a day like this." He grinned, a playful smile hard to resist. Melvina tried and failed. "Well?" he asked again.

Melvina nodded. "Want to take *my* car?" she asked, waiting for him to fluster.

"Terrific idea!" he exclaimed. "And the top comes down?"

Melvina gave in to his exuberance. It was no use trying to drag him down—he kept popping up like a buoy.

"Hey, Sal," he called. "We're going into town. Wanna come?"

Sal rolled her head from side to side in lazy negative.

Hank turned to Melvina, jerking a thumb over his shoulder. "Hard at work. Bob calls it 'Sal's perennial tan.'" Hank lowered his voice confidentially and bent toward Melvina. "He says she cheats and uses a sun lamp. She manages to stay that color all year round. Listen, give me a minute to get some clothes on. I'll meet you at the car."

Melvina circled the house, ducking under the boughs of a lilac bush. She paused to inhale deeply, and the fragrance compelled her to throw back her head, exult in so lovely a day.

"Do you think it's okay to leave Dadavi outside?" she asked Hank when he joined her.

"Sure. Sal will keep an eye on her." Melvina made a doubting face. "She *likes* that cat—or haven't you noticed?" Melvina shook her head. "You don't read her very well, do you?" added Hank, cocking his head to one side.

"I didn't think you knew her very long yourself," remarked Melvina, releasing the convertible top.

"I haven't. But Bob has. He said two things about Sal: 'Her teeth are in her tongue,' and 'Don't underestimate her.'"

"One out of two isn't bad," said Melvina, shifting the car into reverse.

"Hey, what's this?"

"Sal's pith helmet."

Hank chuckled and fiddled with the hat. "One size fits all," he proclaimed cheerfully, settling it on his head. He braced his hands on the dashboard. "Okay, I think I'm ready for anything."

Melvina obligingly hit the gas and zipped the car down the long driveway at a brisk backwards pace. "Did anyone ever tell you you're a bit of a clown?" asked Melvina, watching him mug terror and sway exaggeratedly with each swerve of the car.

"Keep your eyes on the rearview mirror or we're done for," he instructed her. They reached the road without incident, and Melvina backed more sedately onto the pavement.

"This way?" she asked as she accelerated the car.

"Uh-huh. Actually, all roads lead to New Milford."

"Really?" Melvina hit the brakes precipitously and spun the wheel to the left.

"Whoa!" yelled Hank, holding on now for dear life, "What the hell are you doing?"

"I like the other way better," said Melvina simply, her casual tone in direct contrast to the violence of her maneuver.

Hank shook his head. "All right. You got me." He looked anxiously at a Mercedes bearing down on them and breathed a sigh of relief as Melvina pulled the car into the other lane. "But admit it. You're as crazy as I am."

"Crazier," she replied.

"Hell, on a day like this, we're all crazy." Hank figured out how to lower the back of his seat and stretched out, tilting the pith helmet down to shade his eyes. "I feel veddy British in this chapeau. Drive on, James," he commanded.

When they pulled into a parking space by the green, Hank clambered out over the door. "You mind?" he inquired politely.

"Not at all," answered Melvina, smiling and doing the same.

"Look, either you can tag along with me or we can plan to meet somewhere, say, the drugstore over there."

Melvina nodded agreement and watched Hank lope off toward the post office. She really had no idea what she was going to do. She stood for a moment by the row of nose-in parking spaces, looking at all the cars and wondering what it was that bothered her about them.

They were not all expensive vehicles, although there were more fancy numbers gathered together than she was used to seeing. The colors were generally tasteful and muted, in comparison to her own bright Caddy. Almost every one of them looked clean and perhaps even waxed. *That's it,* she thought. *None of them are beat up. There's not a dent, or a twisted bumper, or even a speck of rust-out in the whole lot of them.* She marveled at the

105

sight. Dozens of cars fit for a two-page color spread in *Time* magazine.

"Huh," she said to herself as she crossed from the green to the row of stores. All at once she knew what had been bothering her about the area since she and Sal drove in on Saturday. "Pretty enough for a postcard," Sal had commented, but that was where the problem lay. Everything, everywhere Melvina looked, was beautiful, or cute, or picturesque. She shook her head. There was something unreal about it, like the castle on George's postcard. There was very little that looked ugly, or shabby, and what little there was looked all the more squalid in comparison.

"So that's what money means," muttered Melvina, "having everything *nice.*" A white-haired woman who was ambling by paused and turned as though she had been addressed. Melvina smiled nervously and hurried on. She shoved her hands in her pockets, feeling not so very nice. She suddenly understood why Sue was puzzled by Melvina's idea that her parents' apartment was in a luxurious building. She began to realize how little she understood about money or the people who had it. She felt a twinge in her stomach, an angry little twist.

She was passing a flower shop, and she stopped to look in. There were emblems in one corner of the window, symbols of the credit cards accepted. "Uncle Lester's MasterCard," she sneered to herself. She checked her back pocket for her wallet and went in. *What the hell,* she thought, *I sure hope Sue likes roses.*

• • •

When Hank came into the drugstore, he found Melvina trying on sunglasses. Even from across the room he could sense her mood of sullen rumination. He paused at the end of an aisle, his hand on a display. *What the hell is eating her?* he thought. He had liked her from the moment he met her, moods and all, but she was a tough little nut, as slippery as a well-oiled Sal when he tried to get close to her. He shook his head. *That crazy thing she did with the car....* She had scared the hell out of him. It had been a near-murderous impulse. He felt as though he had brought it to the surface, somehow. What was it about him? He knit his brows, scared of her, scared for her.

Melvina turned and noticed him. She waved. Hank smiled and waved back, starting toward her.

"How do you like these?"

106

"Great. Now you and Sal'll look like two black-eyed peas in a pod."

Melvina turned back to the mirror, giving him an unexpected nudge in the ribs. "I saw you skulking over there."

Hank laughed nervously. "Just thinking about what I could think up for us to do so I could avoid going back to work."

"Well?"

Hank turned and scanned the store. "I don't know. Tennis? Frisbee?"

Melvina shook her head. "Can't play tennis. Hate Frisbee."

"You don't seem to like swimming, either—I told you I thought I could find you a suit."

Melvina shook her head. "Not in the mood. And anyway, Sal rules the backyard. I'm sure she'd love to get clipped with a Frisbee or splashed by my cannonball."

Hank chuckled. "Boy, has she got you trained. Let's see...." His eyes took in the store again, searching. He noticed a display nearby and moved toward it. "Hey, how about this? You want to fly a kite?"

Melvina trailed after him. "That'd be fun." Her face lit up at Hank's suggestion. "The only thing is," she added somberly, "it wouldn't work. There's no wind."

Hank reached into the stand of rolled up kites and selected one. "Come on, don't be that way. If it's kites you like, we'll fly a kite. It doesn't matter whether there's any wind down *here;* it's what's up *there* that counts. All we have to do is go up on a hill, take a good running start, and off she goes!" He made an upward swooping motion with his hand. "Well, what do you think? Game?"

Melvina nodded, uncertain, but more enthused than he had seen her yet. They made their way to the checkout counter with her sunglasses and his kite.

"Let me get you those," he offered gallantly, snatching her shades. He waved away her protest. "Consider 'em aviation equipment."

• • •

He was in his after-lunch kite-flying ensemble of tennis whites and Adidas ("Adds a little decorum to the proceedings"). He was striding up the hill at a pace taxing to Melvina's shorter and less-exercised legs. "What a day for a launch!" he proclaimed, waving his free arm.

Melvina was carried along by his enthusiasm, vaguely aware

107

that he was playing it for all it was worth, mildly annoyed at his well-intentioned emotional manipulations. "Do you really think we'll get it off the ground? I don't even feel a breeze."

"Bah. You have to understand the aerodynamics of kites and angels, very small birds and hot air balloons. Faith! That's the *modus operandi*—only thing that holds 'em up."

Melvina twisted her mouth into a wry little smile, huffed between scampers, "I'm not so sure about kites, but maybe you do know a thing or two about hot air balloons...."

He laughed. "And you're scared of Sal? Another five, ten years, and no one's gonna be able to get near you."

They were just reaching the top of the hill, and the view left Melvina speechless. She gaped at the panorama of the valley beneath them—the silver ribbon of river threading in and out of sight, the distant hills, the pristine spire of a Congregational church—it was the perfection and completion of all the glimpses she had ever had of hilltop vistas. "You guys live ten minutes from *this?* How can you not spend all your time up here?"

Hank shrugged. "I come up here some. Not too much—that'd ruin it." They moved off the narrow paved road and climbed through the fence into a field. "I guess," continued Hank, "I've always thought that a view like this was God's reward for climbing up hills—and mountains."

Melvina chuckled. "My legs are going to reward me tomorrow."

"Well," asked Hank after a moment's rest, "are we going to do this or not?"

Melvina got up. "I guess so. But there's still no breeze." She stuck her finger in her mouth and held it up. "Nothing."

Hank was checking out the path he planned to run. "Yeah, but at least you can't get too mad at me for luring you up here."

"So how do we do this?"

"You hold it over your head and run a few steps after me, then let it go." He spun around. "Wait a minute! We can't do this yet. We haven't named it." Hank met Melvina's skeptical look with a steady gaze. "It's important. Every ship's got a name, every rocket, plane...."

"Okay. All right. What do you want to call it?"

"I don't know. You got any ideas? Think of something, someone, beautiful and good. Something that deserves to be commemorated."

Melvina thought. She thought of Sal and dismissed the idea.

108

She thought of Sue and balked, embarrassed. She thought of Arlene and her kites, Julie and her smile, and remembered that Hank did not know them. She thought finally of Ramona, her impulsive kindness, her calculated flirtations—she smiled.

"You got someone, right?"

"Well, maybe. I don't know. It's just she...."

"Well?"

"I don't know.... You ever meet Ramona? Ramona Stevens?"

"Sure. Lovely woman. Excellent choice."

"Really?"

"Yup," nodded Hank, "ought to get this old thing right off the ground." He held the kite aloft and handed it to Melvina. "I christen thee," he intoned, poised like a sprinter, "the Good Kite, Ramona!" With that he was off, tearing across the field, Melvina straining to keep up and then giving up, letting go of the crossbar of the kite.

Almost as soon as she let go of it, the kite did an ungracious nose dive, jabbed Hank in the back, and fell to the ground. "Forget it, Hank!" she called. "No good."

Hank halted, looked sheepishly over his shoulder, and gathered in the string. "We try again!" he exclaimed.

They chose a different direction and were off. No luck.

Hank climbed onto a rocky knoll and held the kite aloft. "You run with it," he suggested. Melvina ran as though her life depended on it, but to no avail. For the next half hour they tried every variation they could think of. They ran from every direction. They ran fast, they loped slow. They tried throwing it up in the air, sailing it like a paper airplane, and tossing it out of trees. They tried relay running with it, and starting out with the kite banging along on the ground behind them. They finally even tried settling Melvina on Hank's shoulders, holding the kite, and running that way. They both fell down.

Hank was laughing. "I can't believe it. What a crapper."

Melvina pulled up her pants leg and looked at her knee. She rubbed around a cut unhappily. "This isn't fun, Hank. This is depressing."

Hank leaned back on his elbows and sighed. "You're just tired, that's all."

"No," said Melvina emphatically. "This is ridiculous. It's never gonna work."

"Melvina, Melvina, Melvina," he said, shaking his head. "You have to have faith. A kite can't fly without that."

"Sure. And it can't fly without wind, either. Wind, you know? Whoosh, blow. Air, Hank."

He rolled his eyes. "You're just being difficult. You get off on that for some reason."

"Hank, I'm just being reasonable. It's not going to fly. I know you've got this mission in life to try to cheer me up, but...."

"Cheer you up? No, not cheer you up. Just jog you out of that self-absorbed haze you've been in ever since you got here. Ever since you got to Philly, from what Sal says."

"What Sal says," repeated Melvina. "What the hell does Sal know? Or you?"

"I know plenty," said Hank, rolling on his side, jabbing in the air with one finger. "I know we've all got our share of problems, and I know there comes a point where you either have to talk about them or let 'em go...."

Melvina stared blankly at him. "Okay," she said, "we've all got problems. I got that. Can we go home now?"

"No!" yelled Hank. "We're just getting started. There's a principle here. We can't give up on poor Ramona."

"I can," said Melvina, getting to her feet. "You stay here if you want. Try to fly what's left of it." She bent over to pluck a blade of grass that had punctured the paper of the kite. "I wish you luck."

She did not look back as she crossed the field, climbed through the fence, and started down the hill. She did not think she could take it. Melvina sighed. There were some people in this world, absurdly kind, who seemed to think there was no burden of love they could not bear. Melvina shook her head. Ramona, Hank. So wanting to save every poor soul that they ended up drowning themselves.

Melvina yawned and stretched her arms. Crazy. The strain of Hank's kindness was too much to take.

By the time Melvina reached the yard, her heels were sore from the shock of each downhill step. It was later in the afternoon than she had realized on the shadowless hilltop. She cut across the lawn to the house and circled it, wandering into the backyard.

Sal was on her stomach, the lawn chair flattened out beneath her, reading a book. She turned her head and peered over her glasses as Melvina approached.

"So? Back from your labors? I looked for your kite."

"We never got it off the ground."

110

Sal shrugged the corners of her mouth. "Didn't think you would. I don't know who's worse, you or Hank."

"Worse?"

Sal gave an annoyed toss of her head. "Trying to fly a kite? Today? Even running around on a day like this is crazy."

"I don't know about that," said Melvina defensively.

"Well, where's Hank, anyway?"

Melvina looked down at her sneakers. "He's still up there. I came back—to get something."

"What? Wings?"

"*Something*," said Melvina firmly, turning around and heading for the house.

Frantically, she tried to think of anything that might help get the kite off the ground. A ladder, a bicycle. She thought of the long trek back up the hill and groaned. Why did she want to help all of a sudden? She thought of the Cadillac, sitting in the driveway, and decided it would be easier to drive. That was it. The car. The car could run faster than the two of them.

Melvina was trotting now, jogging on sore feet around the house. She was excited, optimistic. This was it.

• • •

Sal came padding out onto the patio. She had a knee-length terry cloth bathrobe belted around her, a cigarette dangling from her lips, and a Scotch-and-water in her right hand. As she walked, she was leaning this way and that, craning her neck and bobbing her head and muttering, "Here cat. Come on, stupid."

There was no sign of Dadavi. She made her way to the chaise lounge, set down her drink, and bent to check under the chair. "Huh," she said, straightening up and casting a nervous glance into the swimming pool. "Good," she added as she settled herself more calmly in the lawn chair. She flicked her cigarette, picked up her glass, and leaned back.

"To read or not to read," she murmured, taking her sunglasses out of her bathrobe pocket and slipping them on. She was about to reach for her book when something above the trees caught her eye. She looked up. It was the kite, a blue diamond bobbing unevenly, high in the air.

"Well, what do you know." She watched it for a minute, disturbed by its movement. It took some time for her to realize that the odd thing was how fast it was moving. It *was* moving. It was jerking through the air. Puzzled, Sal stood up from the chair and walked backwards away from the pool, stepping gingerly over the lawn toward the back of the house.

When she was far enough away to have a chance to see what was going on, she lowered her gaze from the kite, following the imagined line of its string. There! Through the trees by the road that wound down the hillside. She caught a brief glimpse of a complicated and improbable tableau: Melvina's car, gaudy and ridiculous, tooling down the road with Melvina, wearing the pith helmet, at the wheel. Sal saw a fluff of white on Melvina's shoulder, and in the back, perched precariously on the top of one of the front seats, facing to the rear, was Hank, his hair blown backwards into his eyes, his mouth open and laughing, his hands hanging onto a kite string for dear life.

Sal took a sip from her drink. She shook her head. She laughed and choked on her mouthful of Scotch. "What the hell," she sputtered, coughing and laughing and coughing again.

• • •

"Okay, Melvina, can you hear me? I think she's really up, now. You can slow it down. That's right, don't hit those brakes too hard or I've had it." Hank kept glancing from Melvina to the sky, adjusting and readjusting the tension on the string. "Great. Beautiful," he said as the car glided to a stop. "Lovely."

They looked at each other, grinning like fools.

"We did it!" exclaimed Melvina.

"I told you we could," said Hank, trying to be gruff, his eyes grateful.

"Can I hold it?"

"Sure."

Melvina twisted around in her seat and took the string. "This is terrific. How long will it stay up there?"

"Who knows?" shrugged Hank. "Maybe forever." He stood up, arching his back. "I'm pooped."

Melvina chuckled. "Not surprising. You were still charging around like a banshee when I got back. Should we bring her in?"

"I guess so."

Melvina looked up wistfully at the kite, bobbing and dancing on the gentle breezes. "Do we have to? Couldn't we just set it free?"

Hank looked uncertain. "I don't know if—"

"That's okay," said Melvina sadly. "It was just a thought."

112

"And a good thought," asserted Hank, causing a penknife to appear with the surprise and speed of legerdemain. Before Melvina could get a word out, the string was cut. Melvina twisted around to look for the kite.

A pair of hands were clapped over her eyes. "No," said Hank firmly. "Don't look. When you set something free, you just have to let it go."

He removed his hands from her face and she looked up at him, his kind eyes, his grass-stained tennis outfit, his bramble-scratched legs. She smiled and shook her head. "Okay, let's get this crate in the yard."

Hank climbed over the seat, scooping Dadavi off Melvina's shoulder. Melvina backed the car up the driveway, her speed safe and decorous. She cranked the wheel around and steered the car in with a feeling of accomplishment. They did it. Maybe it was impossible, but they did it anyway.

The three of them pulled up by the house breathing the air of victory. They were drunk with their successes, and their imagination filled the quiet arbor with brass bands and confetti.

"Not bad," smiled Melvina, turning off the ignition. She got out of the car and came around to where Hank stood with Dadavi. She threw a comradely arm around his waist and he answered with an arm around her shoulders. They marched toward the door.

As if to concede their victory, Sal was coming around the side of the house towards them. She was wearing a bathrobe. Her steps were nimble and swift. Melvina noticed something in her hand. It was blue and broken and dripping with water.

"You two lose something?" she asked as she came up before them, her arm outstretched, holding the kite.

14

A Problem with Morale

"I said to him, 'Jack, I think you're scared of the wrong things. The first thing you do is get your ass to a doctor and find out what's going on—*then* you worry about what Ron's going to think.'" Bob paused with his empty coffee cup in his hand. He stared into it in a still-sleepy, slightly confused way, and reached across the table for the coffee pot. "Another cup?" he asked Sal.

She nodded. "But I didn't think it was the kind of thing you could get off a toilet seat, if you know what I mean."

Bob hunched his shoulders. "No, but—oh, hell, everybody's scared."

Hank came out of the kitchen and sat at the table, shaking his head. "That's the worst part. Everything we don't know acts like an ink blot—we project our worst fears onto it. And then, of course, there's that lovely chorus of Moral Munchkins, chirping about the 'wages of sin'."

"Just what everybody needs, huh?" Sal frowned and lit a cigarette. There was a pause in the conversation. Three pairs of eyes dropped somberly to a distracted view of the tablecloth.

Before anyone could gallantly pick up the discussion, Melvina came bouncing into the breakfast nook. She was already washed and dressed, Dadavi jauntily perched on one shoulder.

"Hiyo," she greeted them merrily.

"Well, what do you know," smiled Bob, "Ms. Early Riser."

"Big doings," she announced by way of explanation. "Unfortunately, we're going to have to blow this joint."

"What?" exclaimed Sal.

"You heard me," said Melvina, seating herself. She looked at Hank, "You guys have been great to us and all, but we really ought to be getting on with our—expedition."

"I thought you had to wait for some friend of a friend to get back from vacation?"

"Yeah, we thought so, but then I got thinking about it last

night. I think we've been really dumb." All eyes were on Melvina. "Well, look," she began, "we know Laura's husband's name is Bill Monroe, and we know he works for the Mirak Corporation over in Kennedyville."

"We do?" Sal looked doubtful.

Melvina rested her forearms on the table and nodded. "Yup, I called Information. The only branch of Mirak in Connecticut is in Kennedyville. Anyway, I called Mirak, and just like you said, Sal, they aren't supposed to give out any information about their employees—military contracts and all that. But the woman I talked to was really pretty nice. I asked if Bill Monroe worked there and she said she couldn't tell me anything, and I explained about my long lost friend Laura, his wife, and she said—now get this—'Well, I'm sorry, but I am unable to confirm that William A. Monroe is presently employed by our R & D department.'" Melvina grinned. "What d'ya think *that* was supposed to mean?"

Hank laughed. "Sisterhood is powerful, little sister."

Melvina turned expectantly toward Sal. "Well?"

"So? Does that really tell us anymore than we already knew?"

Melvina gave her head several short vigorous nods. "It tells us that this isn't another dead end. He's there. He works there, and even if they won't let us inside, sooner or later, he's got to go in and out.... See what I mean?"

"So you want to go all the way to Kennedyville...."

"We'll end up in Boston anyway."

"Where *is* Kennedyville?" asked Hank.

"I checked a map. It's near Moosup, Connecticut...."

"You mean Moodus?"

"No, Moosup. It's next to Plainfield."

"Oh, you mean Plainville."

"*No.* Plainfield. Don't you even know your own *state?*"

Hank lowered his head in mock shame.

"You're talking about eastern Connecticut," Bob explained. "That's not really part of the state. There's been talk of sawing Connecticut down the middle—in order to create more shoreline."

"Yeah," added Hank, "then they'll tow Rhode Island and eastern Connecticut out to sea, and Rhode Island will finally get to be an island—"

"I was thinking more of a penal colony," suggested Bob.

"Godforsaken, huh?" asked Sal glumly.

"Doesn't matter," said Melvina firmly. "We just go there, ask around Mirak, and we're on our way…. Are you with me?"

Sal looked doubtfully at Melvina. Melvina stared back, her chin set and stubborn. Sal rolled her eyes toward Bob. Bob looked back, his brows knit. Sal turned and looked at Hank. Hank shrugged and glanced at Melvina. Sal sighed. "I guess so," she said in a little voice.

• • •

I-84 east to Hartford was easy. It was a limited access highway, and midday traffic was light. Sal fell asleep somewhere around Farmington, leaving Melvina to navigate the dread Mixmaster on her own. There were a few hairy moments of numbered routes flying onto and off the interchange, but with no major calamities Melvina made it east of Hartford to a point where there was no more highway.

"Shit," she muttered, pulling over to the side of the road to consult a map. She could not decide between the numbered routes. To add to her confusion, I-84 kept popping up and disappearing like the rippling back of the Loch Ness monster.

She finally gave up and decided to just keep pressing eastward. The countryside became more rural and the houses less prepossessing the further she went. The roads wound along gently rolling hills that were less high and sharp than those on the western end of the state.

The landscape lacked the manicured look of western Connecticut. Here the foliage ran wild, the lush growth of trees and bushes and weeds tumbling down very close to the edge of the road. At some points broken down stone walls held back the tumult, and at others the trees arched over the road itself, forming a cooling green canopy.

"It's a little like home," she murmured to Dadavi, who was sleeping quietly in her lap.

Melvina sighed. It brought back to her other roads she had traveled, other times in her life, and she found a kind of familiarity and comfort even in the sagging sheds and porches of the farms she passed. Sal would not like it, of course. She would make arch comments and unhappy faces, Melvina was sure. But for now, while Sal slept and Melvina meandered in and out of states of greater and lesser directional confusion, the road was Melvina's, and her thoughts, and memories, were her own.

116

• • •

The summer after Melvina shot John Dunford was the last summer she went to Farm Camp. Bravely, perhaps foolishly, she had decided to go, even as local tongues still discussed the event. She may have been naïve enough—and she certainly was young enough—to think that at camp, where she had always been welcomed and fairly well-liked, things would not have changed much.

The story officially given out called the shooting an accident, the clumsy mistake of a clumsy girl fetching her brother's gun for his friend. No one believed it. Perhaps this was because that year had been a bad one for accidents involving guns.

When Ralph Brolly was found with his shotgun in his mouth and the back of his head blown off, his mother had called it an accident. A local wag had commented that, well, yes, he figured young Brolly was just about stupid enough to try cleaning his gun barrel with his tongue. And then of course there had been a double murder a couple of towns over. Mrs. Smith and Mr. Jones had been found in bed together, quite bloody and quite dead. Mr. Smith at first denied any knowledge of the shooting or their affair, but when it was demonstrated that he could be placed at the scene of the crime, he had broken down and admitted that he had, in fact, shot them. However, he assured the authorities (and whoever else would listen) that it had been nothing more than a tragic accident. He insisted he had just wanted to scare them. The local wag had an easy time with this accidental shooting—which had required four bullets to do the job.

On the matter of the Skittle-Dunford shooting, there was really more room to see it as an accident. Melvina was only eleven, and Dunford had survived, more or less. However, it happened that Melvina's mother—*not* Lester's mother, the local folks would sagely add—Melvina's mother had been transferred to a state mental hospital shortly after the shooting. Heads were seen to nod. Now, the first Mrs. Skittle, you could not have found a nicer, more Christian woman, but the second Mrs. Skittle—well, people in town had figured out her problem a lot quicker than those doctors.... You know how these things go, people said, shaking their heads. Poor old George Senior, they added, giving Melvina a sideways look.

The reliable local wag just smiled and suggested naughtily that John had asked Melvina for a blow job, and the little innocent thought he said a 'blow-away' job....

117

When Melvina arrived at Farm Camp, it did not take her long to catch the general direction from which the wind was blowing. At taps that first night there had been no one who would take her hand in the Friendship Circle. In her first class of Beginning Swimming (which she was bravely attempting for the third time), she was buddied up with a first year camper who promptly headed for shore screaming that Melvina was trying to drown her.

Melvina was hurt. There were friends from last year who ignored her and others who shyly said 'hello' and tried to explain about how their mothers had forbidden them to speak to her. There were new kids who followed her around at a safe distance, staring and comparing notes. There was even, one evening as she made her way alone, a trio of little boys who followed her, jeering and calling. She finally stopped and spun around, sizing them up and deciding that, while separately they were no threat, together they might give her trouble.

"What do you want?" she barked, hoping to sound tough.

The boys giggled. The littlest one, a pint-sized first year camper, one of those hyperactive crowd pleasers, wiggled his fanny at her in a spastic little dance.

"Go on, Larry," the ten-year-old urged him.

"Hey, Melly," the littlest boy called, "want to shoot me?" To the crescendoing hilarity of his cohorts, he dropped his shorts around his ankles. Emboldened further, he waved his penis at her. "Well?" he asked.

Melvina suppressed a sigh. In the darkness her face reddened, her eyes filled with tears. It was not this particular crew. Maybe it was the older boys who kept asking her if she were going to sign up for Riflery. Maybe it was that girl in her Basic Electricity class who asked if she was planning to construct an electric chair when she got home. Melvina blinked her eyes and chewed unhappily on one side of her mouth.

"Hey, Melvina," chirped the boy again, "you gonna shoot me?"

Melvina rubbed her nose with her hand. "Listen, Larry," she said quietly, "sometimes I don't have a gun with me." She paused and the boys whooped boisterously at her response. "But when I don't," she went on, speaking with ominous slowness and clarity, "sometimes I just—*bite* 'em off." With that she made a run at the boys, an unexpected move that sent them scattering off into the night. All except Larry, who got tangled in his pants and his panic, falling to the ground.

Melvina had not meant to run as far as where he was, but there she was, all at once, standing over him. Anger was welling up inside her, near to spilling over, when she looked down at the little boy and saw him cowering abjectly, consumed with a very real terror.

Melvina swallowed hard. "Go on," she said, almost crying. "I'm not going to hurt you. Get out of here."

He scrambled up and clutched his pants and ran away, leaving Melvina alone on the darkened path, sobbing silently to herself.

• • •

It was not until the third day of camp that Laura came up to Melvina and spoke with her. "Not having much fun, are you?" she asked, falling into step beside Melvina as though resuming a conversation broken off moments before. "I'm sorry I haven't come by, but—you know the C.I.T. thing, they keep me pretty busy."

"Sure," said Melvina, her voice somewhere between sarcasm and resignation.

"I mean it. Listen, I'd like to see you." Melvina rolled her eyes. Laura stopped on the trail and turned to face her. "I really do want to talk with you. How about Quiet Hour? We could get together and take a walk. Huh?"

"I have to be in my cabin," said Melvina warily. She had become nervous about the least infraction of rules, afraid any violation would lose whatever sympathy the counselors had for her.

"Don't worry about that," replied Laura with a wave of her hand. "I'll mention it to Jan if you want. No problem."

"Really?" asked Melvina, incredulous, deeply impressed by the orbs of authority and power within which Laura now moved.

"Really," answered Laura warmly. "Okay?"

Melvina nodded and smiled, realizing with a start how long it had been since she did that simple, happy thing with her mouth.

• • •

When lunch was over, Melvina hiked from the Central Lodge to her cabin. She found Jan reading a magazine on her bunk. "Uh, did Laura talk—?" she began uncertainly.

"Oh, hi, Skit, what're you doing here? I thought you were going for a walk."

"Uh, yeah," said Melvina, "I just wanted to check with you."

Jan waved her out the door, leaving Melvina one of the few

119

people not confined to cabin for the next hour. It made her feel both free and lonely, privileged and cast aside. She shoved her hands in the pockets of her jeans and hunched her shoulders as she strode toward Laura's cabin.

Laura was waiting outside. "Here you are," she said with forced joviality. "I was beginning to think you stood me up."

"Nah," said Melvina shyly, "I don't have enough friends to do that."

Laura threw an arm around Melvina's shoulders. "Rough, huh?"

Melvina tried to sound indifferent but failed. "I guess I wasn't ready for it."

Laura nodded. She steered Melvina toward the lavatories. "There's a trail back there we can pick up."

"You really know your way around," said Melvina, trying to make conversation, bridge the gulf of a year's absence, Laura's new status, Melvina's disgrace.

"Yeah, well, I've been here every summer since—it was my second year they put in plumbing."

Melvina smiled. "Old timer, huh?"

"Yep," said Laura, screwing up her face to look like a crone.

They laughed and looked at each other. "It's good to see you," said Melvina. "I was beginning to think you...."

"No!" said Laura emphatically. But as she spoke, she turned her eyes away. "The whole thing weirded me out when I heard about it," she admitted. She pressed her lips together and lowered her face. "But I don't want to start avoiding you."

Melvina struggled to keep her face impassive. She felt the burn of red in her cheeks, tears in her eyes. When they reached the woods, Laura let go of Melvina's shoulder. It was a relief to busy herself with clambering over stumps and under branches, fighting the brush as they headed for the trail.

They finally broke into the clear space of the path. "Let's go this way," suggested Laura. They walked in silence. "You know," she said at last, "it's not like the staff hasn't noticed what's going on, I mean, how the kids have been treating you." Melvina said nothing, drew her mouth into a pinched straight line. "They'd really like to help, Melvina. They really would." She glanced at Melvina for a reaction. "They thought it might help if someone talked with you, tried to find out what's going on...."

Melvina stopped in mid-step and turned to face Laura. "So, they picked you, huh?" Her voice was flat, uninflected.

"It wasn't like that. They asked me 'cause I know you pretty well and all. But I said 'yes' because I *wanted* to." Melvina's eyes blazed for a moment, and then the fire disappeared, was suppressed with a careful exhalation. "Will you talk to me, Melvina?" Laura's eyes were pleading.

"Sure," said Melvina casually, turning back to the trail and moving forward, "what do you want to know?"

Laura sighed and started after her. "All right, then, what happened? Did you really—shoot somebody?"

"Must have," said Melvina shortly. She looked at Laura. "I mean, last year, we were best friends, now...," she paused, "now we know each other 'pretty well.'"

Laura grabbed Melvina's shoulder, jerked her around. "Come on! I didn't mean it like that. I just...." she broke off.

"I just thought," said Melvina slowly, "maybe—it's like everyone else." She stopped and looked at Laura. The pain on Laura's face was obvious. "I'm sorry," said Melvina, looking at the ground. "I...." She said nothing for a moment. She shook her head. "It was awful."

Laura patted Melvina's shoulder tentatively. "It was an accident, wasn't it?" Melvina stared down and off to one side, her eyes transfixed, her face grave and unmoving. "Wasn't it?"

"I don't know," said Melvina. She shook her head. "That's what Dad and Lester say."

"What happened?" asked Laura, her counselor facade dropping away. "Why did you—shoot him?"

Melvina looked at the ground. "You know what?" She paused. "That's the first time anybody's asked me that." She kicked a tree root with one foot. "I guess everyone figures they know." She slipped her toe under the root, pulled on it hard. She fell backwards, but regained her balance, kicking the root savagely. "Bad blood, right?"

Laura shook her head. "Do you want to talk about it?"

"I don't know what to say."

"Try," said Laura, reaching toward Melvina, trying to turn her face toward hers.

Melvina jerked her head away. "It's so embarrassing. I.... The whole thing is really stupid, that's all. I didn't know what was going on." Laura said nothing. Melvina sighed. "I was waiting for Dad and Lester to get back. We were going to see Mom, you know, and they had to get a—something for the truck. So, I was waiting. I put on this stupid dress, you know, Mom liked it, and

121

then I heard the door, and it was John...." Melvina's face was red, her voice child-like. "I don't know if I can talk about this." She looked imploringly at Laura, who looked back, her eyes mild, waiting. "John came in, you know, to wait, and I went out in the kitchen and I came back in the living room.... John started saying some things, you know, compliments and stuff, and I wasn't paying attention to him...he's always around, you know, with Les, like...family." Melvina stopped again. She hunched her shoulders and twisted her lips together. "I don't know."

Laura looked at her for a minute. Thoughtfully, she asked, "Did he—do something to you?"

Melvina nodded. "I was too stupid to know what was going on. I just got scared, you know? He was hitting me when I tried to get him to stop, and...."She shrugged. "I didn't know."

Laura shook her head. "So...you got away?" Melvina nodded. "And you...?"

"I got Lester's gun. The one he keeps loaded. I...I don't know what I was thinking. I just thought he'd go away. I didn't want him to...." Melvina began to sob. Laura gathered her into her arms and held her tightly, Melvina crying on her shoulder.

"It's okay," said Laura. "It was an accident. I know you didn't mean to." Melvina wept more violently. Laura pressed Melvina's head against her shoulder with one hand. "Really. It's all right. It was one of those things. It...it was almost like self-defense." Laura stood and held Melvina as she cried, swaying her body back and forth ever so slightly, waiting patiently for the flood to end.

Half an hour later Laura and Melvina were on the ground, Melvina's head in Laura's lap. Melvina was wiping her eyes and blowing her nose on an over-used scrap of tissue. "Feeling better?" asked Laura, pushing a few sweaty curls off Melvina's forehead.

Melvina nodded. "I'm sorry."

"No," said Laura firmly, "you needed to talk. It must be hard with your...."

Melvina looked up suddenly. "She's not crazy, you know. She's got like a tumor."

Laura nodded. "My mother says there's a lot of small-minded people in this world."

Melvina agreed. She looked back toward Camp.

Laura dug into her pocket and pulled out a wristwatch, dangling it from its strap. "We have to go back," she said.

Melvina got up and offered Laura a hand. Laura got up, pausing to bow. "Thank you, m'dear."

Melvina giggled. It felt better now. It almost felt right.

They walked along the trail without speaking. "Hey," said Melvina finally, "is it really okay that I told you all that stuff and everything?"

Laura gave Melvina a shove. "Of *course*."

Melvina gave her a playful shove back. "But—are you going to have to tell the staff—about it?"

Laura looked at her. "Not if you don't want me to."

"It's embarrassing," said Melvina, wiping the end of her nose with the side of her hand.

"I understand," said Laura. "I have to say *something* to them, but...," she shrugged "...don't worry."

"Well," said Melvina brightly, "it can't get any worse."

"Mm," said Laura, all at once deep in thought. After another few minutes they had cut off the trail and back up toward the latrines. "One more thing," said Laura, stopping. "There's something I...want you to know."

"What?" asked Melvina. She was relaxed now, the first time Laura had seen her that way.

Laura turned to face her, grabbing Melvina firmly by the shoulders. "No matter what happens," said Laura sternly, "here or anywhere else, now or later on, I want you to remember something: you're a good person, Melvina Skittle, you're a good person and a brave person. There's nothing wrong with you." Melvina squirmed in Laura's grasp. Laura shook her like a rag doll. "Listen to me! You're not crazy, and you're not alone. I'll always be your friend, no matter what. Understand?"

"Sure I do," said Melvina, uncomfortable and confused. "Why are you...?"

Laura shook her head. "Just listen to me. I know this place. I know what it's gonna be like for you. Mel, they're never going to let you live this down. They'll never let it be easy on you...." There were tears in Laura's eyes. "And I'll probably never see you again...."

"What do you mean?" asked Melvina, alarmed.

"Listen to me. Whether I'm here or not, I'll always remember you. You can always come talk to me. You've been my best friend, Mel, and you always will, no matter what."

"But...?"

Laura cut her off. "I love you, Melly," she blurted, and

123

hugged her, impulsively kissing her on the forehead and then, more boldly, on the mouth.

Melvina was stunned. Before she could say or do anything, Laura turned and left, her figure disappearing wraith-like into the brush. Melvina stood where she was, her lips burning, her senses reeling.

Her head was still spinning as she climbed the hill to her cabin. Puzzling over everything, she looked for her supply of Kleenex as soon as she got to her bunk.

"How ya doin', Skit." It was Jan behind her. "Got a cold? You spend most of your time in that Kleenex box."

Melvina's conversation with Jan was repeated almost word for word the next morning when Melvina got up.

"I think you ought to check it out with the nurse," Jan suggested in a more than suggestive voice.

"I don't have a cold," Melvina protested.

In spite of Melvina's opinion, she found herself bundled off to the infirmary. The camp nurse, like Jan, was all kindliness and concern, and before Melvina knew what was happening, she was packed up and sent out to wait for her brother.

"That's funny," said Lester when she climbed into the car, "you don't *look* like you have a cold."

"I know," said Melvina, who was just beginning to figure it out, realizing that Laura had been sent, not to find out the truth, but to warn her of the staff's solution to its morale problem.

Melvina had sighed, sinking into the seat of the car. Then, as now, her eyes had not been on the road or houses they passed on the way home. Her eyes had found pain and solace in the green underbrush, where she could almost make out the disappearing figure of her conflicted and confounding friend.

15

Letters from Camp

Sal was standing by the checkout counter of a five-and-dime, waiting for Melvina to select her poster board and Magic Markers. The older woman behind the counter examined her with a bland and inquiring stare.

Sal winced and turned to the racks of key chains and postcards sitting on the far side of the cash register. Sal spun the display of postcards idly, silently cursing Melvina's indecisiveness and wishing they were back in the car.

The lettering on one of the cards caught her eye, and she paused, picking it up and smiling. The picture on the front was a rather unremarkable view of a very ordinary highway bridge, the kind traveled daily with hardly any notice that it is a bridge at all. The caption, however, proclaimed: "The Brooklyn Bridge." Puzzled, Sal turned it over and read that it was, indeed, a photograph of the Brooklyn bridge of Brooklyn, Connecticut.

Sal chuckled. She half-turned, as though to show it to someone beside her, and remembered she was alone. She shook her head and moved along the counter, placing the postcard in front of the surly cashier. "I'll take this one," said Sal, half-expecting her to smile and say, "Oh, yes, we sell a *lot* of these."

But no, the woman merely flipped the card over twice and said, "Fifteen cents."

Sal rooted in her pocket, discovered she had no change and decided to comment on the card. "Gee," she said, trying to sound innocent, "so that's the Brooklyn Bridge...."

The cashier peered at the card through the bottoms of her glasses and nodded, "Yes, that's what it is."

Sal reached for her wallet, shaking her head in wonderment. "It's smaller than I thought it was."

The cashier shot Sal a suspicious look and glanced a second time at the card. "Nope. That's the same size it's always been."

Sal suppressed a gale of laughter, desperately missing Ramona, imagining her there beside her, clutching her arm in agonized self-control. She laid a dollar on the counter.

"You're not from around here, are you?" the woman asked slowly, staring fixedly at the dark skin on the back of Sal's hand.

"Uh, no," said Sal quickly, a wave of discomfort washing over her. She cast a glance toward where Melvina had disappeared. "I think I'll wait outside," she said quietly. She noticed that the woman had given her ninety-five cents in change, but she said nothing, just scooped it up and turned away in embarrassment.

"You forgot your—purchase," the woman informed her.

"Oh, th-thank you," Sal stammered, grabbing the card and heading for the door.

Dear Ramona,

Haven't called cause not sure what in hell's going on. Find self in beaut downtown Kennedyville, CT. Wld you believe 'Hotel Wauregan'? Mel making signs—explain when call, prob'ly Boston. If you grant lg'st things can be learned fr smallest details, I'll sum up this place: saw woman coming down street w/2 kids, one in decrepit stroller & one (barely) toddling. Woman pregnant, looked under 18 over 45, if you get drift. 1st thought 'Oh, she's out w/sibs,' then realized was mother. Jolt: w/one hand pushed stroller, other hand? Thumb in mouth.... Mel's right at home. I'm NOT.   *Love, S.*

Melvina unlocked the door of the hotel room. It was dark inside. Sal, sitting against the headboard of one bed, betrayed her presence by the glow of her cigarette, the clink of ice in her cup. Melvina switched on a lamp.

"How'd it go?" asked Sal, squinting at the light.

"Not bad. I got the lay of the land, found out what time the desk jockeys go in in the morning. I even met a guy who thinks he knows him by sight."

"Good," said Sal, taking a sip. "All that and you made it back here with your virtue intact."

Melvina harrumphed noncommittally. "Sure you don't want anything to eat?"

Sal shook her head. "I'm fine."

"Getting there, anyway," commented Melvina with a glance toward the bottle on Sal's bedside table.

For a moment Sal did not answer. Then she said, "I don't know why we couldn't get two rooms."

"What a waste," said Melvina, shrugging. "Even this. Look at

126

it—two double beds." She shook her head. "We should have gotten a single. We could have shared the bed."

"Like hell." Sal stubbed out her cigarette and reached for the pack.

"What's the matter?" asked Melvina, flexing her eyebrows, "Afraid I'd bite?"

Sal lit her cigarette and threw the match at the ashtray, hard. "You try biting me and I'd break you in two." She paused to take a drag on her cigarette. "You'd leave here by airmail."

Melvina shook her head. "Friendly, aren't we?"

Sal tossed a couple of ice cubes into her cup. "I just like to be clear about these things."

Melvina nodded, her eyebrows raised. "That's clear, all right. Of course, I can't think of much else to do around here." She paused, casting her eyes around the room. "And it couldn't be worse for you than *that*." She pointed at Sal's bottle.

"Oh," said Sal, pouring another dollop into her cup, "I can't think of a nicer way to spend an evening in this dump."

Melvina furrowed her brows, her expression softening. "You really don't like this place, do you?"

Sal shook her head vigorously. "I hate it. It's depressing. Everything's cheap and ugly and ignorant." Sal paused, as though searching for words. "Today, in that store where you got the poster board...."

"Yeah, you've been acting funny ever since we left there. What's up?"

"Nothing," said Sal, hunching her shoulders. "Forget it. I just hate this place."

"I think I know how you feel," said Melvina, "that's how I felt at your friends' place. I mean, Hank and Bob were nice enough, but that—whole area gave me the creeps. Oh, well, payback's a bitch. I got mine, you get yours...."

Sal cocked her head to one side. "You seem tense, too."

"I am. I'm excited and I'm scared." She paced the room restlessly. "This is the closest I've come to finding her. It's like, I don't know, waiting for a bomb to land."

Sal nodded sagely, jerking a thumb toward the bottle. "You're welcome. I'm not *that* insistent on drinking the whole thing myself...."

"No, thanks," said Melvina, perching on a desk chair backwards. "I'm not good with the hard stuff. I'd probably have one sip, jump you, and get thrown out the window."

Sal laughed. "You've really got a problem, don't you?"

"Ha, ha. It's not funny. I mean, don't you ever get...?" Melvina looked at her sideways.

"Well," replied Sal, staring into her cup, "if I did, I think I'd keep it to myself." Melvina slapped one hand against the side of her chair. Sal startled, then relaxed. "Excuse me," she said, "so sorry I'm not a pedophile." Melvina gave her a wary, puzzled look. "I don't do children," she explained.

"I'm not a...oh, forget it. You're mean."

"Me? I'm not the one on a search for my long lost love, running all over the countryside making passes at everything that moos."

Melvina made a frustrated clucking sound and sighed. "She's not my 'long lost love,' she's just a friend. Why does everybody keep thinking that's why I'm looking for her?"

"Maybe it has something to do with your personality," suggested Sal lightly, emptying her cup. Melvina watched Sal's methodical drink mixing ritual, less steady than before, and said nothing. "It's too bad you didn't discover this insatiable sex drive of yours a little sooner. You could have approached Ramona. She's most obliging," Sal paused, glancing at Melvina, "and not terribly fussy."

Melvina's face darkened. "You're disgusting," she said, inflecting the words with her anger.

"I'm not disgusting, I'm just drunk enough to be honest. I'm also a prude. I know that's shocking in this day and age, but there you are." Sal paused to crush her cigarette in the ashtray. "I get so *sick* of people thinking that just because I'm a goddamned homosexual that means I have to be into every kink in town. You name it, whipped cream, orgies, chains—the minute you admit you're gay everyone thinks you're open to anything." Sal frowned. "Well, I'm not. You're welcome to be as heroically promiscuous as you can manage. Your morals, or lack thereof, are your own. So are mine. Is that okay?" Melvina stared at her in disbelief. "Well?" reiterated Sal.

"Oh, sure," nodded Melvina mechanically.

"Just because we're two lesbians in one hotel room does not mean I'm obliged to sleep with you, does it?"

"No," said Melvina, holding her hands up and away from her.

"Thank you," said Sal curtly.

"And *thank you*," said Melvina with gusto. "Little Melvina may think you're full of horseshit...." she began. Sal opened her mouth to say something. Melvina held up a finger. "*But* she also hopes your well-developed sense of moral superiority keeps you snug and warm tonight."

Sal closed her mouth and reached for another cigarette.

Melvina turned down her bed. "If you set yourself on fire," she muttered, "am I permitted to smother you with a blanket?"

"Don't bother," growled Sal, taking a healthy swig.

"I won't," said Melvina, turning off the light.

16

Catnap

Whenever Sal had drunk too much while out with Ramona, she always woke the next morning to find herself in her own bed and her own pajamas. She had thought she possessed a superhuman ability to go through the motions of getting undressed even while under the influence of an excessive amount of alcohol. That next morning she realized this was not the case. She woke to find herself sprawled across the bed, on top of the bedclothes and still fully, if not neatly, dressed.

"Shit," she muttered, coming to. "Damn," she said when she tried to open her eyes. Her head was a mess. It ached, it throbbed, it seemed to extend an unusual distance in every available direction. Her eyes were no better. They burned, they were coated with grit. They were not even functioning properly.

What Sal thought she saw when she opened her eyes was most peculiar. With her head almost hanging off the far side of the bed, her gaze was directed at a corner of the room. What she thought she saw was Melvina's kitten, Dadavi, standing on her head.

Sal squeezed her eyes shut and lay very still. She could hear Melvina in the bathroom. She could see moiré patterns dancing on her eyelids from the morning sun shining through the window. Good. Sal cautiously opened her eyes a second time.

Damn. Dadavi was still there, the crown of her head resting flat on the floor, the rest of her body awkwardly trying to move forward into the corner, paws flailing. Sal shook her head, crying out at the pain and wave of unpleasant visceral sensations this motion caused. She put her hand to her forehead and struggled off the bed. "Melvina," she called feebly when she thought her legs would not hold her. She sat down on the bed abruptly, relieved to find she had not missed it. She leaned forward and held her swimming head steady in her hands, blinking at Dadavi. She was not seeing things. The cat was lodged on her head in the corner near Sal's bedside table.

Sal cautiously cocked her head to one side. The strangest part was the way Dadavi's legs kept moving, as though the cat were unaware of the obstacle she had encountered or the unusual position she was in. "Melvina!" Sal called sharply. The sound of running water stopped. The bathroom door flew open, banging against the wall.

Sal struggled to straighten herself, to let go of her head and twist around to look at Melvina. She was standing in the bathroom doorway, wearing only her jeans and a towel around her neck. She held the ends of the towel by her waist in a gesture that was a cross between a stance of bravado and one of modesty. Her face was wet. "What is it?" she asked in an unfriendly voice.

"I... could you do me a favor?"

Melvina shifted her weight. "What?"

"Could you go downstairs and get me a cup of coffee?"

"I'm in a hurry," said Melvina, turning away.

"I know," said Sal, each word an effort, her voice cracking. "Just... please? I have to get ready to go with you anyway."

Melvina spun around. "I thought you'd want to sleep it off."

Sal waved an unsteady hand. "I... look." Sal pointed in the general direction of Dadavi.

Melvina craned her head forward and took several steps into the room, moving toward the bed. "What the.... What's she doing?"

Sal tried to speak and produced only a croak. She swallowed with difficulty. "Could you...?"

Melvina turned on her heel and disappeared into the bathroom. She returned with a styrofoam cup that was three-quarters full. "Here," she said. "It's still hot." Sal reached for the cup with a trembling hand. Melvina snatched it away. "Wait a sec," she growled, stalking back to the bathroom.

She returned in a moment with a cold washcloth. "No!" cried Sal, recoiling.

"Shut up," said Melvina, grabbing her behind the head. With her other hand she mopped Sal's face, ungently but thoroughly. "Give me your hand," she instructed. "Now the other one." Abandoning modesty, she whipped the towel from around her neck and wiped Sal's face and hands. She leaned forward to lift an eyelid. "Jesus," she muttered, sitting back on her haunches. "How the hell can you do that to yourself?"

Sal did not answer.

131

Melvina passed her the cup again, steadying Sal's hand with her own as she raised it to her lips. "Better?" asked Melvina. Sal nodded.

Melvina turned toward Dadavi. She paused, watching her. "Weird," she said, leaning forward to pick her up. She lifted the cat gently and tried to hold her to her chest. The cat continued her strange movements. Melvina shook her head and turned back to Sal, setting the cat on the bed beside her.

"No," said Sal, too late. The cat immediately started moving, quickly crawling over the side of the bed. She landed on her head on the floor.

"Ouch," said Melvina, reaching out to pick her up again.

"Don't," commanded Sal, setting aside the coffee cup. "Leave her alone. Watch her."

Without a word, the two of them leaned forward, watching the little cat move along the floor. Her movements were unceasing and mechanical, her head held low and at a peculiar angle. After moving forward several feet, Dadavi ran head-on into one of the legs of the bed. She never flinched and did not stop or alter her walking motions. She stayed where she was for nearly a minute, pushing futilely against the obstacle.

Finally, she stumbled past the bed, more by accident than design. She resumed moving forward, changing direction only when she ran into the wall. There she shifted direction so that she followed it, her head pressed against the baseboard, continuing until she collided with a corner of the room. Here she again attempted to go forward, her head twisting under her until it was upside-down, the movement of her legs continuing even once she had managed to invert her body.

Melvina turned to look at Sal. "I've seen her do some strange things," she began, "but...."

"Bring her here," said Sal, her voice stronger now.

Melvina fetched the cat. "What do you think?" she asked.

Sal held Dadavi's face between her thumbs, peering intently into it. Shifting her grasp so that one hand held her unwilling head still, Sal moved a forefinger carefully towards Dadavi's eye.

Sal's trembling finger touched one of the cat's whiskers lightly, and the cat winked. Sal gave an exasperated sigh. Bracing her elbow against her knee, she tried again, bringing her finger closer and closer. Finally she paused and then retreated. The cat never blinked.

"Damn," muttered Sal. "Here," she said, handing Dadavi to

Melvina, "hold onto her."

"What is it?" asked Melvina.

"Hold her right there," said Sal, returning from her whatnot bag with a pen light attached to a key chain. Melvina was having trouble keeping the restless creature still. "Try turning her upside down," instructed Sal.

Melvina turned the cat onto her back, at which point she calmed a little, twisting her head further and becoming almost still. Sal played with her pen light and the cat's eyes for a few minutes, flashing the light into one eye and then the other, sweeping it back and forth. Again she gently moved her finger towards Dadavi's eyes.

"The pupils respond," she muttered to herself, "but she doesn't see my finger...."

"Huh?" inquired Melvina.

"Nothing, but listen, we have to take her to a vet."

Melvina looked from the cat to Sal and back. "Are you sure? You know how she gets sometimes."

Sal gave Melvina a shocked and disapproving look, "Yes."

Melvina twisted one of her wrists around to look at her watch. Dadavi began her restless, mechanical movements once again. "But if I don't get down to Mirak pretty soon...."

Sal glared at Melvina. "I can take her," she said finally. "I'll drop you with your—sign, and then I'll come back to pick you up."

Melvina looked at her uncertainly. "You think you're okay to drive?" Sal nodded. "The Cadillac?"

"I'll manage."

Melvina shrugged. "If that's what you want to do...."

Sal looked at her in puzzlement and disbelief. "You don't understand. That's what I have to do."

• • •

Nine-thirty. Melvina looked from her watch to the phone booth. She glanced up and down the road, hoping to see Sal and the car. Nothing. The parking lot was full of cars and empty of people. All swallowed up by the buildings beyond the high fence. She missed her companions, the blue collar grunts with their lunch pails. They had pointed out Bill Monroe to her, and one of them, an ill-shaven man with a box of Marlboros poking out of his shirt pocket, had gone right up to him, had said, "Mr. Monroe, I've got that little lady I told you about, your wife's friend."

133

They had made it easy for her. Monroe was nice, a handshake that still tingled in her fingers, a hello that reverberated in her ears. Now she had Laura's phone number in her pocket, an available telephone, all the time in the world.

Melvina pinched her lips between her teeth. She wondered what she was waiting for. It was not until she entered the phone booth, slid the door shut behind her, that she wondered why the hell she was doing this. She wished Sal would come, she wished they could go back to Hank, or Sue, or kind Ramona. She wanted to run away. With the receiver in her hand she peered through the streaked and graffitied glass of the booth and decided she had nowhere left to run.

She dialed, spoke with the operator, heard rings and the click of the receiver being lifted. "Hello? Laura? Laura Maynard? Hi, this is Melvina, Melvina Skittle. I don't know if you'd remem.... Yeah, hi!" The voice on the other end of the line, sleepy, surprised, caressed Melvina's panic, soothed it. "It has been a long time, yeah. Well, I happened to be up this way, you know, and I'd heard you were up here, and I thought, gee, why not.... Yeah, I will be coming up to Boston, I thought maybe, if you're not.... Uh-huh, that'd be great. Well, I'm on a little trip, kind of a vacation, yeah. Would you really? Wonderful. I'll need directions, and...."

Melvina's own voice sounded as far away to her as Laura's, as unreal. She thought about Bill Monroe, that grown-up man who said Laura had spoken of her, and it felt very strange. Laura, barely in her teens, no, older than that, grown up, married. Melvina was confused. She felt far away, mechanical, as she spoke and laughed and reminisced. She felt as though she were in her car, driving very fast, chasing this familiar voice, blind to the road, unable to see the thing, the large thing up ahead that chilled her heart, that was coming at her. She could feel it coming.

• • •

Sal brought the car to a halt in front of the Mirak parking lot. Leaning forlornly against a phone pole was Melvina's hand-lettered sign, but Melvina herself was nowhere in sight.

Sal pulled the car over to the side of the road, put it in Park, and turned on the four-way flashers. Exhaling slowly, she slumped in the driver's seat, letting her forehead rest against the wheel. She felt awful. Every action, every gesture, every word she had uttered in the past two-and-a-half hours had required the marshaling of all the strength she had left inside her.

Her head ached. Her eyes burned. She felt exhausted and yet miserably far from sleep. Every joint and every muscle reminded her of the role each played in her simplest actions. "How the hell can you do this to yourself?" Melvina had asked. "Yeah, how," Sal wondered aloud. She felt immensely old.

"Guess what?" It was Melvina's voice at her elbow, Melvina at the window beside her. "We're going to Boston!" she announced, her voice the most cheerful Sal had ever heard.

"I know," replied Sal flatly. "You can drive," she added, starting to clamber into the passenger seat. "The Connecticut turnpike's only a couple of miles from here. You go down...."

"I know," said Melvina, opening the driver's door. "I already checked that out." She climbed in and fastened her shoulder belt, pulling the car away from the curb with alacrity. "Well," she went on, "don't you want to know what happened?"

Sal gave her a weary look, spiked with what little anger and wonder she could summon up, but Melvina did not glance her way.

"I found Bill Monroe. Talked to the man himself. I explained everything and he was very nice, gave me Laura's—their— address and phone number and everything." Melvina turned to Sal for a reaction, but Sal absorbed herself in staring at something outside her window. "Anyway, I called her right up from that phone booth back there," Melvina gave a jerk with her thumb over her shoulder, smiling triumphantly, "and talked to her. Can you believe it? We found her. We really did it." Sal said nothing. Melvina frowned momentarily and then went on. "I arranged to meet her at her house tomorrow afternoon."

Sal did not reply. She reached down to fiddle with a cardboard box between her feet.

"Well? Isn't that good?" Melvina glanced over at Sal and saw her lifting Dadavi onto her lap. "Oh, hello there. How's she doing?"

"Not well. There's a big animal hospital in Boston that's supposed to be pretty good. The vet made arrangements for me to take her there."

"Well, that's good," said Melvina cheerfully. "Nothing but the best for our little friend."

Sal gave Melvina a dark look. "Melvina, this isn't good. The vet's first suggestion was that he put her to sleep."

Melvina started. "What are you talking about?"

"She's functionally blind," said Sal crisply. "Yesterday she could see and today she can't. That's not good."

"But maybe that's why she's been acting so weird," said Melvina, her voice defensive. "I mean, she can live if she's blind, can't she? It's not that bad, is it?"

Sal shook her head. She looked at the cat, quiet now with her head lolling unnaturally over the edge of Sal's lap. "It's not just that. Her equilibrium's crazy, half the time she can't seem to stop moving.... Those are—well, something's wrong with her brain." Sal glanced at Melvina and realized she was not paying attention. There was a bright gleam in Melvina's eyes, and her hands tightened and relaxed on the steering wheel in response to some sequence of thoughts or feelings completely invisible to Sal.

Sal shook her head and did not bother to say anything more. She felt angry and abandoned. She thought to herself that now that Melvina had located her precious Laura Maynard, everyone and everything else was fading into the background. Stroking the white cat absentmindedly, Sal toyed with the idea that Dadavi was, quietly and ever so obligingly, fading right away, a pale Cheshire cat with not even a smile to leave behind.

• • •

Sal woke up when Melvina stopped to ask for directions. She did not remember falling asleep, and her first thought was of Dadavi, the worry that she may have gone off on one of her compulsive perambulations. She was relieved to find the cat still more or less lying in her lap.

"I saw you at the toll booth, trying to drive while you read your map," an auburn-haired businessman was saying. "That's why I figured I'd better pull over when you stopped." He smiled. "I wouldn't want you driving very far like that—you could be a menace."

Melvina tried to look abashed and failed. "So, you mean this isn't the right exit?"

"No, what you do is...." Sal stopped listening and leaned back. The faint Bostonian lilt to his voice was soothing. She closed her eyes and composed herself for whatever might lie ahead. The range of possibilities did not seem broad or encouraging.

"I got it now," said Melvina, rolling up her window. "What a nice man!" she remarked as she pulled out from the curb. "Little

136

things like that make me think there's hope for this world."

Sal squeezed her eyes shut and held her tongue. She saw no point in raining on Melvina's illusory parade.

In her occasionally haphazard and generally relaxed way of piloting her car, Melvina brought them to the animal hospital. Sal stuffed Dadavi into the cardboard box and folded down the flaps. She was not really surprised when Melvina suggested she wait for them in the car, and Sal offered no resistance. Idly, she wondered whether or not Melvina would even be there when she came out.

The front side of the modern brick building looked very much like most hospitals she had seen. There were signs directing one to the Ambulance Bay, Admissions, and so on. She smiled to herself as she pushed through the glass double doors, imagining an improbably clad Great Dane behind the Information Desk.

"May I help you?" inquired a most un-dog-like lady in spectacles.

"Yes, I have an appointment to see a, uh, cat neurologist?"

"Name, please?"

"Uh...." Sal hesitated, unsure whose name the woman was requesting.

"Yours," said the woman curtly. Clearly, she did not find such confusions humorous.

"Deevers. Sal Deevers."

"And the...patient's?" The woman was peering over the counter at the cardboard box.

"Dadavi. That's D-A-D-A-V-Y, or I, I think." The woman looked at her disapprovingly. "E?" suggested Sal. "I'm sorry. She's not my cat. I...."

"You will be assuming payment?" The woman uttered these words with a finality that informed Sal that she was navigating choppy seas.

"Uh, yes," said Sal, hoping she had said the correct thing. The woman inquired as to address and telephone number (Sal's), description and date of birth (Dadavi's), previous visits to the Hospital (Sal's or Dadavi's), and droned on through a list of questions that made Sal wonder whether or not she and Dadavi would ever be waved on—and whether or not Dadavi would survive that long.

When Sal was finally released, she was instructed to walk to another desk. She reported her presence there, was checked off a Master List, and was sent to the Billing and Payment Department. At Billing and Payment Sal waited in line with her cardboard box and whiled away the time by perusing a notice which explained that the making of plastic patient information cards would save the hospital and the patient's owner inestimable quantities of time during present and subsequent visits. Sal read this particular notice ten times before she was halfway up the waiting line.

When finally seated in Billing and Payment, Sal was quizzed about her Means of Payment in addition to the demographics which she had rehearsed at the Front Desk. There were moments when she wanted to scream and wave poor Dadavi around. There were others when she wanted to throttle Melvina for not being there with her goddamned credit cards when Sal needed her. At the last there was just exhaustion and excessive gratitude when she was finally allowed to return to Desk number two.

"Hello again," said Sal, handing in a wad of papers.

"Fine," said the woman behind the desk. "If you'll just have a seat until we call you."

Sal gave her watch a concerned glance. She had arrived half an hour before her scheduled appointment, and it was now half an hour past the appointed time. Sighing, she picked up the cardboard box and walked to the waiting area.

Taking a seat, Sal looked around at the array of cats and dogs in the waiting room, some impatiently waiting for routine examinations, others nobly enduring the pain of obvious injuries. She looked into her box at Dadavi, so still, almost fetal in the position of sleep she assumed. Sal's brows knit. She felt a surge of frustration, nearly tears. These other animals, frisky, whining, were clearly of the living. But Dadavi? Sal cupped one hand protectively around the back of the white cat's head. She found herself wishing that Dadavi would go back to the stage where she fought Sal's restraint, where she would once again ramble disconcertingly around the room on her strange sojourn. This is worse, thought Sal, but despite her touch the cat did not stir.

• • •

Sal was called twenty minutes later. Rising, she clutched the box to her chest, her arms stretched around it, her eyes impassive. She marched resolutely in the specified direction. Hers was the only measured step along a hallway that was crossed and busily recrossed by the white-clad staff. She paused by a door, her eyes checking the name on the chart in the plastic holder. Deevers, Sultana L., Ph.D. Sal entered the room.

There was a wooden bench along the wall near the doorway, and Sal sat down on it, resting Dadavi's box beside her. She looked around the empty room. There was a large steel table, its finish gleaming dully through an antiseptic glaze. On the far side of the table was a desk. Above, on the wall was a series of triangular plastic holders like the one outside the door, and the emptiness of the holders, as well as the orderliness of the desk, gave the room a barren look. Sal sighed. The room was painted white, completing its feeling of desolation.

The door opened and a white-coated woman went over to the desk. She was stoop-shouldered and old, the kind of person Ramona had once described as "on the sinking side of seventy." She snatched several wisps of paper from the desk and scurried back across the room and out the door. Her movements were spry but imprecise, suggesting that the motor that drove the machine was stronger than the thing itself.

Sal put her head back and regarded the ceiling. With one hand she stroked the sleeping cat. She became aware of some piece of a Christmas carol that was dancing around the edge of her consciousness. She hummed a bit of it and then tried to remember the words. No luck. The melody playing through her head was not from the beginning of the song, that much she could tell. She tried to go back to the beginning and remember it.

The door opened once again. Sal looked around. It was the same woman who had gone in and out before. This time she was advancing toward Sal, one hand extended.

"Dr. Deevers? How do you do, my name is Hepzibah Creely."

Sal rose and shook hands with the woman, wondering if this were the cat neurologist she was supposed to see. "You're...?"

"Yes," said Dr. Creely, smiling and nodding. The smile set off a chain reaction of wrinklings and crinklings across the woman's face. "I'm afraid you've pulled the 'B' team. There aren't very many of us, and no one else is available just now. I'm semi-retired."

Sal smiled back uncertainly, reaching into her jacket pocket for an envelope. "The veterinarian who examined Dadavi sent along this letter. He said he didn't know if his observations would be much help, but...."

"Fine, fine," said the doctor, taking the letter and retreating toward the desk. "Just give me a few moments with this and then we'll have a look at—Dadavi?"

Sal nodded and sat down. Hepzibah Creely proceeded to scrutinize the letter. Sal scrutinized the doctor for a moment, then lost interest. She put her head back and closed her eyes.

"Well," said the old woman's voice, "which is the patient?"

Sal jerked her eyes open and her head forward. Hepzibah Creely stood in front of her. For the first time since waking Sal became aware of how she must look, her ghastly pallor, her rumpled clothes. Embarrassed, she reached into the box and lifted out Dadavi without a word.

At Dr. Creely's gesture she rose and carried the cat to the examining table. "She's quiet now," she said. "She's been pretty deeply asleep for, oh, more than three hours."

Creely nodded, turning her attention to the cat. She ran a friendly hand over Dadavi's head and commenced her examination. Now her movements were steady and sure. Sal marveled at the variety of neurological questions Creely could ask of the cat—and to which she could elicit answers.

"You know something of the nervous system? He said your observations were astute."

"Just human neuropsych," mumbled Sal. "I wouldn't have any idea how to get this kind of information from an animal, without equipment...."

Creely shrugged. "Can you hold her up—that's right." She was moving the cat back and forth across the table, allowing just one or two limbs at a time to touch the surface, support weight, and she watched their movements carefully as she repeated the manipulations.

Sal shook her head, marveling at the woman. Something about both her knowledge and her cheerfulness bolstered Sal's sagging hopes for the first time that day. Silently, she rooted Dadavi on, cheering inside whenever the cat demonstrated a reflex or responded to a stimulation.

The bubble burst when Creely finished. She stepped back from the table, leaving Dadavi in a somnolent heap. She shook her head. "I can think of at least seven different things." She began ticking off viruses, injuries, poisons, and pathological conditions. "I can't give her more than a twenty percent chance of survival—and that's not saying whether she could ever be any better off than...," she pointed "...this."

Sal pursed her lips. "Do you think it's worth trying? Is she in

140

pain?"

"No," said Creely, her face rumpled with concern. "She's not in pain. There is some damage, but I can't tell you whether it's reversible or not. I just don't know. I could work her up. We'd know a lot more in a day, day-and-a-half. I do think it would be worth trying to find out what it is, but I can't offer you much re-assurance...."

Sal waved a hand. "I understand. Any guesses?"

Creely puckered her brow. "Well, I'd guess hydrocephalus, ex-cept the history isn't right. We'll see." She turned back to the desk. "If you're going to admit her, I'll have to write up some...." Creely's voice trailed off as she busied herself with forms and lab slips.

Sal leaned over the examining table and curled an arm around Dadavi's sleeping form. The Christmas carol played wordlessly through her head as she held the cat, hoping for a purr, trying not to cry.

She had a strong feeling of déjà vu that waxed and waned along with the tune of the Christmas carol. It was something about the clinical paraphernalia of the animal hospital, the white hair of the veterinarian, her feelings of helplessness and guilt....

With a sharp intake of breath, Sal remembered visiting her mother in the hospital at Christmas time, remembered all the bureaucratic foolishness of the hospital and the funeral parlor, remembered how hard January had been, back at school. She squeezed her eyes shut, ashamed, remembering how she had never acknowledged her mother's race—or life or death—to her friends at college, how she had gone along with her father in burying her mother's memory along with her body.

"There we go," said Creely, getting up from the desk. "I won't be available after tomorrow, so I'll give you a call in the early evening, perhaps late afternoon, to let you know where things stand. Oh, you don't have a phone?"

Sal took the pile of slips and forms that Creely handed her. Her voice, when she spoke, was unsteady, "Uh, not yet." She stopped to clear her throat. "When I get a room, can I call and leave the number?"

"Fine," the doctor extended her hand once again. "I'll have someone take her over to the ICU—for observation. I wish I could offer you more hope."

"That's all right," murmured Sal distractedly. "Thank you."

141

She hesitated a moment more by the table and then turned to leave, trying hard not to think about her mother. The music that played in her head swelled and faded by turns, like waves breaking on a beach, insistent, relentless. Sal tried to shake it off, wondering if she could possibly make it past the antsy, lively cats and dogs in the waiting area without sobbing hysterically. Just a damned cat, she thought emphatically, as she turned and crossed the lobby.

It was all at once that she recognized the figure waiting for her by a pillar and remembered the words to the Christmas carol she kept hearing. It was Melvina leaning against the marble, her arms crossed and shoulders stiff in her tough-guy pose. Some part of Sal let go, in anger and gratitude and relief. She passed a hand over her face, reached blindly for Melvina, and clutched a steadying arm as a single tear slid down her face. Ignoring the chaos of the waiting room, she could hear at last the words to the song: Above thy deep and dreamless sleep, The silent stars go by.

17

Recreation and Revelation

What Sal had planned after her shower was a nap. When she came out of the bathroom, however, she found Melvina perched on the edge of a bureau, possessed of all the ease and comfort of a bobwhite clinging to a telephone line in a gale wind.

"Nervous, hm?" Sal asked kindly. She was grateful to Melvina for not saying anything about how she had acted at the animal hospital, and she was determined to try to be as gentle with Melvina as Melvina had been with her.

Melvina gave her a lopsided grimace and a nod of her head.

"Hungry?"

"Yeah," said Melvina with gusto.

"Well, the afternoon isn't over yet. What do you say we go out and grab a bite to eat and take in the sights?"

Melvina smiled. "I thought you'd want to lie down."

Sal shrugged one shoulder, inclining her head to that side. "I'm beat, but I'm nervous, too. I'm not sure I could sleep. It's all down to waiting now, isn't it?"

Melvina hopped off the chest of drawers. "Yup. I don't see Laura till tomorrow, and we won't hear about...." Her voice trailed off. "It doesn't seem like one day. So much has happened."

Sal nodded, turning toward her suitcase. "And now, everything's slowing down. Waiting...."

"...Is awful," interjected Melvina with vehemence, bouncing on one of the beds. "So, where are we going?"

Sal reflected a moment, folding a shirt. "Well, I know my way around pretty well. I went to school here. Of course, that was a long time ago. You ever heard of Harvard Square?"

"I've heard of Harvard," volunteered Melvina.

Sal nodded, smiling to herself. "Well, Harvard Square is an interesting place—at least it used to be. They say Al Capp—you know who Al Capp is?" Melvina shook her head. "Well, he supposedly got his characters—he was a cartoonist—from the people who used to hang around the Square."

Melvina looked at her blankly.

"That's okay," said Sal, "why don't we check it out?"

Melvina had her jacket and was out the door before Sal could close her suitcase.

• • •

"You're never going to find a parking space for this boat," observed Sal. "Make a left."

Melvina followed Sal's instructions and brought the car into a parking garage. She halted the Cadillac by the gatekeeper's booth and accepted a ticket from the man. "Thanks," she said, stuffing it over her visor and putting the car in Drive.

"Hey," called the man, "don't put that there. There's lots of people would slit that rag top to get that ticket."

Melvina pulled down the ticket. "This?" she asked.

Sal grabbed it. "You just worry about missing the pillars. I'll take care of this."

"Why would anyone want it?"

Sal rolled her eyes. "Lower their parking tab. It'll be okay out of sight." Sal popped open the glove compartment and stuffed the ticket in. "That was close," she observed as the car rounded a turn onto the ascending ramp. "I don't think this thing was built with Cadillacs in mind."

Melvina shook her head, her eyes attentive to the gloom ahead. Once the car was securely berthed and locked, Melvina and Sal began retracing their path down the concrete ramps. Melvina shuddered. "I'm still not used to these places. Like some kind of, I don't know, car crypt."

"You got it," nodded Sal. "Not a bad turn of phrase. Can you picture the archaeologists of some future age, marveling at the edifices we built to house cars?"

"The Great Pyramid of—Cadillac!" exclaimed Melvina.

Sal nodded. "I always worry about that when I read about ancient cities. We have this tendency to see the past and the future through the ideas of our own culture."

Melvina's eyebrows went up as though she had just run head-on into a Profound Idea.

Sal smiled. "Doesn't take much to keep you amused, does it?"

"But that's neat," expostulated Melvina.

"Well, it's an idea," noted Sal dryly. "I suppose they don't have many of those back in Kentucky."

Melvina made a face. "They have lots of ideas. Maybe not

144

about too many things, but...." They both chuckled as they came out into the street.

"This way," said Sal. They walked up until they came to Massachusetts Avenue, just beyond the Square. Sal paused to get her bearings. "That's right," she said, turning in the direction of the traffic jam near them.

"What's in Harvard Square?" asked Melvina.

"Oh, bookstores, lots of bookstores. Restaurants, coffee shops. Other stores. Mostly, it's people. Couples strolling, making the scene. Academics wandering around, waxing intellectual. That kind of thing."

They passed a rare books shop, a camera store, a foreign bookstore, a run-of-the-mill bookstore. "Whew," observed Melvina, "you're right. I've never seen so many. Could we go in one?"

"Sure, I figured we'd check out the Coop. There are others that'll be open later. Or do you want to eat first?"

Melvina opted for the bookstores. "This is amazing!" she announced, riding up the escalator in the Harvard Coop. She was in her glory. Sal's chief pleasure was in watching her romp around, as excited as a three-year-old and just as curious. It was a kind of naïve and wolfish hunger that took hold of Melvina, the hunger of a mind that had somehow survived boredom and cant, starvation and ridicule, to emerge miraculously open and alive.

It reminded Sal of the way Ramona had been when she first met her, a crazy combination of irreverent sass and passionate yearning for knowledge of any kind. She remembered the first birthday present she had ever given her, a slim volume. She remembered Ramona bouncing around the room as though she had just been given the key to the city.

Sal smiled to herself. There had been an unguarded quality to Ramona then, a vulnerability, a sincerity, that Sal had not seen in years. Ramona still had a look of concern, a manner that promised sincerity, but those were just her stock in trade, a winning facade fashioned upon the shell of who she once was. Sal sighed, watching Melvina launch an assault on a display of paperback books. For the first time she felt a spark of tenderness toward Melvina, and with it a pang of loathing for herself.

Melvina did not slack off until they had visited three more bookstores. Sal grimaced in the last one, busying herself with a best-seller after Melvina strode up to the cashier, seated in a booth above the level of the rest of the shop, and inquired loudly,

"Pardon me, but could you direct me to the lesbian books?"

Sal groaned inwardly and reddened, wondering how many of the patrons had noticed Sal come in with Melvina. "Haven't you ever heard of tact?" she remonstrated once they were back outside.

"What do you mean? I just thought I'd ask. You said they had every kind of book in Harvard Square, but I haven't seen many lesbian books."

Sal sighed. "You're right, I guess. How dare you go around destroying my illusions? I always thought they had every book worth reading."

Melvina patted Sal's shoulder in consolation and insisted on carrying their bag of books. Sal relinquished the parcel, noting to herself that only two or three in the bunch were hers.

Melvina spent most of their dinner looking through her new acquisitions, pouring over book jackets and tables of contents. "I never would have guessed at your scintillating dinner table conversation," remarked Sal.

"I'm sorry," said Melvina, making a valiant effort to extricate herself from one of her books and failing.

Sal amused herself with rereading the wine list and eavesdropping on the other diners. "I'm putting gravy on that if you don't put it away," she finally said.

Melvina made a great show of reluctantly stowing her booty and resigning herself to Sal's company. Sal responded by delivering a grumpy oration on the Decline of Simple Politeness. All in all, there passed one of the most copacetic interludes that Sal and Melvina had managed to date.

It was a relief to both of them, and they left their table reluctantly. On the other hand, it did not surprise Sal that only ten yards from the restaurant, Melvina went and ruined everything.

"What is it?" asked Sal, glimpsing a change in Melvina's coloring.

"I—don't know. I don't feel too good."

Sal shook her head. "You've been wound up like a spring."

"I'm sorry, I...." Melvina slowed her steps.

"Look, why don't you just sit down here. I'll get the car." Sal guided her to the news stand on the corner, wheedling permission from the reluctant hawker for Melvina to rest on an empty crate. "I'll be right back. You hang onto your books."

Sal struck out along Mass Avenue in the direction of the side street where the parking garage was located. Fumbling with the

146

car keys she walked quickly. She got there in less than ten minutes. "Idiot kid," she muttered to herself, "she's just too excited."

Sal started the Cadillac and backed it out carefully, taking the down ramps with extraordinary care.

"Ticket?" asked the man in the toll booth.

"Oh, yes, wait a minute," Sal muttered. She leaned over and opened the glove compartment. She switched on the light and began digging through the junk accumulated there. She took out maps and wads of Kleenex, sunglasses and change, dumping them all on the seat. "Hold on," she called to the impatient gatekeeper. She pulled out another bunch of maps, the car's registration and owner's manual, and, finally, the parking garage ticket, which had fallen down behind everything else.

"There we are," she said as she handed it to the man, trying to sound cheerful. "Okay?" she asked as she handed him money.

Sal put the car in gear, turned out the light, and began to move forward. With a jerk she hit the brakes. Putting the car in Park, she turned to the pile on the passenger seat. She picked up the light brown envelope and stared at the typewritten words visible through the plasticene window. She shook her head. Switching on the light and ignoring the car that was honking at her, Sal removed the slip of paper from the envelope.

It was the registration, all right. And it was made out in the name of Melvina S. Skittle.

18

Telling Secrets

It wouldn't have done any good to ask her about it, thought Sal. She just would've come up with some new and improved lie. That was not all there was to it, of course. There was also the fact that it is difficult to cross-examine someone who greets your arrival with a waif-like "I whupped my cookies."

I'd like to whup more than your cookies, thought Sal, pacing the motel room. She paused to squint at her travel clock. Two a.m. Sal stubbed out her cigarette ferociously. *It doesn't make any sense. Why would someone lie about something like that?* She glared in the general direction of the sleeping Melvina. Even through the shadows, Sal thought she could make out a cloud of curls, wafting angelically above an unwrinkled brow. *She has got to be some kind of pathological liar.* Sal gave her head an angry shake. "You think you've taken us all over the hurdles, don't you?" she muttered.

There was no answer, not even a restless groan. Sal lit another cigarette and inhaled deeply, trying to remember everything Melvina had ever said about herself. It did not amount to much. Tapping her lighter against her chin, Sal turned slowly on her heel and looked toward the pile of clothing at the foot of the bed.

"Hm," she said to herself and walked over. She picked disdainfully through the heap until she found Melvina's wallet in a pants pocket. She hefted the plump accessory with one hand as she moved toward the window, spreading open the wallet where the light from a streetlamp trickled between the curtains.

She did not hesitate. She felt not one pang. If Melvina and Melvina's cat were going to keep her up all night, Sal figured it was as good a time as any to start finding answers.

● ● ●

Sal awoke in the early afternoon. She could see Melvina fretting in front of the bathroom mirror, pausing to check her watch. "The big day, huh?"

Melvina startled and glanced at her over one shoulder. "Hi. I thought you'd be asleep till I got back."

Sal rolled over and reached for a cigarette. "No such luck." She tapped the filtered end on her thumbnail. "You don't want me along for moral support?"

The face that looked at Sal the second time was plainly nervous. "Oh. I—thought you'd want to stay here. Aren't you going to wait for—a call?"

Sal stretched and yawned. "Whatever you say. Any idea how long you'll be?"

Melvina shook her head. "But I probably ought to get going. I checked it on the map, but...."

"Randolph, didn't you say? That shouldn't be too hard."

"Yeah, well.... I better get going." Melvina came out of the bathroom with a hairbrush clutched in one hand. She paused to transfer the contents of the pockets of her jeans to the corduroys she was wearing and then picked up her jacket. "You be okay?"

Sal nodded. "Have a nice time."

"Thanks. Wish me luck." Melvina was already at the door.

Sal glanced down momentarily, opening her mouth to speak. When she raised her eyes to the door, it was closed. Just like that, Melvina was gone. "That was fast," Sal sat up and swung her legs over the side of the bed. She shrugged, yawned, and checked the clock. *Time for a cup of coffee, maybe even a walk*, she thought. She stood up and leisurely began to dress. There was no hurry. She could tell it was going to be a long afternoon.

● ● ●

The call came sooner than Sal expected. She was lying across the bed, trying to find her place in the novel she had begun at Bob and Hank's, when the phone rang.

"Hello? Dr. Deevers? This is Hep Creely."

Sal pressed the receiver into her shoulder with her chin as she reached for a postcard, stuffing it into place as a bookmark. She pushed the book aside and sat up, wondering idly why this woman was so respectful of Sal's title and so indifferent to her own. "Yes?"

"I have some sad news for you." Creely paused. It was the kind of pause Sal knew to be very polite. Let it sink in. The kind of pause compounded of equal parts consideration and dread. "Your kitten, Dadavi, died this afternoon."

Sal reached toward her book, wondered which postcard she

149

had used as a bookmark. "I guess it's...just as well." She sighed.

There was a rustle of papers. "The cause of death may have been secondary, but her EEG—extensive, bilateral damage. Hydrocephalus, it looks like, fluid pressure on the brain. A typical course, but...."

Sal made a small noise of assent, nodding her head.

"Even if she'd survived longer, I'm not certain there would have been much we could have done for her. We don't get to see too many of these—they're usually put to sleep undiagnosed."

"Yes, I guess with cats...."

Dr. Creely paused. Sal heard the sound of a deep breath. "Listen, um, what I'd like to ask you for—I know it's hard, but—well, I'd like permission to have an autopsy done on Dadavi. We'd like to understand what happened."

"I, uh...." said Sal, thinking of Melvina.

"As I said, we don't see too many. We'd like to learn all that we can, be able to help the next one."

"I, well, yes. I don't see anything wrong with...."

"If you'd like to think about it...."

"No, that's all right. I think it's a good idea. Would I be able to find out...."

"Yes, it would take several months for all the tissue...."

"I understand," interjected Sal, not wanting to imagine it. "Um, I'll be going back to Philadelphia. How do I get in touch with you about the results? Do I phone, or...."

There was a pause on the other end of the line. Sal heard a sound somewhere between a chuckle and a cough. "No. I'll be leaving today to go play patient myself. I won't be on staff any longer."

"I'm sorry to hear that." There was an awkward moment's silence into which Sal finally blurted, "Tests?"

This time she was sure she heard an amused, throaty sound. "Um, no. More like treatments—sort of."

"Oh, I'm so sor...."

"No." Creely spoke emphatically. "Don't be sorry. I feel much worse for your little Dadavi—and for you. It's obvious you loved that kitten very much."

Sal said nothing. Vividly, she recalled the sure and knowing touch of the doctor's veiny hands upon the sleeping cat. That was only yesterday. It could not be that now Dadavi was gone, and soon the doctor herself....

"It's not so bad, really." Creely's voice was quiet. "I...." She

150

broke off as though unsure whether to continue. "Do you have a few minutes? Can I tell you about something that happened to me?"

"Sure," said Sal. She stared down at her book, felt the hand that held the receiver begin to perspire.

"Well, I had scarlet fever when I was a girl. I was very ill." Creely paused as though to allow Sal to cut her off. After a long moment, she continued. "It came on very suddenly. All at once this fever, my mother wringing her hands. When my father arrived they bundled me up and he took me off to the doctor. It was a long trip, I remember that much. It was cold outside, and I kept my face buried in his coat as he carried me. I don't think I looked around at all until we were going up the street where the doctor lived. There was a strong wind blowing, and I remember it stung my eyes when I opened them."

Creely paused once again, and Sal wondered whether she should say anything.

"At least I think I opened them. I was ill, it's hard to say. I saw the strangest thing. There was this old woman, Mrs. Drummy, hurrying down her porch stairs all excited. She was just in a house dress, despite the cold, a house dress with a blue and white checked apron. The ties were hanging down behind her, waving in the wind—like kite tails, I thought. That was the strangest part. She was a lean, bony old thing, stepping right along, bowlegged, unsteady, with her big washerwoman hands clutching the sides of her apron. She seemed frail enough to blow away in the wind. I said, 'A kite, Daddy!' and I pulled my hand out of the blankets to point at her. I remember he turned around, trying to stuff my little arm back in, and he looked and said something, I don't know, 'Gonna catch her death out here, looking for a cat.'

"That was the end of it, as far as he was concerned. He didn't look again, but I did. And it seemed to me, as I watched that odd figure, that old woman making her way up the sidewalk to the top of the hill, as though...." Creely paused, searching for words, "as though she had—risen, little by little, uneven at first—like a kite, catching the wind. At first I thought my eyes were playing tricks on me, or the wind, or the fever—I wasn't a completely daffy child—but then it really seemed to happen. Because when she reached the top of the hill, she didn't disappear over it. Instead, she seemed to rise up and up, floating off on the wind, higher and higher. I called to my father but he didn't seem to

151

hear me. I wanted him to see what I saw, a kite with blue-and-white checked tails, and later, an eagle, soaring."

Creely stopped again. "Then what happened?" asked Sal.

"That's all I really remember. For days. Days of fever and delirium I watched that old woman, a kite, an eagle, flying away." She paused for a long time. "I came out of it. I survived. I wasn't the same child, but I was alive. I had this—feeling, that what I'd seen, what I'd watched, was death. Even when I got older, and came to mistrust a child's recollections—and fevered at that—I never lost the sense of revelation I had that winter afternoon." She trailed off.

"I, uh," Sal broke into the silence uncomfortably, "I'm not sure I...."

"All at once it made sense to me why people get bony and small with age, skin wizening into finest paper, sinews into string. Age is just a kite maker, readying the soul to fly. It helped me to understand that death is a part of a process, not some big thing in itself.... I don't fear death, I never have. That's what I started out to explain. The only sad thing about death, is its circumstances. When it's cruel or unjust, premature."

Sal thought about Dadavi, she thought about Hepzibah Creely. She did not agree.

Creely went on all of a sudden. "Not being afraid of death doesn't stop you from fearing other things, from fearing life."

"What do you...?"

"Oh, I used to be afraid I wouldn't do things well enough." She laughed. "Later, that I'd do them too well."

"Too...?"

"If you hold the strings too tight, Dr. Deevers, you never get off the ground."

Sal said nothing.

"Well," said Creely abruptly, her voice hearty, "you have been most patient with my ramblings. It's a privilege of age, isn't it?" She paused once more. "I've never told anyone about that. I guess I thought they'd think I was crazy. It's funny, though, isn't it, how we keep a secret until we've got no one left to tell." There was another pause. "Well, you can direct your inquiry about the autopsy to—let's see, Dr. Staunton. He'll be handling it. Got that?"

"Yes, I...."

"I've enjoyed talking with you, Dr. Deevers. Again, I'm very sorry about your cat. Goodbye."

Sal heard the receiver on the other end click. She sat with the phone held away from her, looking at it with her brows raised. "That was odd," she said.

Sal reached over to place the receiver in its cradle, thinking to herself that Creely was a queer old duck. It was just as she was setting the receiver down that the first wave hit her. As if struck a hard blow, Sal felt herself sliding off the bed, one hand still on the telephone. It hit so hard, so fast, that she could not be certain just where this grief was coming from, or whom it was directed toward. Dadavi, Creely? Her mother, herself? She glanced down at her hands, noting for the first time how they resembled her mother's, folded placidly in the casket. "I don't need this!" she cried as her knees hit the floor, her last words before her sobs made it impossible to speak.

• • •

"Oh, Jeez," said Sal. *A hangover*, she thought. *Was I drinking?* She pushed her torso off the bed with arms that trembled. Her eyes felt clean. *Visined*, she thought, but her eyelids and face felt puffy and hot. *I must have fallen asleep*, she thought, steadying herself on the edge of the bed.

She rose and teetered into the bathroom, pulled back from the face in the mirror. "I was crying," she informed herself, adding, "It's good to have a nice cry now and then." She bent over the sink, splashing hot water on her face and neck. *If it's so wonderful*, said a voice in her head, *how come you never do it?*

"Fuck off," said Sal to no one in particular, reaching for a towel. She pointed an accusing finger at her reflection in the mirror, "You're going to have to give up clean living before it kills you." She threw the towel over her shoulder in a superior manner and turned her back on her reflection.

"Where the hell are you, anyway?" she asked Melvina's jeans, "Off on another two-day spree?" She marched over to her bedside table to check the time. She shook her head and sighed, sitting down on the bed.

About time to call ol' Ramona bones, she thought. After a short skirmish with the front desk, she managed to put through her call. She hummed as the phone rang, wondering momentarily why she was in such a good mood.

"Hello?" she inquired, breaking off her humming abruptly, "That you?"

"Why, hello stranger," replied Ramona. "For a moment I

thought this was just your average obscene phone call."

Sal smiled at the familiar voice. "Obscene, maybe. Average, never. Thought it was about time I let you know what was happening."

"What's happening?"

"Well, let's see. We found Laura Maynard, whoever she is. Melvina's supposed to be talking to her now."

"Where are you?"

"Boston."

"Whew, you've really taken the tour, haven't you?"

"Yeah. It's good to hear your voice."

"It's good to hear yours." There was a momentary pause. "So, tell me everything. What happened, how'd you find her, how are you, anyway."

"Well, I'm okay. Melvina's her usual strange self...."

"I have some things to tell you on that score, but go on."

"She was pretty nervous this morning about seeing Laura. I'm afraid I have some bad news about her cat—you remember Dadavi?"

"Yeah, what's wrong?"

"She's dead."

"What?"

"Yeah. Hydrocephalus. That's...."

"I know. That's a shame—I feel terrible. I should have known, she acted so strange, sleeping all the time...."

"That's how I feel. Of course, we all commented on it. Skittle just kept saying that was normal for her."

"How's she taking it?"

"She doesn't know yet. I'm not sure how she'll—she's been very strange about the whole thing. Indifferent, almost, or—I don't know, denying...."

"Yeah. That doesn't surprise me, though—what rotten luck! That can't be a very common thing for a cat...."

"It's not."

"The poor kid."

"Poor kid, my ass. You haven't seen her operate like I have."

"Maybe not, but...."

"The hell with her. How are you?"

"Oh, I'm okay...."

"Doesn't sound it. What's up?"

"No big deal. Oh, did you hear that Julie's found someone to move in with her?"

"So that's it."

"No, it's just that Julie has a lot of room, what with Sandy off at school most of the year...."

"Sure. When did this one bite the dust?"

"Come on...."

"How are you feeling, Ramona?"

"Like shit—So what else is new?"

Sal said nothing for a moment. "I'm sorry to hear it," she said quietly.

"Oh, hell. I think I'm losing my touch, Deevers."

Sal smiled. "Never. The graveyard they bury you in...." She laughed, "Hell, where they try to bury you—is gonna be a lively place."

Ramona chuckled thinly.

"I wonder if I can get a plot with a view of the proceedings," added Sal, dead-pan meditative.

"Oh," said Ramona, trying to work up to banter, "you'll always be welcome in my plot...."

"Down, huh? Well, look, I think we'll be back tomorrow...."

"Tomorrow?"

"Yeah, if I can corral Ms. Libido, I think we'll head back tomorrow morning, bright and early. I'm sick of Skittle and her moods, and her Laura, and her poor dead cat. I want to come home."

"You've been gone a week," said Ramona in a small voice.

"Too long. Maybe we can plan to rendezvous at Peaks, how's that sound?"

"What time?"

"We should be back early. How about right after work, okay?"

"Sounds good."

"Yeah, we can catch up on everything then."

"Great. Uh, listen, maybe I ought to fill you in on what I've been up to here. I was watering your plants when Sue White called. She was looking for Melvina."

"Oh, really?"

"Yes, we had a most interesting conversation. She's a smart little cookie...."

"Mm...."

"...Very concerned about Melvina. It wasn't very hard to pry out of her what she'd pried out of Melvina...."

"Really." Sal's voice had a cool edge to it.

"There you go again, Sal."

155

"I just think she's had a little thing for you ever since she met you in the bar."

"I'm just irresistible. Anyway, that got me pretty curious again, and I made some phone calls. Got lucky this time—or just smarter."

"Yeah?"

"Are you sitting down?"

Sal stood up. "No. Why?"

"Sit down."

"Come on, Ramona...."

"Do it. I know you. I really think you ought to sit down and compose yourself...."

"This is silly. Anyway, I think I...."

"I don't think you do. Trust me, Sal. Sit down."

• • •

Melvina turned the corner and looked for the house number. There it was. Pink, as promised. Melvina hesitated and then parked the car by the curb. She switched off the ignition and dropped her hand to the seat beside her, groping for the reassuring warmth of Dadavi. She remembered.

Melvina swung open the door of the Cadillac, steeling her nerve as she climbed out. She ran a hand through her curls and tucked in her shirt. She put on her sunglasses and took them off. She hooked one bow of the sunglasses over the placket of her shirt. Squaring her shoulders, she strode up the concrete walk to the house.

"Well, hello," said Laura, opening the front door. she was wearing a pair of nondescript slacks under a bulging maternity top. "Isn't it awful?" she exclaimed, her voice exasperated. "We are planning to have it painted. Any color but pink. Of course, Bill thinks they could have gotten more for it if they'd bothered to paint it first...."

Laura opened the door wide and stepped back. Melvina climbed the two steps and came through the door. She was relieved to have her eye level higher than Laura's uterus. "Hello," she said shyly, as Laura closed the door.

"Hi," said Laura uncertainly. "I'm so surprised to see you."

"Yeah, well, like I said, I figured since I happened to be traveling through...." She glanced down at her feet and back to Laura. "It's been a lot of years."

"Yes! I was just figuring it out last night. Bill asked me. It's

156

been—ten years?"

Melvina nodded and smiled. "I'm almost surprised you remember me."

"Remember you? Jeez, Melly, that's ridiculous. You weren't a forgettable person.... Look, what are we doing standing here? Come on in and sit down. Can I get you something?"

"No, no, that's all right." They were moving from the foyer into the living room. There were two couches, facing each other, on either side of a fireplace. A low coffee table stood between them. Melvina chose a couch and sat down.

"Lemonade? I just made a pitcher—I'm having some."

"Okay, sure." Melvina looked around at the unfamiliar furnishings while Laura went into the kitchen. It occurred to Melvina that there was no reason why anything should look familiar; she had never been inside Laura's family home. Melvina hunched her shoulders as though to ward off a chill. Despite the very ordinary decor of the place, despite Laura's hospitality, Melvina felt out of place and ill at ease. She felt a child in an adult's world, or worse, like an adult stuffed into a child's game of House.

"Here we go," announced Laura, returning with pitcher and glasses on an aluminum tray.

Melvina accepted her glass, meanwhile searching for scraps and rags from which to construct a conversation. "This is a nice place you have," she ventured.

"Except that it's pink," iterated Laura.

Melvina kept her eyes on Laura and nodded, her bobbing head feeling like that of a puppet. "It's really not so bad," she suggested, watching Laura's face contort with disagreement. She smiled mischievously, "Of course, I wasn't sure I should park my car right in front of it...."

Laura guffawed. "Quite a picture, huh? Good layout for House Beautiful."

Melvina smiled, considering the possibility that if Laura mentioned the color of her house one more time she would scream.

"So, how have you been?"

"Okay," replied Melvina, sipping her lemonade.

"I, uh, I heard your brother was in a bad accident."

"Yeah."

"That was quite some time ago, wasn't it?"

Melvina nodded. "Almost six years. No, more than that."

157

"My mother wrote me about it. Sent a clipping, I think. Was he hurt badly?—Oh, I'm sorry. I...." Laura flustered. She apparently remembered what his injuries had been.

"It's okay," said Melvina.

"That must have been so hard...."

Melvina shrugged. "Between taking care of him and trying to support us...."

"Wasn't there a lawsuit?"

Melvina nodded. "Dragged on forever."

There was a lapse in the conversation. Laura looked down to one side. Melvina dropped her gaze from Laura's face and encountered her pregnancy once again. Melvina shifted uncomfortably. It did not feel right. Nothing felt right. They were not children anymore; they did not know one another. Laura's fetus seemed to loom between them, like trying to talk over a boulder.

Laura looked up and saw Melvina looking at her belly. She smiled and patted it. "Pretty soon."

Melvina nodded, trying to smile.

"It must be very hard for you with your brother—paralyzed like that."

"Yeah.... It was hard since he didn't have insurance. I worked two jobs for awhile...." Melvina shook her head. Her voice sounded dull and mechanical to her, far away.

"Well," began Laura perkily, "how's he doing now?"

There it was. It was not the way Melvina thought it would be at all. Her arms felt like wood. Slowly she said, "He's...dead."

"Oh," said Laura, the utterance ejected from her as if by a blow. "I'm sorry to hear that. You were always close to him, if I remember...." Melvina said nothing. After a moment Laura went on, "I suppose after all you both went through it was a blessing in a way...."

Melvina did not respond. She sat looking Laura straight in the eye.

"When...." Laura hesitated, "did it happen?"

Melvina moved her lips to speak. They felt thick and rubbery. How odd. She felt a kind of distant concern. This was not right. She could feel herself becoming more rigid and heavy, as if she were turning to stone. She politely got out her reply after a great effort, "Almost two weeks ago."

Laura startled a second time. "I'm so sorry to hear that," she repeated, her eyes wide.

Melvina wondered idly whether or not Laura's house had a

basement. It worried her. She could feel herself becoming heavier and heavier, sinking into the couch. She could easily imagine it getting worse, imagine her body plummeting through the couch and floor below, creating a mess in the basement, the centerpiece of which would be too massive to remove. Melvina glanced up at the ceiling as if to buoy herself. "It was suicide," she said, her monotone echoing in her ears. Far away she could hear Laura gasp. "He killed himself the only way he could." She paused, wondering how much more the couch could take. "He bit through an electrical cord with his teeth."

19

The Rules of the Game

Melvina spun the wheel of the car, angling it into one of the few available parking spaces. She hit the brakes abruptly just as she was about to clip the next car. Sighing, she shifted into reverse and backed up. Hack, hack, hack. Sooner or later it would fit, but the nearness of the car parked behind her insured that she would have to work at it. Melvina wondered whether she would live that long.

Finally, the Cadillac was nestled between its neighbors. She turned off the ignition and dropped her hands from the wheel. The only feelings she could summon up were exhaustion and dread. She felt old, her limbs heavy as oak. She felt foolish. *What now?* she thought, *What was the point?* She tried to remember, and could not. She felt as though she had spent a long time pushing toward the final exit door and had found it, too, locked. Melvina sighed. How, she wondered, could she explain it to Sal? *Hell, Sal won't care. She'll just be annoyed.* Ramona? That one was tougher. Melvina considered the possibility of just starting up the car and driving away.

Her lips compressed themselves into a wide, straight line. She was too—tired. She felt she had no place to go and no energy left to get there. *Maybe it won't be too bad.* She considered. Maybe Sal would leave her alone, more pleased the quest was over than curious about what had happened. Melvina opened the car door. *That's right. It'll be okay.* She even thought that Sal's unintrusive company might be a comfort.

Melvina stood by the driver's side, gazing at the empty car. There was no Dadavi to cradle in her arms, unwind from around her neck, perch on her shoulder. Melvina knew that there never would be again. Sal, she decided, was the crazed optimist. Melvina knew death when she saw it coming. She had seen it enough. She was the Typhoid Mary, the magnet, the carrier. Her love was a curse, her kiss was contagion. She thought of Sue and shuddered.

She shook her head, remembering. How gently Melvina had tucked the blanket around Lester that last time! How thoughtfully she had told him just where she was going, how long she would be gone! How sweetly she had rearranged the cord of the reading lamp as he requested! How loving an accomplice she had been! Melvina slammed the car door.

She could not tell anymore whom she hated most. She pointed her mask of a face at the ground and propelled herself toward the door of the lobby. She did not look to either side as she walked through. One hand fumbled with the room key as she came down the hallway. She sighed as she fit the key to the lock.

The room was dark. She flipped on the light but did not see Sal. Puzzled, she scouted the room and bath. No Sal, no note, no clue. Sal's suitcase was there: packed, latched, and standing ready on the floor. *Would she have left without her luggage? No,* thought Melvina, shaking her head.

Melvina tossed the room key onto one of the beds and sat down in a chair, her knees apart, arms dangling between them. *Where did she go?* Melvina had had the car; Sal had given no warning. She leaned back in the chair and remained there for a long time.

It has to be a drink, she decided finally. *Sal must have gotten thirsty and gone out for a drink—or a bottle.* Melvina nodded. That had to be it. There was something just slightly reptilian in Sal's nature, a disinclination to stir from a warm and sunny spot unless she really needed something. *A drink,* thought Melvina, *is the only thing she'd want that much.*

Melvina waited. She sat in the chair a few minutes longer and then stretched out on the bed. She lay there like wood, unbearably weary, unalterably alert. She waited some more.

She made herself lie there an hour. After that she got up, paced, rattled empty drawers looking for some clue, something to do. Melvina was deeply engrossed in a doodle of a crashing airplane when Sal finally walked in. "There you are!" she exclaimed, looking up, her relief sounding almost like pleasure. She noted this and adjusted her voice accordingly before demanding, "Where the hell have you been?"

Sal stood just inside the entrance to the room. Her gaze was alert and level, her bearing regal and self-possessed. *She doesn't look drunk,* thought Melvina. Indeed, her summer suit looked as neat as it had, unworn, in the suitcase; her collar points brushed her lapels with symmetrical, even fastidious grace. Sal was not drunk. Melvina's ball-point hovered over the piece of paper in mid-mark. She considered. No, Sal was not drunk, and for once she was not even pretending to ignore Melvina.

Under that steady stare, Melvina began to feel more naked than she had in Sue's apartment. "Where were you?" she asked timidly.

In reply Sal reached under the flap of her coat pocket and slowly raised her hand in front of her. Foop! Like a magician at a children's party, Sal produced an object in the fingertips of her upraised hand. It was a whitish rectangle, its corners rounded. It was a credit card. "I decided," she said casually, "that it was time you treated me to a nice, big dinner."

Melvina set the pen down. She rested her hand stiffly over it. For a moment she flagged, thought, *What the hell is this?* Then she sighed and answered, "I'm sure Uncle Lester will be thrilled."

"There is no Uncle Lester," Sal said evenly. "You made him up."

Melvina glanced down at the sheet of paper and then back at Sal. "I never said there was." Sal began to say something, but Melvina cut her off. "I mentioned an uncle at Peaks because I didn't want to go into everything. It was Ramona who saw Lester's name on the credit cards and invented Uncle Lester. I—I just didn't want to sit there and tell everybody my business."

"Oh. I see," said Sal, pulling her lips back into a peculiar smile. The fingers that held the credit card arched so that one corner tapped against her teeth. "It wasn't our business. It was our business to take you in, and trust you, and feed you and *clothe* you, for Christ sake, and share you with our friends, and comfort you when you had nigh—"

"All right. All right! I was wrong, I'm sorry. It's just— my brother died just a few days before I got there. I was confused, I was upset—I wasn't ready to talk about it...."

Sal's eyebrows arched. "Of course.... But you were ready enough to lie through your teeth, ready to tell us you had no money—" Sal laughed "—No friends. Ready to sucker us in, get us involved in your adolescent wild goose chase...." Melvina shook her head. "You didn't just exploit us, you got us to exploit our friends. You made a fool out of me, a fool out of Ramona...."

"That's not true!" Melvina was on her feet now, hands clenched at her sides. "That's not how it was. I never—"

"Really? How come you never flashed *this* little baby around?

162

Her and all her friends?" Sal waved the credit card. "You never offered to help with even the least expense.... You sponged off me, and Ramona, and poor Sue!—You got a little more than room and board out of *her,* didn't you?—and Bob and Hank...." Melvina was shaking her head violently. Sal made an exasperated sound. "Well who do you suppose paid for this room?"

"I'll pay for it," said Melvina dully.

"Sure. You and all that plastic." Sal flicked the card across the room at Melvina. It bounced smartly off her chest.

Melvina snatched up the credit card and threw it at the bed. "Sure. Me and all that plastic. Is that all that matters? Is that the only thing you care about?"

Sal nestled her hands in her jacket pockets. "I thought," she said lightly, "that we were discussing your good points."

Melvina shifted her weight from one foot to the other. "Ha ha. Very funny. Funny old Sal.... How'd you...."

"About the money? About Lester leaving you his rather— sizable settlement? I called Ramona today. We had a nice little chat. She also told me all about a conversation she had with your buddy Sue." Sal raised her eyebrows knowingly and nodded her head for emphasis. "So there's no use lying anymore. About anything. We are all, as it were, on to you."

"On to me?" Melvina leaned forward. "What are you talking about? Sue and Ramona don't..."

"If they've got a brain between them, they agree. You've been nothing but lies, nothing but trouble. If you had to chase all the way up here just to pour out your traumas to some clown you knew at camp...."

"That's enough!" Melvina took a step forward. "You don't know what you're talking about...."

Sal stood her ground. "Oh, yes I do. I didn't have to talk to Ramona. I'd figured most of it out myself.... I found your registration, *your* registration, when I was looking for the garage ticket back in Harvard Square. I should have known! What kind of a—person, would go out and spend that kind of money on a— car like that? That's what I asked Ramona, I said...."

"You don't understand," said Melvina hopelessly.

"I most certainly *do* understand. I understand deception, I understand parasitic exploitation, I understand what a *waste* it is to spend that much money on a monstrosity like that."

Melvina sat down heavily, her hands limp in her lap, her eyes on her hands. "You don't understand anything." There was a pause. Sal held her position by the door, waiting. Melvina shook her head in a barely perceptible arc, her mouth drawn into a frustrated line. Finally, she looked at Sal. "Is that all that matters to you? The money and the car?"

Sal said nothing.

"Jesus. The car doesn't matter, the car was a joke. I never even...."

"A joke? You and your demented brother spent that kind of money on a *joke*?" Sal's tone was outraged and incredulous. Her eyes blazed.

Melvina came to attention. She glared right back at Sal. "Yeah, dammit, a joke. That's all, it was just...."

Sal bit her lower lip and shook her head. She hooked her forefingers in her side pockets and held her arms akimbo.

"You don't understand! After my brother's—accident, he gave up, he just didn't want to live. I don't know how it started—it was the lawsuit, that's right, the lawsuit. We played this game, that's all. Made up stories about what we'd do if we got the money. Can't you understand that?"

Sal shook her head impassively.

"It was like—I don't know. Lester said that if we ever got a lot of money, we shouldn't blow it...."

Sal laughed out loud.

Melvina made a disgusted face. She heaved a sigh. "He said we should do just one crazy thing. That's all. It was like a joke. We kept adding on more things, making it more silly.... We planned, see, about how we'd get this car, right? And then we'd take off, you know, Lester and me."

Sal shot Melvina a questioning look. "Wasn't your brother's neck....?"

"I know! I know it was crazy. I know now, anyway.... Lester knew. I didn't. I didn't see it coming. I didn't realize he was just hanging on so that—I thought— And then, when we won the suit, and he ordered the car, you know, like a surprise—and he was so happy, talking about how he could send me to college like he'd promised he would, and about how we could take a vacation, get the hell out of there...." Melvina's voice trailed off. Her eyes were focused on something far away.

Sal cleared her throat.

Melvina looked back toward her, continued. "He used to say that car was his work of art, the only thing he ever made, his tribute to...life.... He said it was foolish, impractical, ridiculous, used too much gas—but would get you where you needed to go...."

Sal shifted impatiently. "In a manner of speaking.... Look, this is all very touching, but....."

Melvina flew out of her chair. "But, but, but! What the hell do you want out of me? Jesus, Sal, you're amazing. My whole god-damned family's dead, and all you can think about is that stupid car. You think I ought to be the happiest person in the world be-cause I've got a shitload of money I don't even want and a...."

"Poor Melvina," clucked Sal, "all alone in the world with only a few million...."

"That's right, dammit!" Melvina's face flushed. "Okay, fine. You're right. All that matters to me is money. The only thing in this world I've ever wanted was money. Right. That's why I did it. That's why I took a gun and shot him. Crept up on my poor, helpless brother and gave him both barrels of a...."

"Get out of here," said Sal. "I'm not in the mood for any more of your creative realities. I know how your brother died, and you're not taking me in with anymore of your stories."

"Stories, huh?" A blood vessel on the side of Melvina's neck looked nigh unto bursting. "I'll tell you a story, all right. You know what it's like to grow up as the town freak? Would you like to hear that story?"

Sal looked away from Melvina's growing frenzy with embar-rassment. "That's enough, Melvina," she said calmly, "I think you should...."

"No! No, I'm gonna tell you a story, Sal, one of my real whop-pers...."

"You need to calm down, control your...."

"You see, I really did shoot someone, Sal, only it wasn't Lest-er, it was his best friend. I took a gun and blew him to pieces—you know what that's like?"

"Melvina...."

"I became a legend in my own time, Sal. You know what fa-thers say to their daughters' boyfriends back where I come from? Do you?"

"Listen—"

"No! *You* listen," Melvina paced around once in a tight little circle. She stopped to point an accusing finger at Sal. "You know what they used to say? They'd say, 'You have that girl back here before eleven, or I'll send Melvina Skittle out lookin' for ya—with a gun!'" There were angry tears in Melvina's eyes as she came up close to Sal, a trembling of the chin that made her look like a frightened child.

"I—uh," Sal groped for words. Her face showed both discomfort and disbelief. She rallied. "That's, uh, I mean —why would you have shot this guy, anyway?"

Melvina peered into Sal's face a moment, then turned away, stamped over to the desk. "Because..." she said it slowly, looking back toward Sal "...the only good Martian is a dead Martian."

Sal clapped one hand to her forehead, gave out an anguished moan. "Jesus, Melvina, I can't believe you....." She shook her head. "You're really unstable, do you know that? You're crazy as a loon."

Melvina bent double over the desk with her hands covering her face. Her shoulders heaved silently.

Sal shook her head. Her face hardened. "Look. Don't run that stuff on me. You're wasting your time. You've had your pick of the softest shoulders on the East Coast to cry on, and you blew it. You used up Ramona...and Julie, and Sue, and Hank—and your imaginary friend in Randolph.... It's all over, Melvina. You played tough guy too long. You've reached the end of the line, and there's no one left but mean ol' me—And I don't fall for any of it."

Melvina lifted her face to look at Sal incredulously. A tear meandered down her left cheek.

"Don't even bother," said Sal threateningly. "I've had it with your lies, your jerking everyone around. It isn't going to work with me. You can just pack up your self-pity, your psychopathology, and go home."

Melvina turned away for a moment. She braced her hands on the desktop and stared down at her tear-stained doodle. "You've hated me all along." She looked up at Sal sideways. "Haven't you?.... Why did you...."

Sal shrugged, slid her hands down in her pockets. "I guess I thought I was doing Ramona a favor. I certainly never counted on getting enmeshed in your childish...."

Melvina whirled to face Sal head on. "Doing Ramona a favor?" Her voice was loud. "You? I'll bet you've never done anyone a favor in your life...." She smiled. "And you've certainly never done much for Ramona. You have got to be the most selfish, self-centered, insensitive...."

Sal straightened her neck and tilted her head upward. "I'm not going to bite, Melvina."

166

She rocked back on her heels just a little.

The muscles in Melvina's neck hardened, her hands clenched at her sides. "You think you're so goddamned superior, don't you? You think you're better than...."

"There, there," injected Sal in her most patronizing tone.

Melvina's eyebrows converged. Her breathing became deep and deliberate. "You—bitch," she said quietly, the force of her enunciation carrying the word clearly. She continued after a moment, "You think I haven't got you figured out? You think I don't know?" Melvina eyed Sal's smooth facade. "The little games you play with Ramona? The way you keep her nipping at your heels?"

"You don't know what you're talking about," said Sal in a deprecating voice.

"You don't think so? You think I haven't seen how you string her along, get her to run interference for you—get her to tell your lies?"

Sal tsked, turning away.

"Talk about lies!" Melvina was getting angrier. She minced out her words in a sarcastic falsetto, "'Oh, Sal's not a drunk. Sal's really—secretly—a wonderful, warm human being!'"

Sal glanced over at Melvina and rolled her eyes.

"That's right, it's just a joke. Nothing I say can bother you, can it? It doesn't matter that I know why you get so bent out of shape when Ramona brings in someone like Julie, why she threatens you.... It's not just that it's a little competition, a real flesh-and-blood person who might make Ramona see what she's been missing. Oh, no. It's more than that, isn't it? Some outsider might come along and mess up the rules of the game, might tromp right in and burst your little bubble, huh? Someone like Julie who might not know the game, who might walk right up to you and spill the beans, huh?" Melvina took a step toward Sal, willed her to look Melvina in the eye. "Right? You never know when someone like Julie might just decide to..." Melvina paused. She smiled slowly. "...To call a spade a spade."

It happened so fast that Melvina had no time to back away. Sal was in front of her, towering over her, her right hand coming up into a fist. Sal's face was expressionless, the color drained out, and the motion of her hand came to a stop as suddenly as it had begun.

Melvina had stiffened. Slowly she shifted her eyes from Sal's hand to her face. "Well?" she asked bravely, her voice pinched in

167

fear. She swallowed and went on, "Gonna go get crazy, Sal? Gonna act like some sort of unstable—liar?"

Sal relaxed her shoulders. Her gaze dropped from Melvina's face to her knees. She looked suddenly weary.

Melvina, watching the anger recede, felt her rage rising even higher. "What's the matter, Sal?" she taunted her. "Lose your nerve? Don't you want to slug me? Come on, Sal, we all know I deserve it, don't we? Don't we?" Melvina jutted her chin forward.

Sal dropped her hand and stepped back. She did not look at Melvina. "That's enough."

"Really, Sal? Are you sure? Don't you think you ought to deck me, Sal?"

Sal shook her head, turned toward the door. She paused for a moment and then turned back.

"Don't I have it coming, Sal?" Melvina's voice was getting louder, more urgent. Her eyes were filling once again with tears. "Isn't that what you *want* to do?"

Sal went over to her suitcase and picked it up. She turned once again and walked to the door, reaching for the handle.

"What are you doing? Where are you going?" Melvina's voice took on an edge of panic.

"I'm just—going," said Sal quietly. "That's all."

"You can't do that," howled Melvina. "You can't."

Sal was beginning to recover her composure. The eyes she turned toward Melvina's were less sad and simply harder. "Yes I can. One way or another, I've always had that choice."

"NO!" bellowed Melvina.

Sal shook her head as she pulled the door open. "The only rule of the game is that there *are* no rules to the game, Mel." She took a step forward.

"Wait a minute!" called Melvina. "Where's my cat?"

Sal stopped in mid-step. She did not turn. "She died," said Sal. Behind her there was only silence. Doggedly, Sal began to move forward again.

"But where *is* she?" came Melvina's voice.

Sal paused again. "Don't worry about it. It's been taken care of."

"No, you don't." It was Melvina behind her, tugging at her arm, pulling her around. "Where is she? What did you do with her?"

Sal shook Melvina off and turned to face her. "I donated her to science. They're going to do an autopsy, they want to understand...."

"No!" yelled Melvina, backing away. "You can't do that. You had no right to...."

"Shh," hissed Sal, glancing into the hallway. "Control yourself. There's no point...."

"You can't just take her away like that. She was mine. Don't I even have the right..." Melvina was crying openly now, the tears flooding her face "...to bury her with my own hands?" Melvina wiped at her eyes. "That's what always happens," she said to herself, "They always take them away. And you never...."

Sal heaved a sigh and turned back into the hallway. "Thank God this is the last of your tantrums I'm going to be privileged to experience." She stopped in the doorway. "I'm sorry, Melvina. I did what I thought was best."

The scream that Melvina let out was bloodcurdling. Sal turned back in time to see Melvina launch herself at Sal, her fists flying, her head low. "I hate you! I hate you!" she screamed, flailing her arms.

Sal raised the suitcase in front of her instinctively, but that did not hold off Melvina's attack for long. Sal was knocked against the open door, stunned, winded, trying to hold back this violent dervish. She tried shoving Melvina away, but she sprang back like a rubber ball. She attempted to hold Melvina off with an outstretched arm and found that it was like trying to hold back a windstorm. She took a measured, therapeutic swing at Melvina and missed, intercepting a hard blow to the midriff in the process. "Melvina," she implored.

"I hate you! I hate you!" Melvina just kept screaming and swinging.

Sal stiffened at a sound across the hallway. Sure enough, a door had opened and a balding head peered at Sal. *Shit,* thought Sal, *just what we need.* "Pardon me," said Sal politely, trying for a cheerful lilt. "Oof," she added as Melvina caught her a second time in the gut.

"Uh...." said the man.

"I hate you!" yelled Melvina.

Sal tried to salvage things as best she could. She grabbed Melvina in a moderately effective bear hug and tried to swing her back into the room. "My daughter," she informed the man glibly. "She's—uh—prone to these—seizures."

The man nodded slightly, craning his neck to get a better look at the kicking and screaming Melvina.

"You're not my mother, you goddamned...."

Sal clapped a hand over Melvina's mouth. "There, there, dear," she said sweetly.

The man shrugged and retreated into his room. Melvina bit Sal's hand. Sal wrestled Melvina back into the room and kicked the door shut, the two of them falling half onto one of the beds in a thrashing heap.

"Ow," muttered Sal as she extracted her hand from Melvina's mouth. "Damn you."

"I hate you," sobbed Melvina, still determinedly slugging away.

Sal wrestled Melvina until she had her generally well-pinned and strongly embraced. Melvina quieted a little, not from choice, her range of movement restricted.

Why the hell didn't I think of this before? wondered Sal. Somewhere in her head she heard a laugh and a voice observing, *It's the last thing you'd think of.* The words, the voice, were familiar. *Carla,* thought Sal. *When did she say that to me?* Sal's ruminations distracted her, and Melvina erupted once again into action.

"Stop it," ordered Sal, tightening her hold, pinning her.

"I hate you, I hate you," mumbled Melvina into Sal's jacket, her anger wearing down into tears.

Reluctantly, Sal decided that self-preservation was the better part of valor. She hauled Melvina further onto the bed and held her position, held her tongue. Melvina was just crying now, and Sal rested an awkward hand on the back of Melvina's head. "It's all right," she said. "It's going to be okay."

"I hate you," snuffled Melvina, the tautness involuntarily ebbing from her body.

"That's right," said Sal soothingly. Her tone brought forth another round of Melvina's battling. Sal wrestled her down again. *How long can this go on?* Sal wondered. *Not long. Sooner or later, she'll just wear herself out, fight herself to sleep.* Sal moved one hand tenderly over Melvina's curls, enjoying the very hypocrisy of it. *That's right,* she thought, *then I can go. I can catch a plane, or a train—hell, a bus. I'll be free of all this. Finally.* Sal rested her cheek on top of Melvina's head and let herself be lulled by the litany of Melvina's waning rage.

"I hate you, I hate you," mumbled Melvina, barely coherent.

"It's all right," replied Sal, cradling the child.

20

Invisible Women

It glinted brightly only a few inches from Sal's left eye. She tried to focus on it, but it was too close. She closed her eyes. The phone rang, and halfway through the first ring the bed lurched. Sal clutched the bedclothes for dear life, only to realize she was hanging onto Melvina's shirt. Melvina was still in it.

"Hello?" It was Melvina's voice. "Yes? What time is it? Oh, I'm sorry, I guess we overslept. Is that all right? Uh-huh. Thank you very much." The phone was placed back on the hook. Sal felt fingertips on the side of her face. "Sal?" Melvina's voice was tentative.

Sal opened her eyes again. She lifted her head, peeling her left cheek off the smooth flesh of Melvina's chest. She glanced down. A few buttons of Melvina's shirt had come undone, one was missing. The silver bird glinted merrily at her.

"How embarrassing," muttered Sal. She looked up at Melvina. "We're still here?" Melvina nodded her head just a little, smiling ruefully. She glanced away. With an effort, Sal began to push herself up into a sitting position. She realized her right hand was resting on Melvina's breast. She snatched it away. "Shit," she exclaimed.

The muscles of Melvina's stomach began to heave. She clapped one hand over her mouth, trying not to laugh. "I'm sorry," she mumbled.

"Indeed," observed Sal, sitting up. She hurt all over. "Jesus." She tried to remove her jacket, a process more painful than she would have guessed.

"Let me help."

"Yech," noted Sal as the jacket came off. "Did you throw up on this?"

"I might have," admitted Melvina. "Can I get it cleaned for you?"

Sal waved an indifferent hand. "Will you help me up?"

"Bathroom?"

"Shower."

Melvina nodded, getting up to assist Sal. They were both pale and unsteady. When they arrived in the bathroom, Melvina seated herself on the toilet. "Uh, I'm going to stay here, just in case you decide to take a nose dive in the shower."

"Do I look that....?"

Melvina shrugged. "Just in case.... We're, uh, kinda past modesty, aren't we?"

Sal braced herself against the sink to pull off a shoe. "I think we passed the boundaries of civility and good taste some time ago."

Melvina winced visibly and looked away. "I'm really sorry," she said after a few moments.

Sal turned on the shower and climbed in. "Let's not talk about it, okay?" she yelled over the roar of the water.

Melvina hunched her shoulders and stared at the floor. "I'm really glad you stayed," she said quietly. There was no response but the splash of the spray.

• • •

"This really isn't necessary." Sal took the tray Melvina handed her through the car window.

Melvina walked around to the driver's side. "We should eat." She noted the face Sal made. "Well, we should try." Melvina climbed into the car. "I see you've got your shades on."

Sal pulled the sunglasses forward and down. She turned to face Melvina squarely. "Notice anything?" she inquired.

Melvina sat back. "I don't remember...."

"Neither do I," agreed Sal, pushing the glasses back into place.

"I'm sorry."

Sal handed her a hamburger. "Stop saying that. Every other word since we got up this morning has been 'I'm sorry.'"

Melvina nodded meekly and reached for her milk shake. "I really lost it, didn't I?" she finally said. She sighed as she salted her french fries. "I don't know what came over me. I've never done anything like that before." Melvina looked at Sal with eyes that were sad and confused.

Sal looked down at her hamburger and pursed her lips. "Listen, I was hard on you last night. You've been through a lot, and it wasn't really surprising you blew up like that."

Melvina looked at her gratefully. "It's nice of you to say that, but I had no right to hit you, scream at you...."

Sal set down her lunch and ran a hand over her forehead. "Look, it's fun watching you crawl around feeling awful, but you're making me feel guilty as hell. The only thing you did wrong was not opening up and talking about things." Melvina started to say something and Sal hushed her with a gesture of her hand. "I haven't been very—accessible. I'm the worst person to have in a situation like this. I didn't help you. I didn't even try. I just goaded you and dumped on you and got jealous when other people reached out to you." Sal sighed. "I realize that I'm a rotten excuse for a human being. And *I'm* sorry."

Melvina shook her head. "No, don't be. Your—last night, you staying with me after everything I said and all, that meant a lot to me. Really." She lowered her gaze. There was an awkward silence. "I didn't mean those things I said. I...."

Sal waved a hand at her. "Of course you did. We both did. We're a couple of stinkers." Melvina smirked. "So what? We're both here. We're the survivors, Mel, you have to remember that. Your brother Lester, my friend Carla, little Dadavi, they're the angels who go floating off for halo fittings. Not us. We get left with all that guilt, all that rage. We get left behind, and we have to learn to live with it."

Melvina nodded. She turned to face Sal. "You know, my head's clearer this morning than it's been in weeks. I can think again. Everything still feels—weird, like it's not really happening, at least not to me, but—at least I'm here."

"Good," Sal squeezed ketchup onto her burger. "So can you tell me why you were so hellbent on finding Laura?"

Melvina shrugged and turned away. "It started when I kind of came to my senses, and I was in the car, heading north, thinking I needed someone to talk to. That's all. Some place to hide. When I came home that day, back in Kentucky, and found the paramedics, and my sister, and they said...." she broke off. "I don't even remember leaving. Nothing. I just, I don't know," she paused. "And then when I got to know you guys, you and Ramona and everyone.... Well, it was embarrassing, and I was confused, and I...I guess it was easier to concentrate on finding Laura than remember why I was, why...."

Sal chewed meditatively. "Mm," she said, swallowing, "I see. Did you really forget what had happened?"

Melvina raised her eyebrows. "I think so. For a while, anyway. It was weird. Like Hank kept being nice to me, and it kept making me think of Les, and then I'd get mad." She shook her

173

head. "I don't think I was very nice to him."

Sal dabbed her mouth with a napkin and reached out to pat Melvina's arm. "Don't worry about it. It's over. You've faced things and now you have to work them through. That's not easy, but you'll manage."

Melvina wrapped up her uneaten hamburger and set it aside. "I felt so alone. That's the only way I can explain it."

Sal made a face as she stuffed napkins and food wrappers into a paper bag. "Well, you're not."

"I know," said Melvina, smiling, reaching out to squeeze Sal's forearm, snatching her hand away to wipe the corner of her eye.

"That's not what I meant," grumbled Sal. "Let's get going." Melvina grinned and said nothing as she started the car and got onto the highway. She glanced over at Sal from time to time, smiling and shaking her head. "Cut it out, will you?" demanded Sal. "I'm not Silas Marner, for Christ sake." She sat up straight, wrapping herself in what dignity she had left, trying to ignore Melvina's sudden certainty of her good will.

"You're not so bad," said Melvina.

"Sure," said Sal, glaring out the window.

"I should have known you wouldn't really go away."

Sal felt a wave of guilt, remembering how reluctant she had been to hold or comfort Melvina, remembering her delight in planning to sneak off as soon as Melvina was asleep. She felt like a skunk, and guiltily, she slid down in her seat a little, pulling her chin in towards her chest. As she did so, her shoe hit something in the footwell. She leaned down to retrieve it. Her pith helmet. She set it in her lap and turned it around. She wanted to change the subject. "So, how did your visit with Laura go?"

Melvina grimaced. "It was awful. She must think I'm the weirdest person she's ever known. I mean, I drop in out of nowhere, tell her all these terrible things about Lester dying. I don't know, she's a good sport. She handled it about as well as anyone could. Did I tell you she was pregnant? I was afraid I'd get her so upset she'd drop the kid right then and there. I think I'm going to have to write to her and try to explain everything."

Sal smiled and said nothing. They were both quiet for a long time. Finally, Melvina gave her head a violent shake. "I still can't accept what he did."

"Lester?" Melvina nodded. Sal shrugged. "I don't know. I might have done the same thing. I just don't know if I could have held out that long, gone through all that—helplessness, hu-miliation—just to make sure you got the money. I'm no martyr."

Melvina shook her head. "He was alive, wasn't he? He still had *something*...."

"Everyone has their own ideas about things like that."

Melvina sighed. "It's true, I guess. He kept saying, 'I'm not a man anymore. I'm not anything.'" She screwed up her face. "So stupid! He said it a lot, I should have known. That, and 'You'll do fine, Mel, if we can just get you out of this town.'" Melvina shook her head angrily.

Sal looked over at Melvina and down at her hat. "I'm sorry about your brother. I'm sure he loved you very much.... It's just—the pain, and pride, may have gotten to be too much for him to see how important he was to you."

They fell silent again. Sal's words resounded in her own mind, over and over, with the monotony of the guardrails that whizzed past them. Pain and pride. Pride and pain. She tried to ignore them. She ran her finger around the cloth hatband of the pith helmet, marveling at the workmanship, wondering where Ramona had gotten it. Ramona and pride. Ramona and pain.

Sal had a sudden urge to put the hat on, pull it down over her ears and try to block out the words. She thought of Melvina and did not. She turned the hat over, examined it, rested it again in her lap. Ramona. She sighed. Last night she had thought of Carla, and now it was Ramona who haunted her. She thought of Melvina's angry accusations, of Hepzibah Creely's strange story. She shook her head. It was all so long ago. For years she had managed not to think about it.

Soon enough she would be seeing Ramona, Ramona who had sounded so vulnerable on the phone. Melvina had implied that she still—or once again—cared for Sal. Could that be? She shook her head. Not after Carla's memorial service, not after the way it had seemed to snap something in Ramona.

She remembered the uncharacteristic sarcasm of Ramona on the way to the service, the way she had laughed as they had inched their way through a traffic jam. Ramona had glanced off to the side and jerked her thumb toward a cemetery they were crawling past. "If we lived here," she had remarked, "we'd be home now." Sal had paled.

It was so unlike her. After the service Sal had paused outside to light a cigarette, wait for Ramona to catch up to her. She had heard the brisk click of Ramona's heels on the pavement, and in one movement Ramona had come up beside her, snatched the cigarette out of her mouth, taken a long drag, and thrown it down on the sidewalk. "That's that, I guess," Ramona had said, exhaling slowly, grinding the cigarette under her toe.

Sal had felt afraid, watching her. Ramona had laughed. "We all make mistakes," she said. She clapped Sal abruptly on the back and walked off without another word. Sal had waited around until she had seen her, later, climbing into Julie's car for the return trip.

Sal shook her head. Whatever fantasies she might have nursed had been demolished in that moment. There was no use in even thinking about it, and yet she did.

• • •

Sal gazed out the window at the maze of concrete that presaged New York.

"Rush hour," announced Melvina. "Our timing's great, huh?"

"Sure is," Sal sang out. She stared down at her safari hat, patted it affectionately, and put it back down in the footwell. "Some copilot I am. You want me to drive for a while?"

Melvina glanced in her rearview mirror as she shook her head. "That's okay. How are you doing? You want to stop somewhere?"

"I can wait till we cross the bridge. Um, you want to stop in the city, maybe drop in on Sue?"

Melvina shook her head. "I'd like to, but not yet. I've got some things I have to take care of, first."

"Home?"

Melvina pursed her lips. "It's not home, but I'm going back."

Sal hesitated a moment and then asked, "For good?"

Melvina smiled, "You're not *that* lucky. No, I've got to take care of a few things, but I'll be back."

"Your brother's estate?"

Melvina nodded. "Mostly, though, I've got to bury my dead."

They were quiet for a few minutes after that. "You'll stop over in Philly, won't you?" Sal asked.

Melvina gave her head a quick shake. "I can't. I should get it over with."

Sal watched the emotions flicker across Melvina's face. "Ramona won't like that."

Melvina brightened a little. "Really?"

Sal nodded.

176

"Well, I suppose...."

"Good. You know Ramona. If you didn't stop, she'd chase you down there and drag you back by your toes."

Melvina grinned.

"What are your plans for the future? Have any?"

"Oh, yes," Melvina pulled out to pass a truck.

"Well?"

"I figure, to start with, that if I could get this professorial type I know to write me a stunning letter of recommendation..."

"Oh, no you don't!"

"...Then, combined with my grades from 'Raccoon Community College,' I might..."

"Uh-uh."

"...Be able to get into a really swell school. Like, say, Cathedral."

"Think again, sister."

"And then, in my spare time..."

"You'll have lots of it, because there's no way I'm going to...."

"...Think again, child molester." Melvina glanced at Sal and guffawed. "You can stop turning funny colors, I was just kidding. No, it'll be great. I can get myself real ed-jih-cated, you know, take all the classes taught by the great Dr. Sal...."

"Please...."

"Anyway, in my *spare* time..."

"That again."

"...I think I'll apprentice in something...."

"Apprentice? In what?"

Melvina paused to consider. It made perfect sense to her, but how could she explain it to Sal? What could she say, that she was going to become an assistant junk lady, a maker-of-small-silver-kestrels-in-training, an apprentice kite maker? She shook her head. Sal would not understand. "Just an apprentice, that's all."

Sal made a short pensive sound. "And what about Sue? What are your—uh, intentions?"

Melvina smiled. "I've got my intentions. Don't worry. I mean, I'm a little nervous about seeing her again. I was—well, a little weird at points...."

"You're *always* a little weird."

"You know what I mean."

Sal nodded. "Well, just don't let it go too long," she suggested. "It's not good to...."

177

"I know that," said Melvina, exasperated, glancing at Sal. She looked back at the road and then over at Sal again. "Come to think of it, there's something I've been wanting to ask you."

Sal raised her eyebrows inquisitively, "Yes?"

"Well, I don't know if I...." she paused a moment. "Uh, would you consider us friends?"

Sal gathered her face into a look of genuine puzzlement. "Huh. Well, if I say 'no,' are you planning to slug me again?"

Melvina looked abashed. "No."

"Do you think it's okay to go around assaulting people?"

Melvina hunched her shoulders. "No never," she said quietly.

"Do you plan to get some counseling and work a few things out?"

Melvina twisted her mouth around nervously. "If you think I should, then...."

"I *do*." Sal gave her a sideways look. "Well, then, I don't know. Maybe."

Melvina asked uncertainly, "Maybe what?"

Sal shrugged. "Maybe someday we could be friends. Why?"

"Well, I just wanted to ask you—whatever happened with you and Ramona?"

Sal sat back. "Me and Ramona? That's ancient history." She paused. "That's already been buried."

"Well?"

"Well what? I don't know. What do you want to know?"

"Why'd you two split up?"

Sal laughed. "We weren't ever together."

"That's not what Ramona says. And it's not what I think, either."

"Good for you and Ramona. I don't know. We had a misunderstanding, I guess. My fault. I had a stick up my ass, as a friend of mine used to tell me."

"Hm. So now you think of her as just a friend?"

Sal shrugged. "Sure. Not *just* a friend, but...."

"Then what?"

"I don't know. A close friend."

"Oh." Melvina considered this. "You don't, uh...."

"No," said Sal emphatically.

"Never? You never wish...."

"I wish lots of things, Mel. I'm a big wisher." Sal looked down the road ahead of them with more than a little uneasiness. "A big wisher."

Melvina glanced over at Sal. "Won't you at least tell me what happened?"

Sal shook her head. "It all happened a long time ago, and it's really embarrassing, and...."

"Come on, you know everything in the world there is to know about me. Why won't you tell me about you and Ramona?" Melvina abruptly dropped her wheedling tone and grinned. When she spoke again, it was with a sly smile, "It's either that or I play my tape over and over again, all the way back to Philly."

Sal groaned. "Not that!"

"So, spill it," Melvina demanded.

Sal sighed deeply. "Well, if you want to hear the whole, morbid, stupid story, I'll try to tell it to you," she decided, "but I warn you, it's long and boring."

"I'll be the judge of that," replied Melvina.

• • •

"It began," Sal explained, "with a phone call from Carla. I was living in a rooming house in Philadelphia at the time, just starting my Ph.D. dissertation. There was a guy down on the second floor who always answered the phone, always complained about it, but still, always answered the phone." Sal smiled, remembering. "What was his name?" Only that was missing: everything else about that evening flowed back with perfect clarity.

"He said, 'Deevers, it's for you,'" Sal laughed. "I went from 'Miss Deevers' to 'Sal' one night when he banged on my door, drunk, to proposition me," she explained. "I went from 'Sal' to 'Deevers' after I turned him down."

"Why was he answering your phone?" asked Melvina.

"Oh, it was in the hallway on the second floor. We all shared that pay phone."

Melvina nodded, looking a little puzzled but encouraging Sal to go on.

"To tell the truth, I was happy to be interrupted. It was Saturday night, and despite my good intentions, I was having trouble getting started on my thesis. Carla was worried because she and Ramona, or 'Moe,' as we called her back then, were supposed to go to a play together. Only Ramona didn't show." Sal paused. "It wasn't like she stood her up. I mean, it wasn't a *date* exactly, although I'm sure Carla wished it was. She had a real thing for Ramona. Anyway, when Carla tried to track Ramona down, she found out that no one had seen her for a couple of days." Sal shook her head.

"Friday had been the first of the month, and Ramona hadn't showed up to pay her landlady the rent. That wasn't like her. Carla was worried, and by the time she got done talking to me, I was worried, too. I told her to call me if she heard anything, and I told her she could use my car if she needed it."

"Huh," said Melvina, "so where was she?"

"Well, a while later Carla called back to say that a friend of May's—do you remember the bartender at Peaks? *That* May—said she saw someone who looked like Ramona going into the Paradise Lounge."

"What's the Paradise Lounge?"

"Well, I didn't really know myself. Carla told me it was a stevedore hangout down in South Philly, near the docks. Not a good area at all. There's a seafood place there today, not much nicer than it was back then." Sal paused to rub the back of her neck with one hand. "Neither of us could believe Ramona would frequent a place like that, but we were really worried about her. So," Sal shrugged, "we decided we'd go down there and see if we could find her...."

• • •

"I think you turn here," said Carla. "This is right. See that sign? Park wherever you can."

"I'll park it," grumbled Sal, "but I'm not sure I'll get out. You really think she'd be in a place like this?"

"Not really," Carla looked around doubtfully.

"You willing to take your life in your hands to find out?"

"Come on, Sal. I'm sure it'll be all right. We'll just make our inquiries and...."

"'Make our inquiries'? Nancy Drew hits the waterfront. I'm not sure I like this at all." Sal set the foot brake and turned off the car.

"Let's go." Carla opened her door and climbed out.

Not wanting to look like a coward, Sal scrambled out and joined Carla on the sidewalk, where they huddled together and looked around. "You suppose these streetlights ever work?"

"Not an election year," observed Carla, striking out toward the bar on the corner.

The windows of the bar were littered with beer signs and a small neon rendering of a palm tree and two dice showing snake

180

eyes. "How clever," noted Sal archly, "Pair-o'-dice. Do we really have to go in?"

Carla shook her head. "This is nuts. She couldn't drink if she wanted to—and this place is definitely not in her league."

"Nor mine," decided Sal, turning away.

Carla hooked her arm. "Uh-uh. We've come this far. We may as well...."

"Let's make it quick, that's all." Sal reached reluctantly for the door.

The entrance way was narrow and they moved through it, past the cigarette machine, in single file. Sal reached the inner doorway and felt heads turn to look at her. Her face reddened. She stopped in her tracks.

The bar ran down the left side of the smoke-filled room and the right side was crowded with tables and chairs, a jukebox, a pool table. Everywhere there were men, mostly middle-aged dock workers, she guessed, and they stared or leered or ignored her with equal boldness.

Carla nudged her forward. Sal took a step, leaning a little to the right, scanning the people sitting at the bar. She halted.

"Oh, boy," said Carla, peering around Sal.

About two thirds of the way down the bar, perched on a bar stool between two enrapt gentlemen, sat Ramona. She was turned so that her back was toward the bar itself, her elbows propped on it, one hand still holding an empty shot glass.

Sal cleared her throat and moved forward, men along the way stepping back or being elbowed aside. "Jeez, we're being overrun," someone commented.

Carla caught Sal's arm. Sal shook her off. As she came down the length of the bar, there could be no mistaking who was sitting there. It was Ramona, all right. Her stockings were torn, her hair was in uncharacteristic disarray, her blouse was open one button too many, but it was Ramona. Frowning, Sal noticed the careless arrangement of her skirt, the glimpse of thigh it afforded. Sal scowled and pushed along more quickly.

"Now Sal," cautioned Carla, right behind her.

Sal ignored her. She was only a couple of yards from where Ramona sat, her indignation waxing, when, all at once, her view of Ramona was completely obliterated. A six-foot-plus form had unfolded itself with uncanny grace and speed from a chair to her right and had interposed itself between Sal and Ramona.

Sal tried to keep her temper. "Excuse me, sir," she said, vain-

181

ly trying to move him aside. He did not budge.

"Uh, Sal?" Carla was tugging at her sleeve.

"I can handle this," said Sal. She looked up at the figure before her. Then she looked up some more. He looked like a sailor. He wore black chinos and a chambray workshirt over a navy turtleneck. He was handsome enough, in a very masculine way: the strong jaw line, the cleft chin, the high cheekbones and dark brows, the heavy lids half covering two very bemused eyes…. Sal started. He was no he. He was a woman.

The creature before her unfolded her arms from across her chest and reached toward Sal with one immense hand. Sal backed away. "What the…."

"Need any help, Arlie?" someone called.

"Nope," replied the giant, smiling.

Carla clutched both of Sal's arms from behind. "Listen," she hissed in her ear, "if you want us to get out of here in one piece—if you want to get Moe out of here…."

"What…do you…want?" intoned the woman slowly.

Carla was pulling herself in front of Sal.

Sal clenched her fists. "What the hell *is* she?" she demanded, "Their mascot?"

"Hush," implored Carla. "How do you do?" she said politely to the woman. "Um, we're friends of that woman over there," Carla gestured vaguely toward the other side of the mountain, "Miss Stevens, Ramona Stevens?"

The woman looked down at Sal, looked further down at Carla. Her eyes narrowed.

"Who is that, Arlene?" came Ramona's voice—unmistakably Ramona's voice—from behind Arlene.

• • •

"Hello? Earth to Deevers?" Melvina was shaking Sal's arm with one hand, her other hand still on the steering wheel.

"Oh, I'm sorry," said Sal. "I was just thinking."

"About the Paradise Lounge?"

"Yeah. That's where she was. Carla and I found her there, drunk as a skunk…" Sal grimaced, "…With Arlene."

"Arlene?" Melvina lit up. "*Our* Arlene? How'd they end up there?"

"God, it was awful," muttered Sal distractedly. "You don't know what Arlene was like back then. This huge, butch—*thing*. She hardly said a word, just stuck to Ramona like a snarling

182

junkyard dog." Sal heaved another huge sigh. "For a while I didn't think we were ever going to get her out of there...."

• • •

Ramona, who was having her cigarette lit for her, leaned forward precariously, peering through the blue haze. "Oh!" she exclaimed. "These are the friends I was telling you about." Her speech was slurred hardly at all. "*You* know," she added in a poorly calibrated whisper, "the really smart ones I told you not to be scared of." Ramona raised the volume of her voice. "This one," Ramona pointed to Carla, "is our next great American poet. And *this* one..." Ramona paused, looking puzzled, then lit up, "...That's right. This one is redefining the social sciences as we know them." Ramona looked solemn. "Let's see, you're taking hard science, on the one hand," Ramona held out one hand, palm up, "and soft science on the other..." Ramona gestured similarly with her other hand "...and you're bringing them together..." Here Ramona clapped her hands together "...to create?" Ramona leaned toward Sal quizzically. "Semisoft science? Moderately-firm-with-orthopedic-support science?" Ramona smiled sweetly and the man to her left helpfully pushed her back onto the stool.

"Good God, she's stoned," muttered Sal.

Carla's face was contorted into a look of concern. "Yes, well," she said, stepping forward, "I wouldn't expect that she'd know how to hold her liquor. How are you feeling, Moe?"

"She holds her liquor *fine*," objected Arlene in that same ponderous drawl. "She's been drinking half the guys in here under the table," she added with not a little pride.

"Right!" agreed Ramona energetically, twisting around to tap her shot glass on the counter.

"Ah, I'm not sure that's such a good idea." Carla laid a gently restraining hand on Ramona's arm. "Have you had any of your pills lately, Moe?"

"Cross-tolerance," Ramona informed her sagaciously. "Booze's no problem."

Carla addressed Arlene. "Have you seen her taking any little white pills?" She illustrated with a closely pinched thumb and forefinger. "She keeps them in a tin in her purse."

"She don't have any purse," Arlene informed her, cocking her head to one side.

"What *is* all this?" Sal's impatience was obvious. "Let's just get her out of here."

183

"She's with *me*." Arlene's forearm barred Sal's way.

"Of course she is." Carla's tone was sweet and reassuring. "It's just that we may have a little problem here. Let's see, how long has she been with you? Are you sure she hasn't been taking any pills?"

Arlene shot an unfriendly glance at Sal and turned to Carla. She considered. "I found her. Thursday night."

"You *found* her? What the hell are you talking about?"

Arlene turned back to Sal. "That's right."

"Where did you 'find' her?"

Arlene shrugged, pouted her lips, gestured vaguely with one long arm. "That way. She was sitting on the sidewalk." Arlene glanced back to Carla. "She didn't have no purse."

"Was she all right? I mean...."

Arlene shrugged. "She was drunker than she is now. She was really gone."

"And you...." Sal's voice had gone up a notch.

"I didn't nothing. She called me." Arlene smiled, a slow process, slightly embarrassed. "She said, 'Hey, sailor, wanna have a party?'"

Sal glared at Ramona. "Is this true?"

Ramona shrugged. "I think you're mad, Sal. Are you mad?" She turned toward Carla, "I think she's mad."

"I had to pick her up and carry her," Arlene said to Carla. "I carried her home in my arms."

Sal squeezed her eyes shut and had a quick and horrifying vision of King Kong carrying Faye Ray.

"And you haven't seen her taking—"

Arlene shook her head. "She kept throwing up and said I'd better give her coffee and walk her around. We were up most of the night, me walking her around." Arlene looked at Sal and smiled just a little. "Most of the night," she added.

Carla put a restraining hand on Sal's chest. "I see. Was she drinking like this last night?"

Arlene nodded. "All the time."

"But she hasn't taken any...."

"What's this business with these pills?" demanded Sal.

"Maybe they're in one of her pockets," suggested Carla, stepping toward Ramona.

"Nope," said Arlene. "I was looking for some way to find out who she was. There's nothing in her pockets."

"What is this all about?" Sal asked Ramona.

"Barbiturates," Ramona stage-whispered, a finger to her lips. "You're not supposed to know. Phenobarbital," she added, only it came out 'Phenobarbitarbital.'

"What is she talking about?"

"Listen," Carla shot a look at Sal and turned toward Arlene, "we've got a problem here. Ramona," she gestured, "our friend, isn't supposed to drink. She takes a lot of Phenobarbital—you know what that is? Well, you're not supposed to mix alcohol with that, see? It could kill her. Do you understand?" Arlene looked a little hurt at Carla's patronizing tone. "I think we should get her out of here. She might have to go to a hospital. She could have a seizure."

Arlene moved a little closer to Ramona, protectively. "She seems all right to me."

"Why does she take Pheno..." Sal hovered between bewilderment and outrage.

"Look, I think you ought to let her come with us. Just for now. I'll give you her number. I'll give you my number. I...."

Ramona patted Arlene's arm. "Hey, I told you they'd come. Didn't I? I knew they would." She looked very pleased.

"Moe, tell her to let you come with us, huh?"

Ramona looked dubiously at Sal. "Sal's mad," she informed the group at large.

"That's okay. Sal's not going to stay mad, are you, Sal?"

Sal glowered. "I don't even know...."

"See? Come on, Moe, tell Arlene you want to...."

"I think I have to go," said Ramona. "They're my friends. We're like the Three Musketeers." Arlene looked crestfallen. "'S all right," Ramona said reassuringly. "We can celebrate the end of my medical career some other time."

Sal looked alarmed. Carla helped Ramona off the bar stool. Arlene steadied her.

"So long!" called Ramona.

"Bye, sweetie," said one of the men at the bar. There followed a chorus of good-byes from various people.

"Tough luck, Arlie," someone observed.

"Let's get out of here," muttered Sal, turning toward the door.

• • •

"I don't quite get it," Melvina said. "She was mixing alcohol and medications?"

Sal sighed. "Ramona never quite admitted it, but I think what happened was that she had tried to—kill herself." Sal

185

twisted her hands in her lap. "She had a secret, a secret she kept from me and just about everyone else." Sal shook her head sadly. "She was an epileptic. Back then that was a lot worse than nowadays—the attitudes, I mean. Here she was, a woman, a lesbian, an epileptic. And she was trying to make it through medical school, which has never been a bastion of liberal attitudes."

"But what happened?" asked Melvina. "Why did she try to...commit suicide?" Melvina stumbled over the words.

Sal squeezed her eyes shut for a moment and then spoke. "She was doing grand rounds on a neurology ward. Do you know what that is? Lotsa big shots, everybody who was anybody was there, and she, well, she threw a seizure. A real beauty, I guess." Sal ran her hand over her hair and rubbed her neck some more. "And I guess she figured that was it. They'd never let her stay in med school."

"Oh-h-h," said Melvina, nodding. "I get it." She was silent for a few minutes. "But wasn't that bound to happen, sooner or later?"

Sal shrugged. "I don't know. She said she'd been fooling around with her medications, changing dosages, pushing around the times she took them. She was caught between a rock and a hard place. The medications made it very hard for her to put in the grueling hours they expected of her without dozing off, and if she cut back the meds, she was increasing the chance of seizures." Sal sighed again. "She hadn't had a seizure in years, so I guess she thought she could get away with it."

"Wow," said Melvina, "no wonder she doesn't like to talk about that stuff."

"Well," said Sal, "that wasn't the worst of it. There were people, like me, who should have been there for her. Only I was too wrapped up in my own stuff." Sal was quiet for a moment. "What happened, I think, was that she took the whole damned bottle of Phenobarb, but changed her mind. I think she went looking for help, maybe got mugged along the way—we're not sure—and landed where Arlene found her." Sal tapped on the armrest with a her fingers. "I hate to admit this, but now I see how lucky it was that Arlene ran into her. It could have been a lot worse."

"Well, what happened once you got her out of the bar?" Melvina asked. She glanced over at Sal and saw her squirming uncomfortably in her seat. Melvina grinned. "Oh boy," she said. "This is the good part, right?"

186

Sal looked away and didn't say anything.

"Oh, come on," insisted Melvina. "You can't hold out on me."

"Oh, yes I can," replied Sal haughtily, gathering her usual dignity around her like a shawl. "Did it ever occur to you that some things are just none of your business?"

Melvina shook her head energetically. "Uh-uh. No way. Remember, *we* passed the boundaries of civilization and something-or-other some time ago. That's what *you* said." Sal said nothing. "Oh, come on, Sal, how am I ever going to understand what went wrong if you don't tell me about it?"

"It's embarrassing," Sal said simply. "It all happened a very long time ago, and I behaved like a real jerk, and I don't want to talk about it."

Before Sal realized what was happening, Melvina flicked on her turn signal and exited the highway. She pulled into the parking lot of a rest area and stopped the car. "Now," she said, turning to face Sal, "you have my undivided attention." She crossed her arms over her chest. "Tell me what happened, or we're never going to get back to Philadelphia."

Sal sighed again.

"That's it," said Melvina, uncrossing her arms and draping them across the steering wheel and the back of the front seat, "take a deep breath and talk about it."

"Well," said Sal reluctantly. "Carla and I had to decide what to do with her. I wanted to take her to a hospital emergency room, but Carla vetoed the idea. She figured that if the pills and booze hadn't killed her by then, they weren't going to. Since Carla was still living at home and she didn't think her dad the minister would be thrilled to see Ramona in her present condition, she decided there was only one other option. It was her idea to take her to my place, so I could keep an eye on her. Of course, the real challenge was getting her up the three flights of stairs to my room."

• • •

Ramona came to after a few moments of the cool night air, but her knees and navigational system were uncooperative. "I'm trying," she said groggily.

"This isn't going to work," Carla informed Sal. "You're stronger than I am, it would help if you'd—She's not going to bite, you know. You *could* put an arm around her. I know it's the last thing you'd think of—" she laughed "—but sometimes it works."

187

Sal gave her full attention to the task at hand. She handled most of Ramona's weight where necessary and worked at keeping up a conversation with her. The talk helped keep Ramona as alert and coordinated as possible. Carla steadied her on the other side and went ahead to unlock the door.

"Here we are," said Sal, plonking Ramona down in a chair. "How're you feeling?"

Ramona looked around, a little disoriented. "Okay."

"Now what do we do?" Sal turned to face Carla.

"I'm not sure. I'm hoping that if the barbiturates and alcohol were going to mix, they'd have done it already." She shook her head. "Damned if I know why she's even alive. She's probably just hung over and drunk as hell right now."

"Would you like some coffee?" Sal asked Ramona.

Ramona shrugged.

"I'll have some," volunteered Carla.

Sal nodded. "How about we give her a bath first?"

"A bath? Now? Don't you think...."

"She's filthy. She needs a bath."

"I don't know. What if she throws a fit in the tub?"

"She seems all right. Wouldn't you like a bath, Ramona? I mean, if she's going to be sleeping in my...."

"Gee, Sal...."

"Who knows where she's been. She...."

"Sure, I'll take a bath." Ramona looked puzzled. "Here?"

Carla raised one eyebrow, looking at Sal, and then got up to draw the water. "Personally," she said to Ramona, "I think it's all a matter of sin and redemption, Deevers-style."

"Oh," said Ramona, still looking confused. "Am I staying here?" she asked Sal when Carla had left the room.

"Yes."

"Oh," Ramona nodded her head pensively. "Who's idea was it?" she asked, "Yours or mine?"

"Carla's," replied Sal, taking some towels off a shelf.

"Oh," said Ramona, looking confused once again.

Sal made the coffee while Carla filled the tub. "At least you don't share your bathroom," she observed when she came out, wiping her hands on a towel. "I'd love to try to explain this to your neighbors."

Ramona was docile and sleepy while they stripped her down and put her into the bath, but the water, although warm, woke her. "Whoa, this is strange," she remarked, looking around.

"We should watch her," stated Sal.

"For therapeutic reasons, I'm sure," said Carla. "Here's your washcloth. You want me to bathe you?"

"She can wash herself. Go on, Ramona."

Ramona looked at Carla, smiled and shrugged. She looked back to Sal, stared her right in the eye, and began, quite sensuously, to soap herself.

"Ha!" exclaimed Carla, "Good for you. I don't know if my heart can take it, but Sal's got it coming."

"Cut that out," demanded Sal.

"I think I'm going to take a nap," said Ramona, yawning, sliding down in the tub.

"Oops, no you don't. I'll hold her up," said Carla, hooking Ramona under the arms from behind. "*You* can wash her." Ramona threw the washcloth at Sal. Carla cocked her head to one side and added, "And I don't think she's half as gone as she looks."

Sal glared at them both, rolled up her sleeves, peeled the soapy washcloth off her shoulder, and bent to the task. Ramona waited until she was almost done to yank her, quite unexpectedly, into the tub.

Carla was laughing so hard she was not much help, and Sal was left to untangle herself and clamber out as best she could.

"Don't you need a bath?" asked Ramona earnestly.

Sal got up off the bathroom floor, slipped on the tiles, and stomped off, leaving Carla to get Ramona out of the tub. By the time they came out, Sal had changed into a bathrobe, regained her composure, and was sipping a cup of coffee.

"There we go, squeaky as the day she was made. Feel better? She even did her hair." Carla sat down in an overstuffed chair and left the bed to Ramona.

The hand that accepted the coffee cup from Sal was shaking perceptibly. "You got it?" asked Sal, not unkindly.

"Think so," said Ramona. She gathered Sal's terry cloth robe around her and leaned against the wall behind the bed. Wet, her hair was even darker, and it cascaded down her shoulders in curls and waves. She pushed the hair back from her forehead with one hand. "What day is it?"

"Saturday. Well, Sunday, now," replied Carla.

"God, did I blow it," Ramona said, looking down at the bed, her hair falling forward to cover her face. "Damn."

Carla and Sal exchanged glances.

"Well, uh, are you feeling any better?" asked Sal.

189

Ramona shrugged.

"Maybe you ought to lie down for a while," suggested Carla.

"I'm not tired," said Ramona, but she set the cup on the bedside table and crawled under the covers.

Sal turned off the overhead light and left a small light on in the bathroom. They sat in the semidarkness for a time.

"Well," said Carla finally, "I think I'm going to go now. Can I take your car? I'll bring it back in the morning."

"Do you really think you ought to go?" Sal cast a worried glance in the direction of the bed.

"She'll be okay. Where are you planning to sleep?"

"Oh, I thought I'd doze in the chair," Sal gestured. "I wasn't really planning to sleep."

Carla smiled. "Well, at least you aren't making her do penance by having her sleep on a mat on the floor.... Not that you'd get very far."

"What do you mean?"

Carla turned her hands palms up and hunched her shoulders. She picked up her jacket off the table.

"You aren't really going, are you?" Sal's voice was nervous.

"Of course I am, and it will be quite all right, really." Carla patted Sal's arm.

"What do you mean?" asked Sal a second time.

Carla threw her coat over her shoulder and peered closely at Sal. She shook her head. "You mean you really don't see what's coming?"

"No, I—What do you mean?"

"Gawd, you're stupid, Sal." She plucked the car keys off the table and opened the door. "Give my regards to Twinkletoes, when she wakes up."

"But wait a minute," said Sal urgently, catching Carla's arm as she stood in the doorway, "What do I do if she...throws a fit?"

Carla laughed and turned toward the hallway. "Don't worry. Just make sure she doesn't swallow her tongue." She glanced back, "Or yours." Carla swung the door closed and left Sal standing there. She reached for the door and heard, faintly, Carla's voice saying, "So much for the Three Musketeers."

Sal let her hand drop and stood back. When she heard the outside door, two flights below, clicking shut, she turned away.

The terry cloth robe lay in a heap on the floor beside the bed. Sal bent to pick it up, her eyes slowly adjusting to the dim light. Ramona was on her side, facing Sal, the covers poorly arranged

over her. Sal glimpsed the smooth line of her shoulder, the delicate curve of her breast. She bent to arrange the covers. Ramona
caught her hand.

Her voice sounded sleepy but sober. "Carla congratulated me.
She said she always wondered how anyone'd ever get you to take
your clothes off." Ramona chuckled. "I wasn't so sure. Not till I
saw this." Her hand reached up to caress the thin material of
Sal's robe. "Silk. And no 'jammies. Nice." Ramona lifted a corner
of the material from the vicinity of Sal's knee. "Not bad."

Sal, who had frozen where she stood, realized that Ramona
was talking about the thigh, not the material. She stepped away
from the bed.

Ramona's fingertips trailed down the inside of Sal's leg as
she stepped away. "That's okay," said Ramona. "Take your time.
Light me a cigarette, will you?"

Sal felt heat spreading up her neck and over her cheeks. Embarrassed, she walked to the table, turned away to light two cigarettes. She picked up her cup on the way back. She handed Ramona her cigarette and took a sip. It was lukewarm.

"It's funny," said Ramona. "With you standing there like that
all I can see is the white of your bathrobe, the end of your cigarette."

"Really?" Sal relaxed, feeling less exposed.

"And your teeth, when you smile. Like the invisible woman.
Sexy," decided Ramona, taking a drag on her cigarette.

"So you think Med School's finished?" asked Sal, her tone casual.

"Yes." Just the word. She added nothing to it.

"Is that why you—took off? Why didn't you come to me?"

"You've been wrapped up in your thesis. I didn't want to...."

"Then why didn't you go to Carla?"

Ramona laughed. "Carla? I couldn't. She's got a crush on me
the size of...." Ramona shook her head. "She'd have been very
happy if I'd gone to her. Very comforting. Lease with an option
to buy. I couldn't have done that to either of us." Ramona gestured for the ashtray, flicked off the ash. "Haven't you even noticed the great triangle? Carla's crush on me, me all soft on
you—you desperately in love with your great god Science, your
vision of perfection and control? I used to think I might be able
to measure up: Ramona Stevens, girl doctor."

"What makes you think you can't finish?"

Ramona inhaled deeply. "I blew it. Seizures on the neurology ward, for chrissake. From colleague to case study in the blink of an eye. No, they've been gunning for me. I don't know how much longer I'd have lasted anyway. Unreliability, I think Helter called it. You'd never know when, in the midst of a Medical Emergency, Stevens would hit the floor and do her routine."

"But maybe...."

"It's a relief, in a way. All that hiding and lying. Everything riding on things I can't control.... I tried though, Sal. I really wanted it. You know that. I really did. I put up with so much...." There was a catch in her voice. She brought her fist down on the bed with every word. "I...just...couldn't...control...everything. I'm sorry, Sal. Don't give me your Elizabeth Blackwell lecture; I know all about the Supergirls, able to leap over large prejudices in a single bound. Sure. But not me. I couldn't cut it." Ramona looked up at her plaintively. "Is that so bad? Do you have to hate me?"

Sal said nothing for a moment. When she spoke her voice was carefully modulated, with perhaps the faintest undertone of nervousness. "The pills and alcohol—that woman said you asked her to give you coffee and stuff. Was that an accident, or what?"

Ramona leaned forward to flick her cigarette again. "I'm not going to say.... You'd just hate me more. But it didn't work, did it? I could fuck up falling down stairs, you know that?"

"But was it...?"

"So I'm not perfect! Is that so awful? I guess so.... When I came to after the seizure, you know what my first thought was? 'How do I tell Sal?'"

Sal said nothing. She searched frantically for something to say, some measure of her feelings, and found none.

Ramona stubbed out her cigarette. "Hell, it's not so bad. Can I have a sip of your coffee?" She cupped her hands around Sal's hand and drank. "Thanks. Yech. So anyway, maybe it's not so awful. Maybe we have something in common besides our dreams, huh?" Ramona waited for an answer. Then she added in a quiet voice, "Why don't you come here and find out?"

Sal shifted the coffee cup from one hand to the other. "I, uh, under the circumstances, I...."

Ramona moved restlessly under the sheet. "Stuff it, Sal. Come here." Sal did not move. Ramona sighed. "I've been watching you tonight. I've finally got you figured out." She paused. "I know what you want better than you do—and I mean that graphically."

Sal still did not move. She felt glued to the spot, all the hairs on her neck standing straight up.

Ramona rolled onto her back. She sighed again. "Okay, the hell with you. Just let me know when you're ready." She closed her eyes. "The only thing I'm sure of, is that you'll be here, sooner or later. It doesn't matter how disappointed you are in me. Hell, maybe that even makes it better. Moralists are the worst lechers, baby. And anyway, I make you hot."

Angrily, Sal took a step forward. Ramona did not move. Sal wondered all at once, if she were really all that angry, if maybe it was not just an excuse to—move closer. Slowly, she set down her coffee cup, straightened up and took another step toward the bed. Ramona ignored her. Sal gazed at Ramona's body as she had not dared to before, even in the bathtub. Her eyes traced the inviting curve of her full breasts, the sensuous line of her belly, the sweet dark curls that covered.... She yearned for Ramona to turn to her, reach out to her.... Ramona did not move. *She's asleep already,* thought Sal, watching the deep, regular fall and rise of her breasts. *I can't wake her,* she thought, *It wouldn't be right,* and yet she took the last step, stood by the bed, her heart near to bursting when Ramona opened her eyes and looked at her.

Sal stood by the bed like a wound spring, her fists clenched around the ends of her bathrobe sash, her arms holding them taut. Ramona fixed her eyes on Sal's, her gaze so brutally direct that at first Sal thought she could not bear it, then, that she could not possibly look away. Ramona reached up, finally, put one finger under the knot of the bathrobe tie, tugged just a little. Obediently, terrified, Sal let go of the ends of the sash and stood foolishly with her hands in midair.

Still keeping her eyes on Sal's, Ramona pulled the knot loose, pulled it out, freed the sash to fall to the floor. Sal stood where she was, waited while Ramona sat up part way, grasped the sides of the bathrobe and pulled them towards her until Sal could feel the material straining against her back. Once Ramona had her that way, caught, she finally moved her eyes from Sal's, slid them down Sal's body. Ramona's pleasure was obvious. Sal tried to swallow, felt a blush spreading over her, closed her eyes.

After what seemed like a long time, Ramona let go of the bathrobe. Fearfully, Sal opened her eyes. Ramona reached up and flicked the smooth material off her shoulders, watched it fall to the floor. Sal took a deep breath. All at once Ramona was

193

there in front of her, stroking her face, kissing her softly, putting her arms around her to draw her down onto the bed.

"I...." said Sal.

"Hush," said Ramona, kissing her on the mouth, her lips warm and full, a gentle pressure Sal could not resist.

Ramona moved away a few inches in order to look at her, her eyes, serious and steady, catching and comforting Sal's frightened gaze. Ramona's fingertips traced the line of her jaw, the angle of her chin, the arch of her throat. Her touch was as light as the brush of her hair over Sal's shoulder, but her fingertips were warm, pulsating with the thrill of discovery that her face did not betray.

Woodenly, Sal raised her arm, brought fingers that felt like lead toward the face she longed to touch. Ramona threw back her head, baring her velvet throat, luxuriating in Sal's caress. It was like an electric surge that passed into Sal, innervating her fingers, her skin. The quiet march of their mutual exploration was disrupted, thrown into an urgent collision of passions that crashed together like two mighty rivers, commingling, swirling and dancing, flooding their borders as one. Sal felt Ramona's hands cupping her breasts, holding them, worshipping them. She felt her mouth, open and wet, kissing her throat. Sal arched away, her hands grasping Ramona's shoulders, her hips pressed against Ramona's. She could feel the heat, mirroring her own, the pulse, the growing wetness.

She pulled Ramona toward her, felt the unbearable sweetness of breast against breast, belly against belly. She bowed her head in joyful agony, kissed, bit, the soft flesh of Ramona's shoulder. Ramona put one hand behind Sal's head, with the other explored the sweep of Sal's hard back.

Sal rolled on top of Ramona, their hips moving together in the jagged rhythm of their hearts, their mouths coming together, open, in counterpoint. Ramona's tongue sought Sal's, made love to it, one moment soft and yielding, the next moment thrusting and hard. Sal tore herself away, her thigh pushing between Ramona's thighs, her mouth passionately journeying over her throat, her breasts. Ramona arched her back, her fingers digging into Sal's shoulders, her leg coming up between Sal's.

It had been more than Sal could bear, and she had rolled over, turned away, her back to Ramona, breathing hard, dizzy, trying to collect herself. Almost immediately she had felt Ramona's breath warming her neck, her words tickling her ear with

194

an urgent, "What's the matter, babe?" Sal had said nothing, welcoming the warmth of Ramona's body, pressed against her back, the feel of her breasts, nipples taut, the brush of her curls against Sal's buttocks. Ramona had reached around and held her, rocking her, gentling the terror until it disappeared.

Finally, slowly, Ramona had rolled her over, and the second joining of their bodies had been even more wondrous than the first, the awkwardness dissolving, the heat even greater. Had there been any part of their bodies that they had not shared and explored? Bold fingers, hungry mouths, a compelling urgency as though there would not be time enough, could not be time enough, in the world of ecstatic moments or blessed dreams for all their love to be molded into flesh. Twenty-five years later, Sal blushed to remember it, Ramona's love tattooed all over her, enveloping her, once again, in a red hot wave.

And must she remember how the dam had broken, how, at the moment of searing release, she had cried out and cried; must she face a vision of herself as that sort of person, a woman who would collapse in Ramona's arms, sobbing in her joy as though she had, somehow, lost something?

Ramona came back to her in crisp flashes: the aching vulnerability of her eyes, the sculpted hollow between her breasts, the undulating waves of contractions across her belly, the sacred moment of revelation when she parted those lower lips with tongue and mouth, discovering a sweet, hot moistness that swelled with her kisses....

• • •

Somewhere in a flat, bald future, Sal found herself rocking back and forth, tears streaming down her face. She ached to feel the ancient sensations draining away, dissipating like lifeblood, leaving only an empty shell behind. She squeezed her eyes shut, struggling to stop her tears.

Melvina put her arms around her and held her, rocking with her, stroking her hair and murmuring, "It's all right. It's all right, now."

They stayed like that for a long time before Sal was finally able to marshal her emotions, beginning to sniffle and stiffen and push Melvina away.

"Hey, cut it out," said Melvina, holding Sal more tightly. "You were there for me. Why won't you let me comfort you?"

Sal stopped struggling and let Melvina hold her a few minutes more. Then she took a deep breath and pushed her gently away. "Enough of this," she said, trying to keep her voice steady. "I'm all right now."

Melvina sat back and looked at her critically. She shook her head from side to side. "I don't get it. It's obvious you really loved her. What the hell happened?"

Sal shook her head, busying herself with the tissues Melvina handed her. "I don't know," she said. "The next morning, I freaked out. I got scared, that's all." She stared distractedly at the pith helmet at her feet. "I was scared of how much I was feeling, how much I wanted her, I—" Sal stopped. "All I can tell you is what I did," she said, resuming the story in a quiet voice.

• • •

It hurt to tell Melvina how she had awoken that morning, early, her eyes flying open in the thin light of dawn like some overexcited child on Christmas morning. She had felt the unaccustomed weight on her left arm, had glanced over at Ramona with a heart filled with joy and misgivings. Was it all right that it had happened? Would the hung-over Ramona of this morning share the feelings of the ferocious and loving woman of the night before?

Sal extricated her arm from under Ramona and propped herself up to gaze fondly at her. Dare she wake her? Could she possibly refrain from reaching out to touch her once again? So beautiful. Sal's eyes sketched the outline of this body that seemed so perfect to her, so exquisite and so holy. Was that a bruise on Ramona's hip? She bent closer. It was a nasty one, deep and wide. Sal thought of Ramona, falling on the sidewalk, succumbing and alone. She ached, wanting to kiss the bruise, mend it.

Concerned, she examined Ramona for any other signs of injury. She noticed the charm strung around Ramona's neck, the bit of silver hanging from a chain, which she had inadvertently kissed the night before, which they had joked about being in the way later on. She smiled. *How lovely, a little bird.* She had assumed that it was a religious medal of some sort, but no, this was nicer. Ever so gently she fingered the chain, trying to catch enough light to examine it more closely. Her movements caused some locks of Ramona's hair to fall away from her neck, revealing yet another bruise, a different one, high up.

Sal frowned and looked intently at it. It was not the sort of bruise one would get in a fall. It was another, coarser kind. The vulgar mark of a certain form of passion, it—Sal stiffened. All at once it occurred to her that she had never seen the silver bird before. All at once she remembered Arlene.

Wide-eyed, Sal sat up, she turned and placed her feet on the floor, her heart racing. Even then, although she had no sensible reason for believing such a thing, she knew that the bird and the bruise and that oversized bitch on the waterfront were all connected. She groped for a bathrobe with clumsy hands and unseeing eyes. She lurched to her feet and steadied herself, fighting the impulse to whirl around, shake Ramona, jolt her from her pleasant reveries as Sal had been jolted.

That woman! That monster! Sal propelled herself toward the bathroom, closed the door, and crouched on her haunches like a wounded animal. It had all been a trick, a game, some diversion hatched out of boredom and despair. Sal clapped her hands over her ears, tried not to hear the echo of Ramona's endearments, Sal's ardent replies.

How could Ramona have done it? How could she have gone from the arms of that—freak to Sal's bed? What Sal had taken to be a culmination of arduously built trust and understanding had been instead a little dalliance, another mark casually added to Ramona's list. Sal swayed back and forth, rocking herself, burning at the thought of her vulnerability—now her shame.

She stayed as she was for a long time, finally sitting against the door, numb, waiting for day to come, for Ramona to awake and leave her bed. After hours, she at last heard Ramona's tread, making her way into the kitchen. It took Sal a while longer to pull herself together, paste on her dignity, dare to open the door.

She managed, tight-lipped, to play out her role, and she was angry enough to carry it off. Ramona required breakfast, more sleep, acknowledgments of her apologies for her imposition. It was a relief when Carla arrived, cheerful and full of energy.

It seemed like forever until she could lend them her car, send them off to pay the landlady, fetch pills, patch up the mess Ramona had made of her life. After they were gone Sal indulged in a good, long cry. A few hours later she found a hypocritical little love note that Ramona had left on the bedside table, and she took immense satisfaction in ripping it to shreds.

• • •

"Pride. Fear. Too much pride," Sal said sadly. "Hell, I'm prob-

197

ably the one who gave her the damned hickey. And what the hell did it matter, anyway?"

Melvina had one arm around Sal's shoulders, and she held her tightly.

"When did I lose my pride?" Sal asked. She gazed out the window, not listening for an answer. "When did the night before become more important than the morning after?" Sal bit her lip. "I lose either way. There's no fool, Melvina, like an old fool." She hung her head. "I guess I was just looking for some excuse to climb back on my high horse and ride away." She smiled sadly. "Swell horse. Just when I need it most, it dumps me in the muck and takes off."

They sat together in the car for a long time after that. Neither of them said much. They just sat, side by side, thinking about things. At one point, Sal cried again and Melvina held her.

"You've got some unfinished business to attend to," Melvina said gently.

"Yes, I know," said Sal. "I know."

21

Return to La Casa Sappho

Bets came out of the storeroom glumly, clicking the lock behind her. She crossed to the bar and rested her hands on it. "You were right," she admitted. "We're almost out."

May slapped her towel down on the counter. "I *told* you...."

Bets hunched her shoulders sheepishly, "I know. I can take care of it tomorrow."

May shrugged one corner of her mouth and relented. "Well, as long as we get them before the weekend...."

Bets smiled, the shy, proud smile of a person who knows she is loved. May gave her hand a surreptitious pat, and Bets turned away, her confidence restored, ready to survey her domain with regal goodwill.

She caught sight of Ramona Stevens presiding over a crowded table and decided to ignore her. Even when Julie Farragut hailed her warmly, Bets passed by, acknowledging the greeting with only a casual wave of her unraised hand. She could forgive and forget, but not that fast.

Bets paused by the door to peek through the window. She was ready to move on when she noticed a pair of longhorns appearing on the right side of her field of view. Bets leaned closer, her apprehension increasing and blossoming into dread certainty. *Oh no,* she thought, *not again.* By the light of day the customized Caddy looked even more dizzy than it had under the pink glow of a weary streetlamp.

Bets shook her head sharply. Was there a hue in God's creation quite as—awful, alarming...? Words failed. Through the tinted glass Bets could make out the girl from Kentucky. *Not this time,* Bets vowed, *I'm not letting her in.*

The car parked right in front of the bar, not bothering to angle in, just sitting there brazenly, blocking traffic if any happened along. The driver of the car seemed to be in animated conversation with someone else inside. After a few minutes she leaned away from the side window. Bets squinted and watched.

In a few more minutes the passenger door opened and some-one got out. It was Sal Deevers. She wrestled for a moment with something, a suitcase. Finally, she closed the door, walking around behind the car. The driver's window rolled down and there she was, that scrawny little troublemaker, calling to Sal, trying to push some sort of sun hat into Sal's hands.

Sal waved it back, they argued amicably, and Sal plonked the hat on the driver's head, giving it a pat. She stood back while Melvina parked the Cadillac. Bets scratched her head. Sal Deevers?

Bets felt a pressure, light enough to be imagined, on one side of her waist, across her back. *Goodness,* thought Bets, *May's been affectionate lately.* She threw her arm around the waist of the woman beside her, and was on the verge of turning and say-ing something when she heard, "See them yet?"

Bets jumped. She could feel the blood rushing to her cheeks as she stepped back, pulled away. Ramona smiled and stepped forward to peer through the window, patting Bets on the cheek as she did so, remarking, "I knew you couldn't stay mad at me."

Bets glowered and retreated, stalking to the bar to retrieve the beer May had automatically uncapped and set on the coun-ter. She saw Ramona pushing open the door and going out to greet them from the corner of one narrowed eye.

• • •

Sal heard Ramona's voice behind her.

"Well, hello, stranger!"

Sal took a deep breath and turned around.

"Where's Melvina, what did you do with her?"

Sal gestured toward the Caddy. "She's parking it. Don't wor-ry, she'll be along." Sal smiled and clapped one arm around Ra-mona's shoulders. "Life's not all beer and skittles, you know— God, how I've been biting my tongue, struggling not to say that. You'll never know the self-control—"

Ramona looked at Sal. "I'll bet. But, uh, you didn't do any-thing to—?"

Sal laughed. "Me? Would that I had given as good as I got."

Ramona searched Sal's face intently. "It's good to have you home."

Sal pushed her sunglasses up her nose and cleared her throat. "I was hoping you'd notice."

Ramona gave Sal a push and they turned toward Peaks as

Melvina joined them. Ramona picked up Sal's bag, insisting on carrying it. Just inside the door, Sal halted when she saw the crew that Ramona had assembled. Arlene and Mary were there, and Julie with someone she didn't recognize, and Sue, and others, more faces than Sal felt up to dealing with.

Melvina rushed forward to hug Sue, struggling good naturedly with the questions everyone threw at her.

Sal shook her head, allowing Ramona to propel her forward and seat her in an empty chair. She sat to Ramona's left, with Arlene to Ramona's right and Julie sitting squarely across from them. *She's called out the shock troops,* she thought. *She's got herself all shored up with the old standbys and she's ready to face Julie with that absurd equanimity, that misguided notion of fair play.* Sal smiled and nodded mechanically at the comments and greetings people were offering. *Just once I'd like to see her throw a tantrum, make a scene, act like she gave a damn.*

"Good to have you back." It was May at her shoulder. "What'll you have?"

Still feeling overwhelmed, like a dreamer returning from distant shores, she put a restraining hand on Ramona's arm. "That's okay, I'll get it." She answered May's question without looking at her. "Whatever Moe's having."

May hesitated. Ramona stared at her and then recovered. Her lips silently formed the question, "Club soda?"

Sal glanced up at May. "Yeah, to start with," she said shortly.

"So, how was your trip?" It was Julie, leaning across the table. Sal nodded. She was grateful when Ramona, with only a concerned glance in her direction, answered for her.

Sal looked over at Arlene. She looked so out of place, now, in a bar. She was a quiet, hulking presence, gentler with age. Arlene gazed fondly at Ramona, protective as always. Under the table, Mary held her hand.

Sal sighed. *Two old war horses,* she thought. *We're the only ones that have lasted, have hung onto her—by the simple strategy of never, quite, having her at all.* She sat back in her chair and sipped her drink and let the sweet cacophony of friends' voices wash over her. It did not, quite, wash away the uncomfortable feeling that she and Arlene were really not so different after all.

"Are you all right?" Ramona gave her an owlish look.

Sal nodded. "I...." she paused, then said it. "I need to talk to you."

"Sure. Now?"

"If you think that'd be okay."

"I guess...," Ramona trailed off uncertainly. Sal, catching the thumbs-up signal Melvina was giving her, realized it was time for her to take the lead.

She rose from the table, nudging Ramona and excusing herself, and strode over to May. "Uh, listen. I need to talk to someone alone for a few minutes, and I was wondering if...."

"How about the upstairs bar," suggested Ramona, joining them.

May shook her head. "You know we keep that locked except for weekends. I go opening that and everyone and their uncle...."

"Aunt," corrected Bets, coming up behind them.

"Yes, I know," said Sal, "but this...."

May was shaking her head, regretfully but firmly. Ramona was stepping back. Sal glanced over at Melvina, feeling helpless and resigned.

Bets stepped toward May. "Don't worry about it," she said gruffly. "I'll take care of it."

"But...." said May.

Bets waved her keys and turned away, motioning Ramona and Sal to follow.

"This is really nice of you," said Ramona as they climbed the stairs. "I know I've given you a hard time, lately, but...."

"This okay, *Sal?*" asked Bets as she unlocked the door.

Sal smirked at Ramona as she followed her through the door, wondering what bedevilment she had visited on poor Bets. "Thanks," said Sal, turning to face Bets and saluting her with her club soda.

To her surprise, Bets gave a bow. "My pleasure," she said. "Just don't touch the booze," she added in a less friendly voice.

Sal flicked on lights and closed the door. She glanced around nervously, taking in the pseudo-Alpine decor, and joined Ramona at a table under a large, colored photograph of clouded mountain tops.

"You on the wagon?" asked Ramona, indicating Sal's glass.

Sal shook her head vehemently. "Don't get your hopes up. As soon as we're done here—I deserve a stiff one."

Ramona nodded, her face impassive. "So," she said.

"So," said Sal.

Ramona leaned across the table and deftly removed Sal's sunglasses. She turned Sal's face toward the light and looked at her. "Nasty, nasty," she remarked, folding the sunglasses and pocketing them.

"I wish it were the only one," said Sal. "I'm sore all over."

Ramona clucked her tongue, raised her eyebrows. "Would you like the doctor to make a complete examination?" she asked.

Sal snorted and shifted in her chair. "One of these times," she threatened, "I ought to call your bluff."

Ramona smiled. "Wanna try it?"

Sal waved a hand at her. "Can't you be serious for once?"

Ramona composed her face into a serious—and unbelievable—frown. Sal made a face at her, and Ramona gave it up. "What happened?" she asked.

"Your little time bomb blew up in my face."

Ramona nodded. "She all right now?"

Sal shrugged. "I'm not here to talk about that. I...." her words stuck in her throat. Sal got up from the table abruptly. "It's too quiet. I can't...."

Ramona shrugged, rose, and headed for the door.

Sal startled and started to go after her when she realized Ramona was at the jukebox. She watched her pause to take change out of her pocket and examine the selections. Swiftly, she inserted coins, punched a few buttons. "There," she said, facing Sal, "instant noise."

Sal smiled. The music began.

"Shall we take a turn around the floor?" asked Ramona, gathering Sal in her arms, leaving little choice.

"You've got the skirt on," grumbled Sal, "I get to lead."

"Like hell," laughed Ramona.

It surprised Sal how well they moved together, how good it felt.

"Why don't we ever do this?" asked Ramona.

Sal shrugged and dropped her arms. She stood back. "Enough of that, we're not here to dance."

Agreeably, Ramona moved off the dance floor, seated herself again at the table. "I forgot," she apologized. "We're being serious."

"Listen," said Sal, sitting down, "I had a lot of time to think while we were gallivanting around. I spent a lot of time listening to Skittle, too."

"I can imagine," Ramona commented, looking mildly amused.

"Anyway, she said we were both idiots, that we...."

"I thought we weren't here to talk about Melvina," said Ramona quietly. "What did *you* say?"

203

"Me? I—I think it's about time we talked about things."

"What things?" Ramona looked puzzled.

Sal took out her cigarettes and laid them on the table. She extracted one from the pack and lit it with an unsteady hand. "I don't know. You and me." Sal began to feel very uncomfortable under Ramona's steady scrutiny. She felt naked, ridiculous.

"You and me? What about you and me? I mean, we're good friends—"

"I know. It's just—we never really talked things out. We were—a lot closer, a long time ago, and we've never...."

Ramona raised one eyebrow. "That was a *long* time ago."

"I know...."

"Our relationship is very different now, has been for a long, long...."

"I know...."

"Hell," exclaimed Ramona, "we're like a comfortable old pair of bedroom slippers. We know each other too well to...."

"I know." Sal could feel her ears burning. She felt like a fool. She glanced around, yearning for some place to hide. "It's just...." It was too late to turn back. She had to speak. "I still feel badly. I was wrong. I was scared...of how much I felt...and I was proud, and judgmental, and...."

Ramona was shaking her head impatiently. "That was a long time ago, Sal. And I never should have made my own forgiveness, my own self-acceptance, conditional on your...."

"And I've been a rotten friend ever since. I've been jealous, and disloyal, and two-faced, and...."

"We were *both* wrong!" Ramona shook her head. "We were young and we were stupid."

Sal placed her hands flat on the table top and rose to her feet. "All right. I may be older," her voice trembled, "but I'm still...stupid. I can't lie or hide anymore, Ramona."

Ramona looked up at her, her brows drawn together.

Sal looked away, the feeling of vulnerability past bearing. "I was wrong then, and I've been wrong since, because I...I love you, Ramona. I always have, and I guess I always will." She turned to face the door.

"What did you say?" asked Ramona's voice behind her.

"It doesn't matter," blurted Sal, her courage failing. She took a step or two and then stopped, one finger resting on the juke box. "There's one more thing." She looked back at Ramona. "That woman in the picture with me? The one when I was little?" Sal glanced at her feet. "Well, she wasn't the housekeeper. She was my mother." Sal started toward the door again.

Ramona's voice stopped her. When she looked back again, Ramona was on her feet. "I know that."

Sal started perceptibly.

Ramona looked down at the table. "I guess I always have. I think I thought I was doing you some kind of favor by never mentioning it. I thought I didn't have to, that I was being enough of a big-hearted liberal by pretending to ignore it." Ramona shook her head, fiddled with Sal's cigarette pack with one distracted hand. "Sometimes," she said, raising her head to look at Sal, "I think we've kept each other's secrets too long and too well."

Sal nodded. She could feel the bands of anxiety that crossed her chest tighten with each breath. "Well," she said with great difficulty, "we've said a lot. I guess it doesn't really change anything, but, still, maybe we need time to—think it over, digest it all." She was moving toward the door again, as toward a haven. She could not imagine how she would make it through, how she could possibly go down the stairs without stumbling, how she could face everyone in the bar without them noticing her nakedness, her utter defenselessness.

She lengthened her stride. There were only a few more steps to the door, to escape, when she could hear Ramona bearing down on her. She reached out toward the doorknob, almost had it in her grasp, when she heard Ramona's voice, close behind her, saying, "Oh, no, you don't," and felt a hand, hard, upon her shoulder, grabbing her, pulling her around.

Oh, shit, she's mad, thought Sal, *here we go again.* She was so sure of what was coming that she raised one trembling arm to cover her face, had already begun to hunch her shoulders protectively when she heard Ramona's voice, as though from far away, booming, "Time to think it over? I've had a quarter of a goddamned century to think it over...."

● ● ●

Bets was sitting halfway down the stairs, having a smoke, surveying the bar below. At May's behest she was hanging around, keeping an eye on things—however it is that one does that through a closed door. She reached out to flick the ash off her cigarette and glanced up the stairs.

Strange. First there was quiet, and then music, and then

quiet again. Once she thought she heard a raised voice, but nothing had followed.

Bets scowled. What she wished would happen is that Sal would take that damned Ramona over her knee and—just then there was a loud noise at the door.

Bets frowned and cocked her head. Years of experience told her that that was the thud caused by the disequilibrium resulting from the collision of two very passionate bodies. She listened intently and heard nothing for a while. *That figures,* she thought. Then she heard some urgent low murmurs, then more silence, then a sound of—gentle laughter, quiet tears?

"Well, wha'd'ya'know?" muttered Bets, grinding out her cigarette. She smiled briefly, imagining once again a deep-flaked-purple Cadillac, a fetching black fedora, a silver-headed cane.... Bets stretched and hoisted herself to her feet, striding down the stairs, calling to May across the room, "Hey, babe...." She paused. Her voice was louder than she had intended. Every head seemed to turn in her direction. The stranger from Kentucky grinned at her. Bets smiled back. "How about a beer over here?"

Born in Medford, Massachusetts, and raised in Plainfield, Connecticut, the author received her B.A., summa cum laude, from Wells College and her M.A. in Psychology from the University of Pennsylvania. She has worked at a variety of jobs, ranging from agricultural laborer and electronics assembler to editor of *Bay Windows*, a gay and lesbian newspaper, and developmental writer for a management consulting firm. In recent years she has served the community as chair of the Greater Boston Lesbian and Gay Political Alliance, host of the cable television show, "Gay Boston," and editor of the *Center Times*, a monthly publication of the Boston Center for Lesbians and Gay Men. She shares a home in Dorchester with her lover, CM Deucher, a lesbian activist and underwater photographer. This is her first novel.

Other books from New Victoria

Mystery-Adventure

Woman with Red Hair—Brunel—The mystery of her mother's death takes Magalie into the swamps and the slums of France, her only clue the memory of a woman with red hair. ISBN 0-934678-30-8 ($8.95)

Death by the Riverside—Redmann—Detective Mickey Knight finds herself slugging through thugs and slogging through swamps to expose a dangerous drug ring. ISBN 0-934678-27-8 ($8.95)

She Died Twice—Lauren—The remains of a child are unearthed and Emma relives the weeks leading up to Natalie's death as she searches for the murderer. ($8.95) ISBN 0934678-34-0

Mysteries by Sarah Dreher

A Captive In Time—Stoner finds herself inexplicably transported to a small town in the Colorado Territory, time 1871. When, if ever, will she find a phone to call home? ISBN 0-934678-22-7 ($9.95)

Stoner McTavish —The first Stoner mystery—Dream lover Gwen, in danger in the Grand Tetons. *"Sensitive, funny and unabashedly sweet, Stoner McTavish is worth the read."* ($7.95) ISBN 0-934678-06-5

Something Shady— Stoner gets trapped in the clutches of the evil Dr. Millicent Tunes. *"The piece de resistance of the season...I think it's the funniest book I ever read."* ($8.95) ISBN 0-934678-07-3

Gray Magic— Stoner and Gwen head to Arizona, but a peaceful vacation turns frightening when Stoner becomes a combatant in the great struggle between the Hopi Spirits of good and evil. ($8.95) ISBN-0-934678-11-1

Adventure / Romance

Cody Angel—Whitfield—Dana struggles for self-esteem and love through her emotional entanglements— with her boss, with Frankie, a bike dyke, and Jerri, who enjoys sex as power. ISBN 0-934678-28-6 ($8.95)

In Unlikely Places—Beguin—While following a dream of exploring Africa, nineteenth century adventurer Lily Bascombe finds herself searching for the elusive Miss Margery Pool. ISBN 0-934578- 25-1 ($8.95)

Mari — Hilderley.—The story of the evolving relationship between Mari, an Argentinian political activist, and Judith, a New York City musician. ISBN-0-934678- 23-5 ($8.95)

Dark Horse— Lucas—Fed up with corruption in local politics, lesbian Sidney Garrett runs for mayor and falls in love with her socialite campaign worker. ISBN-0-934678--21-9 ($8.95)

As The Road Curves—Dean—Ramsey, with a reputation for never having to sleep alone, takes off from a prestigious lesbian magazine on an adventure of a lifetime. ISBN-0-934678-17-0 ($8.95)

All Out—Alguire—Winning a medal at the Olympics is Kay Strachan's all-consuming goal until a budding romance threatens her ability to go all out for the gold. ISBN-0-934678-16-2 ($8.95)

Look Under the Hawthorn—Frye—Stonedyke Edie Cafferty from Vermont searches for her long lost daughter and meets Anabelle, a jazz pianist looking for her birth mother. ISBN-0-934678-12-X ($7.95)

Runway at Eland Springs— Béguin—Flying supplies into the African bush, Anna gets herself into conflict with a game hunter, and finds love and support with Jilu, the woman at Eland Springs. ISBN-0-934678-10-3 ($7.95).

Promise of the Rose Stone —McKay—Mountain warrior Issa is banished to the women's compound in the living satellite where she and her lover Cleothe plan an escape with Cleothe's newborn baby. ISBN-0-934678-09-X ($7.95)

Humor

Cut Outs and Cut Ups A Fun'n Games Book for Lesbians—Dean, Wells, and Curran—Games, puzzles, astrology, paper dolls—an activity book for lesbians ISBN-0-934678-20-0 ($8.95)

Found Goddesses: Asphalta to Viscera—M. Grey &J.Penelope—*"Found Goddesses is wonderful. I've had more fun reading it than any book in the last two years."* —Joanna Russ. ISBN-0-934678-18-9 ($7.95)

Morgan Calabresé; The Movie—N. Dunlap- Wonderfully funny comic strips. Politics, relationships, and softball as seen through the eyes of Morgan Calabresé ISBN-0-934678-14-6 ($5.95)

Short Fiction/Plays

Secrets—Newman—The surfaces and secrets, the joys and sensuality and the conflicts of lesbian relationships are brought to life in these stories. ISBN 0-934678-24-3 ($8.95)

Lesbian Stages—"Sarah Dreher's plays are good yarns firmly centered in a Lesbian perspective with specific, complex, often contradictory (just like real people) characters." ($9.95)ISBN 0-934678-15-4 —Kate McDermott

The Names of the Moons of Mars— Schwartz—In these stories the author writes humorously as well as poignantly about our lives as women and as lesbians. ISBN-0-934678-19-7 ($8.95).

Audiotape read by author **The Names of the Moons of Mars** ($9.95) ISBN 0-934678-26-X

History

Radical Feminists of Heterodoxy— Schwarz—"Numerous tantalizing photographs that accompany the warm lively narrative of the women and the times in which they lived." ISBN-0934678- 08-1   ($8.95) —Th eWomen's Studies Review

Available from through your favorite bookstore or

Order directly from New Victoria Publishers, PO Box 27 Norwich, Vt. 05055